I0823336

RICH PEOPLE IN SANTA BARBARA

"These are two wonderful, engaging novellas about the all-but-secret world of Santa Barbara society of the not-so-distant past. These people are still around behind their gates and high hedges. Beneath the snobbery and scandal, there is something eerie, something noir. Elizabeth Gilchrist knew this world well, and she writes of it with sympathy, humor, and ruthless honesty. A great read."

—**KENT ANDERSON**, author of *Sympathy for the Devil*, *Night Dogs*, *Green Sun*, and *Liquor, Guns & Ammo*; Recipient of Prix Calibre 38 1998; Finalist for the Los Angeles Times Book Award 2019; and Awardee of the 2019 Grand Prix de littérature policière

"A smell of eucalyptus and salt air, morning fogs, mountains in the distance, lust, adultery and unsolved murders. If Raymond Chandler's Los Angeles has been called "the great wrong place," Elizabeth Gilchrist's Santa Barbara runs a close second. She is its bard. Her selection of period details is impeccable, her wit and judgment playful and subtle. Her wealthy characters, seemingly proper and socially responsible, listen to the best jazz, eat the most sensible food, drive the hippest cars, and move in an atmosphere of entitled amorality and dread."

—**PHILLIP LOPATE**, author of *Two Marriages*, editor of *Art of the Personal Essay*

RICH PEOPLE IN SANTA BARBARA

Two Novellas by

Elizabeth Gilchrist

RARE BIRD
LOS ANGELES, CALIF.

Rich People in Santa Barbara is a work of fiction. Santa Barbara is, of course, a real place, but the Santa Barbara of "Montecito Peak" and "The Polo Club" is seen through the prism of the author's memory and imagination.

THIS IS A GENUINE RARE BIRD BOOK

Rare Bird Books
6044 North Figueroa Street
Los Angeles, California 90042
rarebirdbooks.com

FIRST HARDCOVER EDITION

For more information, address:
Rare Bird Books Subsidiary Rights Department
6044 North Figueroa Street
Los Angeles, California 90042

Set in Minion Pro
Printed in the United States

10 9 8 7 6 5 4 3 2 1

Library of Congress Cataloging-in-Publication Data available upon request

For my father
John Wesley Gilchrist

MONTECITO PEAK

1990

CHAPTER ONE

Struck by Lightning

One afternoon in January, on her way home from a *Concours d'Elegance* committee meeting at her daughter's school, Barbara Palmer stopped by the Montecito Garage on East Valley Road. Montecito was becoming more built up, but East Valley Road was still a quiet country road lined with pittosporum hedges and stone walls, with big houses hidden from the road down long driveways. If there was a line of cars at a stop sign, you wondered what the event was. The Montecito Garage was located at a curve in the road a half mile or so from Montecito Village. The house Barbara inherited from her grandmother was another half mile farther on.

Barbara and Mike Brooke, the owner of the Montecito Garage, had known each other since they were children. Mike was one of the children whom Barbara's grandmother rounded up to play with Barbara and her sister when they came up from Pasadena to visit. She would send them to the horse show with her chauffeur. Whenever their grandmother remarked of Mike: "There were three presidents at his grandmother's wedding. One sitting and two former. Alas, his father spent all the money," as she was fond of saying, Barbara and her sister would make hoity-toity faces at her behind her back. Mike's father was an architect who wore silk scarves and a beret, and he seldom got a commission.

The garage had been there since the twenties. The original white-stucco-and-red-tile-roof building still stood. The garage office had the original chairs for customers, chrome and leatherette—a rip on the seat of one of the chairs had been mended with duct tape. The hydraulic lifts in the service bays were new, however—only a few years old. Across the cracked concrete pavement, there was an I-beam prefab steel building outfitted to work on racing cars. Texaco had long since stopped delivering gas to the glass-globe gas pumps in front of the garage, but deliveries were still made to a 500-gallon gravity-flow fuel tank on a stand by the metal building.

Mike had always been into cars. At Santa Barbara High School, he ran with the car guys; he worked at the Montecito Garage in the summers. The Vietnam War was going on then. All of the guys Mike knew who went to Vietnam came back fucked up. For nothing, as Mike saw it. He went to Cal Poly in San Luis Obispo and majored in civil engineering. Mike's senior year at Cal Poly, he applied to a graduate program, with the idea of continuing his student deferment. The same week that he got the letter informing him that he'd been admitted to the graduate program, the first draft lottery was conducted. His number was 349. He was never going to be drafted. Soon after, the estate of one of his great-aunts was settled and he got a cashier's check in the mail for three hundred thousand dollars. A few days later, the owner of the Montecito Garage decided he wanted to retire and offered to sell the garage to Mike. And so, Mike, three months short of his BA, quit college on the spot and bought the Montecito Garage.

Barbara parked her red Volvo station wagon under a dusty pepper tree next to an old green pickup truck with board sides, the back of the truck piled high with fishing nets. FRESH WISH COMPANY was lettered in white block letters on the faded green of the driver's door. The truck belonged to a fisherman buddy of Mike's. The front brakes were metal on metal. Mike had told his friend he'd give him the bro rate for a brake job. But he couldn't get to it right away. Barbara walked across the concrete parking area to the garage. The glass-globe gas pumps reminded her of Montecito the way it was when she was a little girl visiting her grandmother.

In one of the service bays, a black BMW that looked like an SS staff car was up on the hydraulic lift; in the other, a yellow 1955 Corvette, the Turbo-Five V-8 model, was backed in. Mike, in jeans and a racing crew jacket, was making a repair on the BMW, standing under the car, his neck craned back, looking up under the engine, doing something with a sprocket wrench. He didn't hear Barbara's approach. She scrutinized the Corvette for a minute, then made her presence known.

"Hello, hello," she said. She had a sweet, emphatic voice. She was wearing a blue-and-white-striped French sailor's jersey and blue wool slacks, and she carried an L.L.Bean Boat and Tote bag, white canvas with navy-blue trim. Her hair was the same honey blonde as when she was a girl.

Mike ducked out from under the front of the elevated BMW.

"Barb Lloyd. What brings you here?" he said, wrench in hand. He called her by her maiden name. Barbara had been married to Rawson Palmer for sixteen years, but people who had known her as a girl still called her Barb Lloyd. Barbara had a large unearned income. Her great-grandfathers on both sides had been robber baron industrialists. There were trusts. There were trustees. There were the family's attorneys. There were investment managers. She lived within her income, her very large income. If anyone asked, she said, "I was born lucky"—and changed the subject.

Mike was a handsome man. He had sapphire blue eyes and dark-brown hair, almost black. Barbara's sister said he had the most beautiful straight nose of any man she ever knew. Mike had never taken his good looks too seriously.

"I have a favor to ask," Barbara said.

"Anything," Mike said. "Within reason. Have a seat."

They sat on red metal porch chairs on the pavement outside the open door of the garage office. There was a smell of motor oil. Barbara took a yellow legal pad and a plastic bag of baby carrots out of her tote. She carried around baby carrots the way some of her friends carried around bottles of Evian water. She still weighed the same as when she was eighteen.

"Would you like a carrot?" she said, offering the plastic bag to Mike.

"No, thanks," he said.

"I'm a great believer in crudités," she said. "Let me tell you the situation."

Her daughter's school, Crane Country Day School, had a vintage car show every year as a fundraiser. A *Concours d'Elegance*. Mike said he was familiar with the *Concours d'Elegance*.

"I know you are," Barbara said. "But what you do not know is that this year I am on the committee."

"It's terribly important to be involved," Mike said. He had a rascally smile.

"It really is," Barbara said, repressively.

"Sorry," Mike said.

"The first two meetings, I didn't say a peep. Not a peep. Today I had a brainstorm. Why not have a fifties section. We all know people who have terrific fifties cars."

"I think I see where this is going," Mike said.

"Everyone on the committee is excited," Barbara said. "I volunteered to come up with a list of possible exhibitors. And it occurred to me that (a) you could help me with my list; and (b) you have a fifties Corvette." She counted off "a" and "b" by pointing her index finger at Mike.

"Affirmative to the first," Mike said. He got up and got the garage Rolodex and sat back down next to Barbara. He flipped the Rolodex, stopping at the entries for garage customers who owned fifties cars. Barbara took notes, writing with a black gel pen in cursive backhand on the yellow legal pad, encouraging him with "That's great" and "Got it." He came up with five names, finishing with "Ron Gamberini—he has that turquoise 1957 Chevy Bel Air with *Veni Vidi Vici* on the dash. 969-3554."

"What about Rawson's cousin's convertible?" she said. "It's like riding in a big comfortable glove. It has those big whitewall tires."

"It's a 1952 Chrysler New Yorker. But he doesn't bring it to me."

"His loss. I have his phone number at home. Now what about your Corvette?"

"The transmission's shot," Mike said.

Barbara put the yellow legal pad and the plastic bag of carrot sticks back in her tote bag—she had eaten three carrot sticks while they talked. She got to her feet and drifted over to the Corvette in the service bay, Mike accompanying her.

"Maybe you could tow it down to the Polo Club?" she said, tracing a curlicue in the dust of the hood with her index finger.

"The cars have to run. That's the drawing card. Get with it, Barbara," Mike said.

"Oh. I guess they do have to run," she said. "You could fix it."

"I'd have to order parts. I've got work backed up."

"The *Concours* isn't until June. Are you saying that if you ordered the parts for the Corvette today, they wouldn't come in time?" She was playful but persistent.

"Barbara, don't be a pest."

"Sorry. What's going on with the land speed record?" she asked.

"We're racing the Lakester at El Mirage in June," Mike said. "Chasin' that record."

The rolling doors of the metal building were up. A Lakester—an open-wheel race car, its body shaped like the fuselage of a Cessna Citation bizjet, gleaming white with a futuristic red streak—was inside. The owner was a boyhood friend of Mike's, a car guy with family money. In high school, he and Mike customized a 1958 Chevrolet with a small-block V-8, a classic drag racing car. Now Mike was his head mechanic and crew chief.

"Exactly how fast can that car go?" Barbara asked, eyeing the race car in its lair, across the parking area.

"It had better go over 324 miles an hour, or we're not in the running."

"Yikes. Well, it certainly looks fast. I have to dash. I'm going into town to pick up the laundry at Ablitt's. The days are so damn short in January. You know how Rawson gets." Barbara could say this sort of thing to Mike without any feeling of disloyalty. He was an old friend. Her tone when talking about her husband was indulgent.

"We all know Rawson," Mike said. It was common knowledge. Rawson had a fit if Barbara was out after dark.

"I'm a saint," Barbara said.

Mike walked with her to her car. Seeing FRESH WISH COMPANY lettered on the green truck, she said, "Remember the Palmer Orchards logo?"

"Jesus, that International Harvester was a junker," Mike said.

"I know. But I loved to drive it."

Mike smiled at Barbara. She had a pretty face—her full lower lip had a piquant charm.

For several years, Barbara and her husband had been in the exotic fruit business. During this period, the horse pasture was planted in macadamia nut trees and the hill behind the swimming pool was terraced for a cherimoya orchard that never materialized. They also bought property at La Conchita and planted a banana grove. They had a farm truck, an old International Harvester that kept breaking down. Mike was pressed into service as the farm mechanic, but he eventually refused to work on it.

He remembered Barbara sitting high in the cab, her blonde daughter seat-belted in the bench seat next to her. He'd installed the seat belts. The Palmer Orchards logo—a photo-realistic rendering of a macadamia nut, a cherimoya, and a short fat red banana—was airbrushed on the door.

"How's Sheila?" he asked.

Sheila was Barbara's sister. She was two years older than Barbara, the same age as Mike. The summer Barbara was fifteen, she and her sister had spent the summer in Santa Barbara. Mike would take Sheila out to the movies and bring her home and kiss her good night, then he'd circle around the house and climb up the wisteria trellis, and she'd let him in her bedroom window. Their grandmother didn't care, so long as the proprieties were observed. Barbara's bedroom was across the hall from her sister's room, and once she tiptoed out of her room and listened at the door.

Sheila's adult life was glitzier than Barbara's. She had a house in Aspen and a house in the South of France, and an international circle of friends. She'd made the scene in New York in the late Sixties and early Seventies. After a brief, spectacularly disastrous first marriage to a man who turned out to be after her money, she had been married for fifteen years to an easygoing guy with a lot of money.

"The last time I talked to her, she said she was a sybarite," Barbara said. She rummaged around in her tote for a baby carrot. "They've rented a villa on Mustique for February. That's when Mick Jagger is there."

"She thinks she's Princess Margaret," Mike said.

Barbara burst out laughing. Mike smiled his rascally smile, amused that he'd made her laugh. Then something was wrong. Barbara was laughing with no sound, her mouth an O. She dropped her tote on the pavement.

A piece of carrot had lodged in Barbara's windpipe, and no oxygen whatsoever was getting to her lungs. It was a silent, peaceful process. No coughing. No gasping for air. Barbara was more bewildered than panicked. Mike had an aura of white light around him. She clutched silently at her throat. Mike recognized the classic sign that a person is choking. He paid attention to public service spots on television. He had never administered a Heimlich maneuver before, but he knew what to do. Acting fast, he got behind Barbara and encircled her in a close embrace. Barbara was starting to go limp at the knees, a dead weight. He made his two hands into a fist and lodged his double fist in the hollow beneath her breasts. He jerked in and up, hard and fast. Barbara's mouth opened with a small *ahhh*, more an exhalation than a cough, and once again she could breathe. The morsel of carrot was on her tongue. Mike released her, and she turned to face him.

There was an enormous silence all around them. In the pale January sunshine in a year when the rains didn't fall, two souls spoke to each other. They stared at each other, looked deep into each other's eyes.

"Everything was turning black," she said.

"I'm shaking now," he said. "Thank you, Jesus. I did it right."

"You saved my life."

He touched a finger to her soft cheek in wonderment. The smell of cucumber soap and Blue Grass dusting powder. The smell of motor oil and of Mike's sweat. They were old friends. Acquaintances, really. Barbara had always been able to see why women liked Mike—and Mike could see Barbara's appeal. But they'd never been attracted to each other. No undercurrents. Now everything had changed. That was before. This was after.

Like magic, they saw each other with new eyes. Lightning had struck. Eros shot his golden arrows. Angels sang. A red-headed acorn woodpecker rat-a-tat-tat-ed on the utility pole. A car drove past on East Valley Road. The phone was ringing in the garage office.

"You should answer that," Barbara said.

"They'll call back."

Mike picked up Barbara's tote and handed it to her. The phone stopped ringing. They stood under the pepper tree with its dusty, weeping-willow leaves.

"I'm never going to eat another carrot in my life," Barbara said.

"That's probably best," Mike said.

"Do you remember when we went grunion hunting?"

"I do remember."

An August night at the dark of the moon. Sheila didn't want Barbara to come with her and Mike, but their grandmother prevailed on Mike to take Barbara along. He was nice to her; she didn't feel like a third wheel. The wan yellow lights along the boardwalk at the Miramar were almost invisible in the foggy night. Tendrils of fog. A group of kids around a driftwood fire on the sandy beach. Six-packs of beer. Sheila stripped down to her bra and panties and swam out to the float. When she got out of the water, Mike gave her his Pendleton wool shirt. Two of the girls had made a thing of racing down to the water's edge to see if the grunion had come yet and running back to report. One boy got drunk and pissed in the fire. An old couple staying at the Miramar had chatted with one of the boys on the boardwalk, and the woman had asked if the kids were having a weenie roast. He thought this was hilarious, and every once in a while, he started a call and response: "Weenie roast!"—"Weenie roast!" Barbara joined in.

It was midnight when the shallow waves glistened with the slender silver fish, the spawning fish squirmed on the wet sand.

Mike and Sheila and Barbara filled their galvanized pail with grunion and went back to the big kitchen at her grandmother's house. Fried in butter, the silvery little fish were perfect crisp morsels.

Mike said, "I remember something you said. A guy who wasn't from Santa Barbara—his family was staying in one of the cottages at the Miramar—said that Santa Barbara was cliquish if you weren't from there, and you said, 'That's not true. We all know each other. And I'm from Pasadena.'"

"Oh dear," Barbara said. Another silence. Then she said, "I really should go now."

"The witching hour," Mike said. "We don't want you to turn into a pumpkin."

"Me and Cinderella."

"You're sure you're alright?"

"I'm perfectly fine. Everything was turning black, and now I'm perfectly fine."

He held the car door for her, and she got in, put her tote on the seat next to her, and fastened her seat belt. "Please get the Corvette running," she said, looking up at him.

"You don't give up," he said. He felt infinite tenderness for her.

"Never!" she said, as she started the engine.

Mike watched her drive away, between the high green hedges. He remembered that Barbara's nose was sunburnt and peeling the night of the grunion hunt.

CHAPTER TWO

The Eucalyptus Tree

Stone gateposts topped by pineapple finials flanked the entrance. Periwinkle groundcover grew under old oak trees. There was still daylight, but the winter light was fading. As she drove up the driveway, Barbara met her husband, Rawson, coming out in their Lincoln Town Car. Their thirteen-year-old daughter, Betsy, was in the passenger seat next to him. The asphalt driveway was wide enough for the two cars to pull up next to each other. Barbara and Rawson rolled down their windows at the same time.

"Where were you?" he asked, his tone only mildly curious. But a muscle in his jaw twitched. It could go either way.

"Sun's already set, Mom," Betsy said, talking across her father. She had her mother's coloring—honey-blonde hair and hazel eyes.

"Oh, for heaven's sake," Barbara said. "I had a *Concours d'Elegance* meeting at Crane." With Betsy, she did her best to make the home-before-dark thing into a silly foible of Rawson's. Daddy's just a little insecure. "We're going to have a fifties section. I went by the Montecito Garage and Mike gave me a list of people who have fifties cars." She didn't say the important thing: I almost died. Mike saved my life. "Then I went into town to pick up the dry cleaning." Barbara had gone over the hill on Camino Viejo to avoid the traffic backed up at the stoplights on 101—the only lights between San Diego and San Francisco. It would be two years before the Garden Street on-off ramp and the underpass at State Street were completed.

"You've been a busy bee. We're going to the Nugget for burgers," Rawson said, amiable now. He hadn't really been interested in where she had been. That was not what it was about. "Do you want to come? We can wait for you."

"I'll stay here," Barbara said.

The Nugget was in Summerland. A hamburger joint with a full bar. You always ran into someone you knew. Ordinarily, Barbara would have gone along, but this evening she wanted to be alone. Partly, she had Mike on her mind. Also, she had something she wanted to do unobserved. Barbara was secretly poisoning a eucalyptus tree on the neighbors' property.

"Bring me a meatloaf sandwich, please," she said.

"Righty-o," Rawson said. He was almost handsome, with sandy hair and regular features, but he had a small mouth, a phenomenon among men of his age in a certain demographic, the result of a fashion in orthodontics for unnecessarily pulling two permanent teeth, the two upper pre-molars, to correct an overbite. Rawson and Betsy drove off in the Lincoln Town Car, and Barbara proceeded on to the house.

The large, square-ish, ochre-stucco two-story Italianate house with its sage-green shutters and an entry court paved with granite cobblestones was a departure from the usual Spanish Revival architecture of its period. Barbara's grandmother had left the Santa Barbara house to Barbara and a ranch outside of Tucson to Sheila. Two separate bequests. She said she'd seen too much argle-bargle with one heir having to buy out the other, or quarrels if the heirs owned the property in common. At the time of her death, Barbara and Rawson were living in La Cañada, not far from Barbara's parents in Pasadena. She'd had mixed feelings about moving to Santa Barbara. Betsy was little, and Barbara liked being near the grandparents. Rawson, however, was gung-ho, and Barbara acquiesced. The move had turned out to be a good thing. Barbara felt at home in Montecito, and people were tolerant of Rawson.

Italian cypress grew around the walled entry court. A della Robbia plate—a Madonna and Child ringed by yellow lemons and green leaves—was in an arched opening over the front door. Barbara drove around to the three-car garage. Each of the three single garage doors had its own automatic door opener. A Cadillac Allanté—a red two-door, two-seater convertible that she'd given Rawson for his fortieth birthday, three years before—was parked in the garage.

"Wow. A red convertible. I love it. Midlife Crisis Caddy," Rawson had exclaimed, but he rarely drove it, and he never took off the removable hardtop. He didn't have the panache to carry off the Allanté. When he drove it, he looked sheepish. She was so used to the red Cadillac in the garage that she hardly saw it. Now, burdened down with the dry cleaning, her tote, and a brown paper grocery bag from Isaiah Brothers, she contemplated the Cadillac. There was a fine film of dust. She imagined Mike driving with the top down. Sporty. Barefoot. As if Santa Barbara was still a sleepy little beach town.

The caretaker and gardeners and the housekeeper were gone for the day. In the kitchen, Barbara stood at the sink and contemplated the view. As long as she could remember, the view from the kitchen window had been of Montecito Peak, hazy purple against the sky. Over the years, however, a blue gum eucalyptus tree in a stand of tall eucalyptus—a windbreak planted at the turn of the century—had gradually blocked it from view, until one day Barbara realized she could no longer see Montecito Peak from the kitchen. This was unacceptable.

Barbara hung the dry-cleaned clothes in their flimsy plastic wrappings in the laundry room, put on an old Fair Isle cardigan, and went out a side door from the butler's pantry, taking with her the wicker basket that she used for cut flowers. Her first stop was the workshop for the property. The workshop was at a distance from the house, down the dirt road that circled around the thirty-seven acres. The door was kept locked, but the key was in plain view on a nail over the door. It was an old frame building with double-hung windows and a wide plank floor. Barbara let herself in and switched on the fluorescent shop light suspended from the ceiling. There was the smell of engine oil

There was a table saw and workbench, and generations of tools—rakes, hoes, loppers, spades and shovels, carpentry tools. An old pedal grindstone was stored in a corner, and an electric water-cooled slow-speed grindstone was on a shop table. The herbicides and pesticides were all together in one area. That corner of the shop had the poison chemical smell of the pesticide/herbicide aisle at the Home Improvement Center. Barbara was a proponent of natural weed and pest control, but, as she said, "Sometimes you just have to nuke 'em."

A pump-action spray bottle on which the caretaker had drawn a crude skull and crossbones with a black felt-tip marker and printed TREE POISON in capital letters was next to a plastic jug of Ferti-Loam Brush and Stump Killer. There was a jumble of protective accessories in a cardboard box—plastic goggles, dust masks, rubber gloves. Barbara put a pair of rubber gloves in her basket, along with the Tree Poison spray bottle and a pair of pruning snips. Then she switched off the shop light and exited. In the gloaming, she walked down the dirt road—the hillside planted with macadamia nut trees on one side, an orchard of Valencia oranges on the other. She walked past the old pump house, a squat fieldstone building. As soon as the sun went down, the air was damp. Smells were more intense. Sound traveled.

She was not unmoved by the beauty of place; she felt the poignancy of the past. But Rawson was the nostalgic one; he was sentimentally sad that the days of the orchards and groves, the pump house, the empty pasture, the Italianate main house, the croquet lawn that always had dandelions—their days were numbered. One day a developer, that sinister entity, would make an offer they couldn't refuse and all this would be gone. Sometimes when he was drinking, he shed maudlin tears for what would be no more.

Barbara found this annoying. Who was this developer? The house and land were hers, as her sole and separate property. Her plan, which she saw no reason to reveal to Rawson, was, in ten years, maybe longer, do it in stages, to develop the property herself. Five-acre plots. Very swank. Underground utilities. Sell the main house with three acres of land as a Montecito estate. It would be fun. Nothing is forever. Her sister was turning the ranch outside of Tucson into a luxury desert resort. Real estate was a time-honored way for each generation to top off the trusts.

The small white flowers of a Victorian box tree filled the air with the smell of orange blossoms. Walking along the dirt road, Barbara thought of Mike. What was going to happen, she had no idea. But her life had changed. She felt a glad anticipation. Her thoughts were all of Mike—his arms around her, the touch of his hand on her cheek.

She came to where the dirt road skirted the eucalyptus grove. This was the property line. There was a long-abandoned archery range, the straw-filled targets fastened to ghostly tree trunks, medieval in the fading light. In other years, new tender green grass and wild oats would have been growing under the trees, but in this drought year there was only dead, dry grass and dead leaves, long strips of eucalyptus bark. Years earlier, one of the biggest trees had fallen. It was a wet winter, an El Niño year, and the ground was saturated. Then one night there was a windstorm—almost a tornado—that toppled big established trees—oaks, eucalyptus, cypress—all over Santa Barbara. The bare gray-white trunk of the fallen eucalyptus, maybe ten feet in circumference at its base, lay where it had fallen, the side branches denuded of leaves by weather and the passage of time. Rocks were still entrapped in the tangle of uprooted roots at its base. When she was little, Betsy had liked to climb on the trunk.

The owners of the stand of eucalyptus were a couple who lived in a midcentury modern house up the hill. Even if they had been outside, they wouldn't have seen Barbara. They could only see the tops of the eucalyptus trees.

Barbara picked her way over the litter of dead leaves and strips of bark to the tree that blocked her view from the kitchen window. It seemed to her that the leaves were already looking a little yellow. Kneeling at the base of the trunk, her basket on the ground, she put on the rubber gloves, then brushed away the litter of dead leaves. Using the tip of the pruning snips, she dug out a little plug of bark to reveal the deep hole that she had made a few weeks earlier with a brace hand drill with a three-quarter-inch auger bit. There were six holes at even intervals around the base of the tree. She inserted the nozzle point of the sprayer into the hole and pumped the handle. The chemical smell of the poison mixed with the menthol eucalyptus smell. Barbara pumped a shot of stump killer into each of the six holes. “Sorry, tree,” she said.

She replaced the plugs of bark, mussed up the litter of dead leaves, so that even if someone had looked the holes were not visible. She peeled off the gloves, replaced the sprayer and her gloves in her basket, stood up, brushed herself off, and walked out of the grove onto the dirt road. She paused to snip a few sprigs of eucalyptus from a low branch to put in her basket for the house. “Sorry, tree,” she said again.

Barbara came from a family of women who believed in taking matters into their own hands.

She could have called Hank and Ann Paine, the owners of the stand of eucalyptus, and told them, nicely, that their tree was blocking her view of Montecito Peak. She could offer to pay to have it cut down. If they said no, then what? Or she could hire the midnight tree trimmers. These were two surfers and a kid who was a gymnast at UCSB who could be hired to take down a tree at the dark of the moon when the owners were known to be away. Barbara knew someone who had actually hired them. The problem with the midnight tree trimmers was that, although they were discreet, they weren’t all that discreet. If they were, how come Barbara knew about them? Much better to poison the tree. There would be a dead eucalyptus tree in her view, but then she could go to the Paines and offer, magnanimously, to pay half the cost of removing it, remarking that, of course, it was a public nuisance. What if it fell on her road when someone was out for a walk?

Obviously, there is a big difference between poisoning the neighbors’ tree and, say, burning down an unprofitable office building on Colorado Boulevard—an act of arson that Barbara and her sister strongly suspected their mother of committing. The arson investigator ultimately attributed the fire to a faulty gas pipe, and the insurance company paid.

CHAPTER THREE

Triumph of the Will

When Barbara came in from injecting the stump poison into the eucalyptus tree, the phone was ringing. She answered it in the home office. The home office—originally the breakfast room—was equipped with a red IBM Selectric self-correcting typewriter and a desktop computer with a floppy disk port. The printer and copier were office quality; the fax machine had a dedicated phone line. Rawson was an early adopter of the personal computer. By 1988, he had their Christmas card list on an Excel spreadsheet, also the addresses and telephone numbers of his fraternity brothers. Fraternities were in decline when he was a student at UCSB, but, swimming against the tide, he had pledged Delta Tau Delta.

The caller was Ted, the young man Rawson and Barbara had hired to manage the bookstore. After they got out of the exotic fruit business, they had a chance to buy the inventory of a rare book dealer in Los Angeles, and they started Bird of Paradise Books. They bought a historic adobe in downtown Santa Barbara, set back from the street in the middle of a block on Laguna Street. It took two years to get the necessary permits to transform it from a private home to a place of business. Barbara had to appear in person before the Architectural Review Board. Endless red tape. But she had persevered. Bird of Paradise Books was now a showplace. Modern firsts in one room, art books in another, another room for Californiana, a shipping room, a full kitchen, an office with the latest office equipment. They hired the garden designer Lydia Graham to design a garden around the hundred-year-old olive trees. There were graveled paths and a stone fountain.

Barbara and Ted's aunt had been roommates their junior year at Katherine Branson's. Ted had gone to Vassar, then he'd been assistant manager at Heritage Books on La Cienega. He was knowledgeable about modern first editions—he put together their specialized catalogs and compiled mailing lists. He asked Barbara if Rawson was there. She said, "Not right now," and he said, "Good. I need to talk to you."

"What's up?"

Did she know that Chas Hanson, a book dealer in Bakersfield, had offered an important hate literature collection to Bird of Paradise Books? Hate literature was a recognized category.

"Rawson showed me the catalog," Barbara said. The cover was red, white, and blue stripes printed on cream. *The Radical Right: Anti-Semitism / Anti-Catholicism/British Israel / Depression Economics / Fascism / Anti-Evolution/Racism, Etc.* There was a tastefully lettered disclaimer: *This strictly for scholarly purposes.* "He wants to buy the collection," Barbara said. "What do you think?"

"I think it's a bad idea," Ted said, in a diffident but firm voice. "If you break it up, you can probably make some money. There's some interesting ephemera—there's a Nuremberg Rally program—and some first editions of fairly important books, but most of it is garbage. A lot of Nazi pornography. KKK propaganda."

He wanted Barbara to use her influence.

"I'll do my best," she said. "You know Rawson."

♦♦♦

When Rawson and Betsy got back, Rawson went straight to the butler's pantry and poured himself a Scotch on the rocks. Things were always better when he had a drink. Not necessarily for the people around him, but he felt better. He'd had only one beer at the Nugget. He always watched his blood alcohol level when he had Betsy with him.

Betsy talked to Barbara in the kitchen while Barbara took her meatloaf sandwich out of its cardboard box and poured herself a glass of milk. A boy in Betsy's class had done a clever thing: he kept getting demerits for forgetting to lock his assigned locker, so now he left it locked all the time and kept his books in a disused locker that none of the teachers ever looked in. Barbara said she'd always liked that boy's style.

Betsy's room was pale robin's-egg blue with white voile curtains and a cork bulletin board over the white student desk. Barbara had decorated it for her. There were two twin beds. Betsy sat cross-legged on one of the beds, her books and spiral notebooks around her, and Barbara sat on the other with her back against the headboard, her meatloaf sandwich and milk on the night table. Betsy had a test in her United States history class, and Barbara asked her the questions in the study guide.

"What was the Dred Scott case and why was it important?"

Betsy recited from memory. She had a good memory. "The Dred Scott versus Sandford case was the most important slavery-related decision in the United States Supreme Court's history. Dred Scott was a slave who sued his master for his freedom, and the case went all the way to the Supreme Court. The Supreme Court ruled that because Scott was black, he was not a citizen and therefore had no right to sue."

"What was the date?"

Betsy thought. "1852?"

"1857," Barbara said, double-checking. "What else did the Supreme Court decide?"

"Ummm." Betsy twirled a lock of hair. "Oh, oh. Wait." She recited: "The decision also declared the Missouri Compromise of 1820, legislation which restricted slavery in certain territories, unconstitutional."

Barbara ate her sandwich and drank her milk. The sandwich was delicious beyond any expectation for a meatloaf sandwich. The potato chips were oily and salty and she ate every single one. She thought of Mike.

"Mom. You're not paying attention," Betsy said.

"Sorry. What did Abraham Lincoln think about the Dred Scott case?"

"He made a speech called the House Divided speech."

"What else?" Barbara asked, consulting the study guide.

"It set the stage for the historic presidential election of 1860."

It took forty minutes for them to go over all the study questions. Most school nights, ever since Betsy was in second grade, Barbara helped her daughter with her homework, while Rawson watched television or made entries on his spreadsheets. Even if they had guests and she'd rather be with the grown-ups, Barbara would excuse herself.

"I have a blonde joke," Barbara said. Betsy wasn't allowed to tell ethnic jokes. But Barbara didn't see anything wrong with blonde jokes. "One blonde was on one side of the river and there was another blonde on the other side of the river. The first blonde yells to the other blonde, 'How do you get to the other side?' And the other blonde yells back, 'You are on the other side!'"

"Mom! That's terrible. Wait, wait…I have one. How can you tell if a blonde's been using the computer?" Betsy started laughing at her own joke. "There's Wite-Out on the screen."

"That's really terrible."

Barbara kissed Betsy. "Good night, sweetie. Remember to do your face."

Betsy had a peaches-and-cream complexion, but since she'd gotten her period, she had pimples on her forehead and enlarged pores on her nose. Barbara had taken her to the woman she went to for her skin. Betsy thought the facials were great—she liked to be pampered—but she was not scrupulous about daily skin care.

"Where's the Getting-Ready-for-Bed Car Wash when we need it!" Betsy said.

They had a running fantasy about the Getting-Ready-for-Bed Car Wash. You push a button and it gets you ready for bed. There was a deluxe model that hung up your clothes.

"If only. We'd make a fortune. I love you," Barbara said from the doorway.

"I love you, too, Mom."

♦♦♦

Rawson was in the game room in his big leather chair watching a video of *Triumph of the Will*. The forty-five-inch big-screen television and a big couch with a tomato-red slipcover created an island of *Gemütlichkeit* coziness. There was a cabinet full of VHS videos and a CD player. The rest of the game room was virtually unchanged from when Barbara would visit her grandmother. The pool balls were still racked on the green felt of the art deco pool table, as if time had stood still, like in *Sleeping Beauty*. There was the octagonal poker table and the poker chip carousel that Barbara had played with when she was a little girl, stacking the chalky poker chips into the round slots.

The sound was turned up. The rousing martial music of Wagner's "Nibelungen March" filled the room. Ranks of Waffen-SS troops, crack military units as far as the eye could see, goose-stepped in formation. Rawson pressed pause. The image on the television screen was of three immense swastika banners.

"I'm doing my homework. I'm meeting with Chas Hanson tomorrow."

"Oh, for heaven's sake," Barbara said from the doorway. "Do we really want to buy an important collection of hate literature?"

"Yes," Rawson said. "Don't be so narrow-minded, Barb. I want to buy the collection."

"It's tacky, Rawson."

"Why do you always have to argue, Barb? Please sit down."

Barbara sat on the couch. *This is my real life,* she thought, feeling how thin and paltry her emotional life was. Rawson hit the play button. The Wagner swelled and German women—Madonnas with blonde braids—waved handkerchiefs and threw flowers to the parading troops in the narrow medieval streets of Nuremberg. A drum corps of Hitler Youth. The high-spirited horseplay of young soldiers in the tent barracks. Leni Riefenstahl's portrait shots of German faces, all noble, all true believers. The film cut to an interior shot of the Reich Party Conference. Joseph Goebbels, with his pinched methamphetamine-addicted weasel face, took the podium. Rawson clicked off the video.

"There's a book that refutes the claim that Hitler was not a true Aryan. It's not true that Hitler had brown eyes."

"Rawson, please."

"Hitler's eyes photographed brown, but really they were dark blue."

They had a whole life together. They had Betsy. They'd had Palmer Orchards. Bird of Paradise Books was a ton of fun. Lucrative, also. She wished Rawson was dead. The sense of optimism, the gladness of spirit that she had felt earlier evaporated.

"The Germans didn't have to lose the war," he said, leaning forward in his big leather chair, addressing Barbara. His eyes were bloodshot. He drained his glass. "They had the best uniforms. They had the best army. They had the best weapons scientists. If Hitler had stayed out of Russia and left England alone—that was what brought in America—Hitler would have annexed Western Europe permanently and the Third Reich would have lasted. Don't go away. I'm just going to get myself another wee drop o' the pure." Rawson heaved himself up out of the chair.

"Maybe not Scandinavia," he qualified. "Scandinavia might have been problematic."

"Sieg heil," Barbara said.

"Don't make fun of me," Rawson said.

Barbara stayed where she was. *Wee drop o' the pure.* Why didn't he just say he was getting another drink? It was like when he said *Righty-o.* She closed her eyes. She felt completely wrung out. In a perfect world, she would tell Rawson the important thing: she'd choked on a carrot and Mike Brooke had saved her life. How it was the most extraordinary thing. She'd tell Rawson that they needed to talk about their marriage. But it was not a perfect world. Rawson came back with another drink and the bottle of Glenlivet single malt. He settled himself in the big leather chair.

"Why did you say *Sieg heil*?" he asked.

"I was participating in the conversation."

"Don't be sarcastic when I'm telling you something."

"I wasn't being sarcastic."

"Please don't patronize me, Barbara. I saw you roll your eyes."

"I didn't roll my eyes." She hadn't. He was right, though. Mentally, she had rolled her eyes. The Nazi bullshit was incredibly unattractive. Even if—especially if—in Rawson's case, it was mostly a fetish. When they were first married, they role-played that Rawson was an SS officer on leave in Berlin before he was deployed to the Eastern Front and she was Lili Marlene seducing him into deserting his unit. She wore a black leather corset that pushed her breasts up and a garter belt with black stockings and an Iron Cross on a ribbon around her neck. Rawson had a cassette tape of Marlene Dietrich—"Lili Marlene" and "Falling in Love Again." He called the portable tape player in the bedroom a ghetto blaster. For a while, Barbara got into it. It was so naughty. But it was a lot of work, and Rawson started to remind her of the boy in her sixth-grade class who didn't have any friends and drew swastikas on his desk. It had been years since she had indulged him.

"I can't afford to get angry," Rawson said. His too-small mouth twitched. The train had left the station. "You said, *Sieg heil.* Why did you say that?"

"I really don't know. It was just something I said."

"This afternoon you were dismissive of my feelings: you had a meeting, you had to pick up the dry cleaning. Such a busy bee. But I didn't get angry. Now I share something with you, and you make fun of me."

"Rawson, I wasn't making fun of you."

"So why did you say it? It was just something you said? That doesn't make sense. That's crazy." He said this in a tone of controlled reasonableness.

Barbara got up and shut the door. It was too late—too late by years and years—for Betsy not to be exposed to this, but she didn't want her, in her sleep, to hear Rawson whinging on.

"Don't walk away when I'm talking," Rawson said.

Barbara sat down again. "I was closing the door."

"You're not as smart as you think you are, Barb."

"Oh, piffle. I don't think I'm smart."

On and on. Rawson drank Scotch and castigated her. He was irrational. What choice was there but to humor him? Something was wrong with him. His father was a drunkard who put his cigarettes out in his mashed potatoes at the dinner table. It was after midnight and Barbara's eyes kept closing. She'd been up since six.

"Rawson, I'm going to bed now," she said and walked out of the room. When he shouted at her to come back, she pretended she didn't hear him.

There was a fireplace in the bedroom. On the mantel, a crystal vase of acacia—puffy tassels of powdery yellow—gave off a faint, sweet perfume. The purity of the acacia's yellow, the poignancy of the scent, gave her pleasure. She was one of those people who are born with the gift of taking joy in the world, joy in the moment.

The first Christmas they were together, Rawson's present for her was a pair of Ferragamo flats. Dark red and French blue. It was hard for her to find flats that fit, and they fit perfectly. For years, whenever he was being pissy, she reminded herself of the perfect shoes.

He was an odious man, though. It made it worse that he couldn't help it. He couldn't help it and he was never going to change. The only thing to do was to go to sleep. In a day or two—maybe even in the morning—Rawson would be as if it had never happened. She got ready for bed and slipped under the covers. It felt wonderful to be in bed. She was so sleepy. As she drifted into sleep, she thought of Mike Brooke. Faintly, almost subliminally, she could hear Marlene Dietrich singing "Lili Marlene" in German, torchy and sentimental.

Downstairs, Rawson played a Marlene Dietrich CD over and over. He might go up to bed. He might fall asleep in his chair.

It pissed him off. Barbara was his wife. She didn't love him. She treated him with contempt. He was in love with her, but she was a bitch. Why was she such a shit?

That night, Barbara had a dark dream. It was night, and she was standing on the sidewalk at the intersection of a secondary cross street and a four-lane roadway in a residential neighborhood, like in the new developments in Simi Valley and Santa Clarita. There was a raised center median and halogen streetlights. Traffic was sparse. A black Mercedes-Benz was stopped at a stop sign on the cross street, across the four-lane roadway.

The man driving had a thick head of white hair and a deeply tanned hatchet face. He was wearing a tan suit. Barbara had been waiting for him. He wasn't anyone she knew. The sedan's right-turn blinker was on. The man gunned the engine and the big sedan pulled out. He swung wide, past the median. Tires squealing, he made a fast right into the inside lane of the far side of the roadway. Against the flow of traffic.

Barbara screamed, "You're going the wrong way." The big black sedan was already out of sight, speeding into the night. The man was going to cause a horrible head-on crash.

Barbara woke up panicked. It was five in the morning, still dark. She switched on the bedside lamp. Rawson was heavily asleep next to her. She sat up in bed and, for the first time in her life, she recorded a dream, writing in a forest-green moleskin blank book with lined pages and a red grosgrain ribbon sewn in the spine for a bookmark. It had been in the drawer of the night table for three years, ever since Dr. Frierson suggested she keep a dream journal.

That same night, Mike had a dream of the Western Isles—an Arcadia of tender green grass like new grass after the first rain. Birds sang with silver voices, and the light was golden. He held Barbara in his arms and kissed her swan's-down neck.

CHAPTER FOUR

Jitterbug Waltz

THE NEXT AFTERNOON, BARBARA and Betsy went by the Montecito Garage. They were on their way to soccer practice. Barbara usually stayed to watch. She'd never been sporty. When women her age said, "Don't you wish we'd had all the sports that girls have today?" Barbara always thought: *Actually, we had entirely too many sports, as far as I was concerned.* But she liked to watch Betsy nimbly dribbling the ball up the field, then passing it with a well-aimed long pass. Mike was in the service bay looking at the yellow Corvette. The hood was up. Barbara rolled down the car window, and Mike walked over.

The excitement of awakened feelings, the glad optimism was still there. *He is my fated true love*, Barbara thought.

"Working on the Corvette, I see," she said, smiling into his eyes, his soul.

Betsy said, "Rumm rumm," making a car noise.

"You better watch it, hot shot," Mike said to her, leaning his head in the car window.

"What's our timeline?" Barbara asked.

"I ordered parts this morning," he said.

"Mom, we're going to be late," Betsy said.

There were high billows of cloud massed over the mountains and the wind was blowing from the southeast. In other years, it would have meant rain, but this drought year the clouds formed and then blew over the town without any rain falling. Barbara said they had to dash, and Mike said he'd be in touch. He watched the red Volvo as it disappeared around the bend on East Valley Road. He'd saved her life and, in that moment, everything had changed. Neither of them quite understood that, going forward, nothing was of their own volition.

♦♦♦

THAT NIGHT, MIKE HAD dinner with Cissy Benedict, his on-again, off-again girlfriend, at her house. A friend of Mike's—his Fresh Wish Company buddy—had given him some fresh halibut, and Mike brought it over for Cissy to cook. Mike was genuinely fond of Cissy. But he didn't love her. He certainly wasn't going to marry her. They'd been keeping company for two years. She was small and vivid with a tight little body and a *jolie laide* chic; she wore horn-rimmed glasses and *L'Heure Bleue* perfume. She had a hundred-year-old Chinese sleigh bed with chipped red lacquer panels.

Cissy wrote poetry and went to the Vedanta temple, somewhat stagily. She did yoga. For years, she'd taught a popular adult education class: Finding Your Voice as a Poet. She wrote articles for local magazines. She always had a man in her life, although she'd never been married. She had, however, been engaged. Years later, she still spoke of the broken engagement as if it was a betrothal in the Middle Ages. Virtually the same as a marriage.

Cissy's house was a rented bungalow on a hill in Summerland with a view of the ocean and the constant sound of the traffic on 101. Beeswax candles burned in a tarnished silver candelabra, and Ravi Shankar played on the record player. Lots of books. Cissy's house reminded Mike of the houses of his parents' bohemian friends on Mountain Drive above Montecito when he was a boy. After dinner, Cissy wanted to talk about their relationship. This happened periodically. The relationship was never going to be what Cissy wanted. Sometimes Mike felt a little guilty.

"I want us to be a real couple," she said.

"We are a real couple," he said. Barbara was at home with her husband, and he was going through the motions with Cissy.

"We are not. I don't want to just have a good time together and then one day look around and it's too late," Cissy said to Mike, sitar music in the background. "I want a big juicy relationship with a future. Just because you had a tragedy in your life, that's not a reason to close yourself off to commitment forever. It was twenty years ago."

Yes, it is, Mike thought, *it is a reason.* Cissy was oblivious to what she was really saying, how unkind she was.

Mike and Victoria had gotten married when she was twenty-two and he was twenty-four. It was a good marriage—they had the same sense of humor; they had the same ideals. Victoria was the secretary and bookkeeper for the boat chandlery at the harbor. She loved to come to work and see the fishing boats and the pelicans, the piles of purple sea urchins on the jetty in the morning. They named their daughter Ariana. Her nickname was Bootie. When she learned to talk, one of her first words was *beautiful*, but the best she could do was *bootie*. For her, all of creation was beautiful: a swallowtail butterfly, a pile of folded towels, a Cecile Brunner rose, her mother's face. She'd pat Victoria's cheek and say, "Bootie, Mama. Bootie."

When Bootie was twenty-two months old, almost two, they went on a vacation to the Montecito-Sequoia Lodge in Sequoia National Park. The thin, pure air of the Sierras, gray granite outcrops, a little lake ringed by pine trees. It was their first family vacation. They were booked into one of the rustic cabins for a week. Bootie chased the gray squirrels with their fluffy tails. "Querrel. Querrel. Bootie querrel," she said. They went out on the little lake in a rowboat, and Bootie was entranced by the trout swimming in the clear water. The next to the last day, after the buffet lunch in the main building, Mike took the binoculars and went for a birdwatching walk. Victoria said she'd get Bootie down for a nap. Bootie was a reluctant napper—Victoria would lie down with her and the little girl would nurse and drift off.

Mike went a half mile or so—not far—up a trail that led across massive granite outcroppings. A pair of Steller's jays screamed at him and dive-bombed him. He turned back, looking forward to telling Bootie about the jays. When he got back to the cabin, Victoria was fast asleep and Bootie was gone. Twenty people joined in the search. Mike was the one who found her body. She'd wandered down to the dock and fallen in the lake. He and Victoria drove back to Santa Barbara with Victoria holding her dead child, her breasts swollen with milk.

It was the end of the marriage.

"I don't think we should see each other anymore," Cissy said, interrupting Mike's thoughts.

Mike said, "You don't think you could wait to break up with me until after our Bonneville Flats weekend?"

The racing team was taking the Lakester out to Bonneville Flats for a trial run, and Mike had invited Cissy to come along. They had a motel reservation at the Nugget Hotel and Casino in Wendover, Nevada, across the Utah border from Bonneville Flats.

"Gee, race cars. Can't wait," Cissy said. She was dismissive of Mike's interest in cars. She didn't get who he was. He was a car guy. A successful car guy. He owned the Montecito Garage, and the Lakester racing team was the real deal.

"Mike. I want to take a break," she said.

"If that's what you want," he said.

♦♦♦

A FEW DAYS LATER, Barbara called Mike at the garage.

"Montecito Lunatic Asylum," Mike answered. "This is the Head Lunatic speaking."

"Head Lunatic?" Barbara said. "Honestly!"

"You caught me."

"Ron Gamberini called," Barbara said. Ron was the owner of the turquoise 1957 Bel Air with *Veni Vide Vici* on the dash. "He's stoked about the car show. His very words. He said he's bringing the Bel Air to you for a tune-up."

"I'll have it purring like a kitten," Mike said. "Barbara, how are you?"

"I'm fine. I just wanted to hear your voice, really. I have to dash."

"Keep in touch," he said.

After they hung up, they both felt an understanding had been confirmed. It was in the hands of Fate.

♦♦♦

A FEW DAYS AFTER that, Mike got a postcard from Cissy. She liked to send notes, postcards, long letters, newspaper clippings, to the men in her life. In later years, she'd send emails and text messages and have a blog. The postcard was a Sierra Club photograph of a cove on Santa Cruz Island—they'd been talking about signing up for a university extension field trip to Santa Cruz Island. On the back, she'd written: *Better a diamond with a flaw than a pebble without.* Mike tacked the postcard up on the corkboard in the garage office and waited for her to call. They'd take a break, and then Cissy would decide they should reconcile.

The next day she called.

"I miss you," she said. "Can we stop taking a break? Will you buy me a drink?"

"Sure. I'll buy you a drink. How about the bar at the Miramar?"

The Miramar was the cottage beach hotel in Montecito. The beach at the Miramar was where he'd taken Barbara and her sister grunion hunting.

"Perfect," Cissy said.

Mike arrived first and got a table by the window. It was a Saturday night, but there were not very many people. Mostly people up from LA who were staying at the hotel, a few local serious drinkers at the bar. The days when young married couples hired a babysitter and closed the bar at the Miramar on Saturday nights were in the past, although the piano player was the same piano player. A Montecito institution. There was a black-and-white publicity photo of him on an easel in the lobby. The photo was at least fifteen years old. Cissy was late, as she so often was. Mike ordered a double bourbon and water.

He watched the door and sipped his drink and thought about Barbara. They'd talked again on the telephone. He had called her at Bird of Paradise Books to give her another name for her list. A short conversation. Before they rang off, she said, "Thank you for saving my life." And he said, "We both know what's happening."

Mike could see the sidewalk in front of the hotel through a gap between the rattan blinds. The Miramar was the Montecito stop for the Santa Barbara Airbus van. There was a little cluster of people on the sidewalk in front of the hotel entrance. The ocean fog was drifting in, and the streetlights on Jamison Lane had halos. The scene was like a Hopper painting. The piano player was playing "Sweet Caroline" when Cissy walked in. She was wearing tight black jeans with a Chinese brocade jacket and red shoes. Mike waved and she joined him. What did she want to drink? She vacillated. Maybe a glass of red wine? Maybe a screwdriver? She decided she wanted a tequila sunrise, and Mike got her a tequila sunrise at the bar.

"Here's to crime," he said.

"Cheers," she said. A votive candle burned in an amber hobnail glass cylinder on the red tablecloth. "You're looking very handsome."

"You're looking very fetching yourself," Mike said. Her *L'Heure Bleue* perfume evoked the voluptuous melancholy of *la belle époque*. He thought of the sleigh bed with the red lacquer panels.

"This isn't an ultimatum," she said.

"That's good. No ultimatums."

"Mike, I want to have children. I'm thirty-seven. I want to get married."

"Cissy, I had a vasectomy."

"You can have it undone. We could use a sperm donor."

She has no idea who I am, Mike thought.

The piano player started playing "Jitterbug Waltz," slow and dreamy, the way the Herbie Hancock Trio played it, and an old couple came out on the little dance floor and started to waltz. She had a dowager's hump; he was bent over. They danced together in perfect rhythm.

It was then that Mike had a vision. Not an actual vision, but something he really saw that was like a vision. Through the gap in the rattan blind, he saw Barbara. The Airbus van to LAX was boarding. People were saying their goodbyes. Barbara was talking to her husband. She was wearing gray slacks and a cherry-red sweater. Rawson was wearing a track suit, a weekender duffel bag over his shoulder, his leather suitcase on the sidewalk. He had the demeanor of a man who was confident that he was correctly dressed for a night flight to New York. It looked like a married-couple conversation. Last-minute instructions, reminders.

Given the circumstances of her life and of Mike's life, to see Barbara thusly was not an extraordinary coincidence. Barbara was there because Rawson and Ted were taking the red-eye to New York on book business. Rawson liked to fly at night—the thrum of the engine, the lights of farms and towns far below in the velvet dark. Bird of Paradise Books had a table at an antiquarian book fair at the Armory, and Rawson and Ted had a breakfast meeting at the Plaza with a couple who were interested in some of the ephemera from the hate literature collection, which Bird of Paradise had not yet officially acquired, but Rawson was not going to be easily discouraged by Barbara and Ted. Barbara had given Rawson a ride to the Miramar. In situations like this, where he would be spared inconvenience, Rawson was perfectly fine if Barbara was out after dark by herself.

Mike watched Barbara and Rawson kiss goodbye, a peck on the lips. Kiss kiss. Barbara admonished him about something. Mike couldn't hear what she said. Rawson made some objection, and Barbara tapped him affectionately on the nose. Cissy had digressed into a tale of infighting at the adult education center.

"I told you that the man who coordinates the adult ed program asked me if I would teach a class on the *Upanishads*?"

"What?" Mike was distracted.

"You don't remember at all. I was really excited about it. I submitted a syllabus. Mike, I really worked hard on it. Now some stupid woman with a PhD—she's an adjunct at the university—has taken my class. I was counting on that money," she said sadly.

"Sweetheart," Mike glanced at Cissy, then looked back at the tableau outside the window. "If you need a loan, I'm glad to help." He helped her with money sometimes. It was understood that the loans were gifts. Men often bailed her out. She saw it as her karma.

Rawson was the last passenger to board the van, as Ted looked impatiently out the window and Barbara stood on the sidewalk. The driver got in and closed the doors, and the van pulled away in the direction of the on-ramp to Highway 101. Barbara waited until the taillights disappeared, then walked over to her station wagon, got in, and drove off. Watching her, Mike was filled with yearning, with love; he wanted to hold Barbara in his arms. She was married. He didn't do married women. No love triangles. Someone always gets hurt. Everyone always gets hurt. He'd been involved with a woman who was married and wasn't going to leave her husband. He was jealous all the time.

"Maybe we don't have a future," Cissy said in a sad little voice.

She wanted Mike to contradict her. He couldn't do it. He felt, in a way he hadn't before, that his relationship with Cissy was ignoble.

The piano player was taking a break, having a drink at the bar. Two tipsy middle-aged women sat down at the grand piano and started to play "Heart and Soul." Mike remembered Barbara and her sister playing "Heart and Soul" at her grandmother's house, side by side on the piano bench. Barbara had the treble.

"Cissy," he said gently. He knew he had to be honest. "You're right—we don't have a future. I don't want to marry you."

"I thought we were trying to work it out. I don't want it to be over. All the men I've ever been with have broken up with me."

"I'm not the person you want. This isn't good for you." *For me, either*, he thought.

"I feel like I'm dying," she said.

"We have some good memories," Mike said. He felt bad. He liked Cissy. "I'll always be your friend."

The piano player sat down at the piano and started playing "Misty."

Cissy stood up. "Go fuck yourself," she said, loud enough so heads turned. A man at the next table caught Mike's eye, shrugged with a smile. *Women!* "Take your stupid house key," she said, slamming the key down on the table. She marched out.

Mike let her go. She'd had one drink. She was okay to drive. He had another bourbon and water and left. Driving up San Ysidro Road, past Montecito Union Elementary School with its terraced lawns and red tile roofs shadowy in the night, he had a buzz on. He wondered what Barbara had said to Rawson when she tapped him affectionately on the nose.

CHAPTER FIVE

We Work Well Together

DOWN BY THE OCEAN it was foggy, but Orion shone cold and bright in the night sky overhead at the Montecito Garage. Mike's house was behind the garage. The house was originally an artist's studio on a sprawling property that adjoined the garage. After Bootie drowned and his marriage ended, Mike sold the house in town where they had been so happy and persuaded the owner of the property to sell him the studio and a half acre of land. He added a very small kitchen, like a ship's galley, in a corner of the big main studio, and up three steps, there was an addition with a bedroom and a bathroom.

He took a shower, made a ham sandwich, got himself a beer, and put on a Fats Domino record—"Blueberry Hill." It was still early. He felt good. He'd done the right thing. He sat on the purple velvet couch that he'd bought at an estate sale and wondered if he was going to call Barbara, now that he knew Rawson was out of town. He thought of the strangeness and sadness and beauty of life.

When the doorbell rang, he thought it was Cissy. This had happened before. They'd quarreled—it was over—then she showed up crying, wanting to talk, they ended up in bed, and they kept seeing each other. Because, if he was honest, it hadn't mattered. Now it did. He considered not answering the door. It would put the period on *It's Over.* But it was a crummy thing to do. Clearly, he was at home. The lights were on. She would be able to hear Fats Domino. His car, a 1978 Toyota Corolla with 220,000 miles on it, was outside the front door. His work truck, a 1988 F-150 Ford, was parked by the metal shed.

He got up and took the needle arm off the record. Braced to take a firm line with Cissy, he switched on the outside light and opened the door. He was in his stocking feet, dressed in worn corduroy jeans and a white T-shirt. His hair was still damp from the shower. With his beautiful straight nose and sapphire-blue eyes, streaks of gray in his dark brown hair, he was a handsome cat.

It wasn't Cissy. Barbara was standing on the porch. Mike's face softened. She smiled back at him, a confiding smile. She had beautiful skin, the fine lines around her eyes aroused tenderness. She smelled of Elizabeth Arden Blue Grass.

"Are you at home to visitors?" she said. She held a paper bag with the Bird of Paradise Books logo—a stylized drawing of a bird of paradise flower—printed on the white paper in dark red. "I promise I won't stay long."

"Jesus, this is a surprise. Come on in." He stood back and ushered her in the door.

She'd been in Mike's house before, during the Palmer Orchards period. The high-ceilinged room had clerestory windows. The Mission furniture, the worn oriental rugs on a concrete slab floor that was painted teal blue, the glass-front bookcases filled with dog-eared paperbacks and hardcover books. There was a twenty-six-inch console television and a long oak refectory table where Mike did his paperwork, piled with stacks of papers and invoices and automotive magazines.

"I brought you a present," she said.

He took the paper bag ceremoniously.

"Would you like something to drink?" he offered. It seemed both like magic and entirely natural for Barbara to be there. "A glass of wine? A beer? Coffee or tea? I have fizzy water."

"A glass of water would be perfect," she said.

"Ice?" *I don't even know if she likes ice in her water,* he thought.

"No ice."

Barbara sat on the velvet couch. There was a round mid-century modern coffee table with a glass top. She studied the objects on the coffee table: a white restaurant china plate (the plate the ham sandwich had been on), an almost-empty Dos Equis bottle, a pile of *New Yorkers*, a hardcover copy of *Chuck Yeager's* autobiography, face down and opened in the middle, next to a television remote, a racing car Christmas ornament—and now the bag with the Bird of Paradise logo. *He's a bachelor,* Barbara thought. It was true. He'd been a bachelor for seventeen years. None of the women in his life had made an impression on his home. Mike came back with two Picardie glass tumblers of water. He sat opposite Barbara in a Mission oak chair with wide wood arms.

"Open your present," she said. Expectantly she watched Mike take his present out of the shopping bag. The gift wrapping was splendid—orange and red bird of paradise flowers on a black background, tied with extravagant curls of gold ribbon. An unsealed envelope addressed to Mike was stuck under the ribbon.

"I wonder what it is," he joked. It was clearly a book.

The gift wrapping was emblematic of Barbara's solution to the problem of how the bookstore could make money. She hadn't liked it that Palmer Orchards was essentially a hobby. A rare bookstore with a limited clientele of serious book collectors would be another hobby business. How to expand the customer base? Barbara started right away to talk up Bird of Paradise Books to people in her social circle—people who could afford modern first editions or rare art books but had never considered them as unique gifts. Or the investment value of an interesting collection. Barbara did things like donate a selection of signed first editions to the Crane silent auction. Word spread. The effort Barbara put into remodeling the adobe paid off. The bookstore became a place where you could bring your friends from out of town. People started to drive up from LA to buy books at Bird of Paradise Books and then go out to lunch on Coast Village Road. Ted was especially good at hand-selling volumes of Californiana. Rawson could be problematic, but everyone knew he was a character.

At no point did Bird of Paradise Books advertise, although there was an article in the *Santa Barbara Independent*, a weekly newspaper with a large circulation.

When Barbara first proposed that they offer complimentary gift wrapping, Rawson said, “That’s stupid. You’re telling me that your mother’s friends are going to buy five thousand dollar signed first editions because we have gift wrapping?”

Hardly the point. Barbara ignored him and bought rolls of the sumptuous wrapping paper. The customer could pick from three different spools of ribbon: gold leaf, orange satin, or black grosgrain.

Mike set aside the card and slid the gold ribbon off, unfastened the wrapping paper. The book was a first edition of *The Great Impersonation* by E. Phillips Oppenheim, its dust jacket in pristine condition under a clear plastic slip-on book cover. The jacket illustration depicted two men—Sir Evarad Dominey, disgraced and dissipated English aristocrat, and the disciplined and patriotic Baron Leopold von Ragastein—at their fateful chance meeting in darkest Africa. The same summer that Mike took Barbara and her sister grunion hunting, he and a friend were into *The Great Impersonation*. Mike had found a copy at his grandparents’ beach house.

Mike examined the book. “This is very cool.”

“We just got it in.”

“My dear sir, I am not the Baron von Ragastein. I am Evarad Dominey,” Mike said in an upper-crust British accent.

“It was either *The Great Impersonation* or *Zip Saunders, King of the Speedway*,” she said.

“This is much better,” Mike said.

“Read the card.”

The card was from a rack of cards at Bird of Paradise, also Barbara’s idea. It was a reproduction of an Oak Group *plein air* painting of an oak grove.

He read the inscription out loud: “You saved my life! Thank you, Barb Lloyd.”

"Mike, it's the most amazing thing that ever happened to me." She recalled the peaceful sensation of no oxygen, the world turning dark, and then Mike's arms around her, the jerk of his fists between her breasts. The wondrous clarity of every word they spoke after she was restored to life.

"It was pretty amazing to watch," he said. "It was one of those times when you think: I better do something fast—and I better not screw up."

"Mike, that's not what I mean."

"I know, sweetheart. We both know what's happening."

There was the feeling that it was raining outside, that it had been raining for days, although it hadn't rained in over a year. Gibraltar Reservoir was bone dry, nothing but cracked mud on the bottom, and in the town of Santa Barbara, tall pine trees were turning yellow and dying. The water table was below their deepest roots. Across the coffee table, they talked, a conversation from the heart. The only light in the room came from a floor lamp with art deco swans and a parchment shade.

"I know about your little girl drowning and that your marriage broke up," Barbara said. "But how do you feel now?"

"I'll tell you," he said. Cissy had never once asked him how he felt. "Weeks, months go by when I don't think about it. It's a story from my past. Then I remember the little person Bootie was, and it still makes me cry."

"Oh, Mike. If anything happened to Betsy, I'd… I don't know… I'd die."

"I remember it as a good marriage. It broke my heart when Victoria left. But we couldn't comfort each other. We couldn't forgive each other.

"Victoria wanted to get pregnant again right away. She didn't want to use birth control; she had the idea that Bootie would come back somehow in the new baby. I did not want another child. Not then and probably never. It wasn't something to negotiate or compromise on. But I wanted to make love—it was a solace. She told me she was taking birth control pills, but she wasn't. She got pregnant and had a miscarriage. All she wanted was to get pregnant again. I got a vasectomy without telling her first. I came home and told her what I'd done. That was the end of the marriage. She went home to Marin and married a lawyer, someone she already knew, and was pregnant at their wedding. They have three kids."

Barbara and Mike were both quiet.

"I was at the Miramar tonight," Mike said. "I saw you put Rawson on the Airbus."

"What were you doing at the Miramar?"

"I met Cissy for a drink. She called me."

Barbara knew that Mike and Cissy were an on-again, off-again item. She and Cissy weren't friends, but they knew the same people. They saw each other at parties, and Cissy had written an article about Palmer Orchards for *Santa Barbara Magazine*.

"Where is Cissy now?" she asked.

"I don't know. At home, probably. We broke up. I broke it off."

"Are you sad?"

"No," he said. "It should have ended sooner. I was fine with the Eastern religion and the poetic pretensions. She wasn't fine with who I was. It really irked her that I have cable TV and watch NASCAR and NBA basketball. The bad thing was, I didn't care."

Barbara said, "It's not the same, but in a way it is. Rawson's fixation that I have to be home before the sun sets? It's only the tip of the iceberg. In a way I don't care. But every day, I feel more contempt."

Other than with her sister, this was the most candid Barbara had ever been about Rawson. The most she ever said to other people was, "Better to stay together and fight." As if they were a normal couple.

Mike said, "What did you say to Rawson right before he got on the van? When you tapped him on the nose? You looked so married. I was jealous."

"I was telling him that I was going straight home and take a hot bath and go to bed, so if he called from LAX and he got the machine, I hadn't been kidnapped."

"An alibi," Mike said in an *ah-ha* voice.

"So shoot me," she said. "I wanted to see you. Betsy's at a slumber party."

They were maybe eight feet apart, the round coffee table between them, Barbara leaning forward on the velvet couch, Mike in the Mission armchair. They felt the power of human love to transcend the isolation that is the normal human condition, to break down the barriers between two souls, so there is a center of joy and communion. The particularity of such a love. The sexual attraction was undeniable, but what was happening between them was irresistible in a way that was not carnal.

Mike said, "I want a marriage that a shared tragedy doesn't turn you into strangers."

Barbara said, "I want to be a beloved companion, not a mental health nurse."

"Why don't you divorce him?" he asked. "Do you love him?"

"He had a grisly childhood. He went to six different elementary schools. They kept having to move because his mother kept sleeping with the neighbors. They rented houses in places like Darien and Brentwood."

Mike laughed. "You're kidding."

"It was very traumatic for him," Barbara said, trying not to laugh herself.

She told him that five or six years earlier she'd seen a therapist. She was trying to understand why she didn't divorce Rawson. Dr. Frierson's office was in a suite of offices with a shared waiting room and receptionist on Oak Park Lane near the Cottage Hospital. Danish modern chairs and a Noguchi lamp. Dr. Frierson was in his forties and wore a corduroy jacket and knit tie.

"He had a framed reproduction of a Bonnard, a bowl of plums, on the wall in his office. My aunt has a real Bonnard in her dining room. A different one. He had no idea of my life. I always felt as if I'd gone deaf when I talked to him."

"Did you have any insights?" Mike asked. "A hell of a lot of people wonder why you stay married to Rawson."

"In a way," she said. "I saw Dr. Frierson three or four times, and then I had a moment of truth: it didn't matter why I didn't divorce Rawson. I wasn't going to. Not until something happened. Not until it was out of my hands. Dr. Frierson said we should explore the element of magical thinking in that statement. What did I think would happen? I said I had no idea and didn't make another appointment."

"Now something has happened," Mike said.

He stood up and held out his hand. Barbara looked up at him, her lips parted. Through the high windows, a silver gibbous moon shone in the night sky. There were clean sheets on the bed. At that moment, the doorbell rang. They hadn't heard a car drive up. Ding-dong. Ding-dong. Then bang bang bang on the door.

"Mike!"—it was Cissy's voice, plaintive, urgent. "It's Cissy."

"God dammit," Mike said. "I'm not going to let her in."

"Mike, you have to open the door," Barbara said, keeping her voice down. "Shall I leave?"

Mike shook his head. *No. Stay*. Their eyes met, and they shrugged their shoulders. *What can you do?*

He opened the door, and Cissy came in in a rush. "Please, can I just talk to you," she implored of Mike. At first, it didn't register that Barbara was there.

"Sure," he said. There was no warmth in his voice.

"Hello, Cissy," Barbara said. She was good at carrying off an awkward situation. Lots of practice with Rawson.

"What are you doing here?" Cissy asked, perplexed. She wasn't suspicious; it just didn't make sense.

"I stopped by to give Mike a present," Barbara said, indicating the copy of *The Great Impersonation* on the coffee table, the Bird of Paradise gift wrapping, the swirls of gold ribbon. "He's helping with the *Concours d'Elegance*. We're having a fifties classics section. Come sit down."

But Cissy remained standing. Swaying a little, her hands clasped in front of her, without preamble, stopping to remember a word a couple times, she declaimed a Rilke poem. It was a bizarre thing to do.

Again and again, however we know the landscape of love
and the little churchyard there, with its sorrowing names,
and the frighteningly silent abyss into which the others fall:
again and again the two of us walk out together
under the ancient trees, lie down again and again
among the flowers, face to face with the sky.

Mike had once been moved by it. Or at least, he'd taken her to bed. Now he was embarrassed for her. He didn't want her to suffer, but he was detached from the spectacle.

"That's a beautiful poem," Barbara said.

"I don't know what to do," Cissy said, starting to cry. "I can't stand it."

"Please sit down," Mike said. He wished she would leave.

"I don't want to sit down." She stood there sobbing, her face screwed up, her breath coming in gasps.

Every time Mike tried to get her to sit down, she shook his hand off and went into a fresh paroxysm of tears. "I loved him. We were going to get married."

She was sobbing too hard to hear distinctly what she was saying. Even so, Barbara and Mike both knew she was talking about her famous broken engagement.

"I always get the shitty end of the stick," she wailed, her breath coming in gasps. "Why are you here?" she asked again of Barbara.

"I brought Mike a present," Barbara said again.

Cissy was hysterical. "He said he didn't love me. He said I got on his nerves."

Barbara had met the fiancé at a Christmas party at a Queen Anne house across from the Mission. Over the mantel there was an oil painting of a clipper ship under full sail with billowing white sails. Cissy showed everyone her diamond engagement ring, and he kept saying, "I told Cissy, let's elope." Every time he said it, Cissy playfully punched him on the arm and said, "I'm not going to Las Vegas and get married in an Elvis chapel."

At the Christmas party, the fiancé told people that he taught writing at Stanford. A novelist who had recently been a visiting professor at Stanford made polite conversation about the Wallace Stegner writing fellowships, and it was clear to all that the fiancé had never heard of Wallace Stegner. The fiancé also told people he was a screenwriter and pontificated about the dog-eat-dog world of Hollywood to a man who was the producer of a popular network crime drama. The producer had trouble keeping a straight face. After the party, people were asking each other: Doesn't Cissy know he's a bullshitter?

Soon after, the fiancé broke off the engagement and left town.

This was Cissy's tragedy. The broken engagement.

Cissy looked about in despair. She addressed Mike: "Now you broke up with me."

"It wasn't meant to be," he said.

"I can't stand it." This was a howl of misery. "Let me stay, Mike. I'm too sad."

Barbara stood up decisively. She handed Cissy a Kleenex.

"Cissy, let's get you home. You should be in bed." This was the Barbara who organized the 1950s classics section in the *Concours d'Elegance*, who was head room mother at Crane Country Day for two years in a row, who was secretly and efficiently poisoning the eucalyptus tree that blocked her view of Montecito Peak. Good organizational skills. The same skills required to manage Rawson came in handy. The part of Barbara that was capable of decisive action in her own self-interest came into play. Mike was taken off guard. He gave Barbara a *What's this?* look.

"How should we do this?" she said to Mike. "Why don't you drive Cissy's car—with Cissy in it—and I'll follow you and give you a ride back."

"We could do that," Mike agreed. He was impressed. Barbara was a force of nature and butter wouldn't melt in her mouth.

"Cissy, do you still live in the same place in Summerland?" Barbara said.

"Yes," Cissy said. Sullenly? Meekly? She was relieved, perhaps.

♦♦♦

On East Valley Road, the eucalyptus trees had striped trunks like storybook trees, gleaming ghostly white in the headlights. Mike was in the lead, driving Cissy's red VW Bug, Cissy in the passenger seat. She had pulled herself together, somewhat. She talked feverishly to Mike about an article tentatively titled "Old Mexican Families in Santa Barbara" that she was writing for the *Santa Barbara Independent*. Mike could see the headlights of Barbara's Volvo in the rearview mirror. The two cars drove past the entrance to Barbara's house, past the stone gateposts with the pineapple finials.

The fog was thick on Sheffield Drive, the steep winding road over the hill between Montecito and Summerland. Barbara lost sight of the taillights of the VW. She felt as if she was driving into another world, as if she were suspended above her own life, as if she might drive off into the void, as she steered carefully. Over the hill, the fog cleared to swirls of mist. Cissy's bungalow was on one of the steep little streets leading down to Highway 101. Barbara parked at the curb on the steep little street; Mike had already pulled into the driveway. Barbara watched him walk Cissy to her door, watched him unlock the front door with his key. Cissy put her arms around him, buried her head in his chest. Barbara stopped watching. She looked at the house across the street, a gingerbread Victorian dating from when Summerland was a spiritualist community. A black cat sat regally on the porch.

Mike said to Cissy, "I can't stay. I'm sorry."

"Please tuck me into bed?" She knew that Barbara was out front in the Volvo.

"Come on, Cissy. Let go of me."

"Goodbye," she said forlornly, stepping back.

"Cissy, I wish you well." He handed her his key to her house. She watched him go back down the front walk and get in the Volvo, then she shut the door. Cissy was not very observant about other people's emotions. It still didn't occur to her that Mike might be involved with Barbara. So rich—and so square. That was what Cissy had said about Barbara on more than one occasion.

"Mission accomplished," Mike said, as he settled into the passenger seat. "That was very smart of you."

"It seemed like the best way to handle it," Barbara said as she started the car. "That really was a beautiful poem. 'Again and again, however, we know the landscape of love.'"

"She recites it for all her boyfriends," Mike said.

"What were you thinking when Cissy was going on about her broken engagement?" Barbara asked.

"Probably the same thing you were. You know what happened?"

"You mean Kip Voorhees paid him off?"

"Yep."

Kip Voorhees, the television producer who was at the Christmas party, was an old boyfriend of Cissy's. He helped her with money sometimes. She'd call him, and he'd leave the cash in an envelope in his mailbox. He did some digging and discovered that the fiancé was not just a bullshitter. He was a con man. He had outstanding warrants for fraud and grand larceny in three states under different names. Kip gave the fiancé ten thousand dollars to break off the engagement and leave town. In return for which, Kip wouldn't alert the authorities. Part of the deal was that the fiancé let Cissy down gently. This he had not done, but the important thing was that he was out of the picture.

On the drive back to the Montecito Garage, the closeness between Barbara and Mike was beyond the erotic. They were friends of the heart. As Barbara steered carefully down the steep curves of Sheffield Drive, through the dense fog, cypress trees looming out of the whiteness, she felt safe in the richness, the possibility, the depth of her feelings for Mike. Mike apologized for Cissy's showing up, for the awkward scene.

"She was upset. She was performing her sorrow," Barbara said. "She really is carrying a torch for that awful fiancé."

She kept her eyes on the road. They came around the curve at Park Lane—her driveway with its stone gateposts topped with pineapple finials was on the left. They both knew no one was home. Neither suggested that they take advantage of the empty house. It was beneath them. Six or seven minutes later, they arrived at the Montecito Garage. Barbara pulled around to the back by Mike's house, out of sight of anyone driving past on East Valley Road, and switched off the ignition. Mike unfastened his seat belt and leaned over to kiss her, brushing his arm against her breasts. Her breasts were soft under her sweater; he felt the lace of her bra. He had a hard-on. It was only ten thirty.

Barbara pushed him away, gently. "I don't want to have an affair. What's going to happen?"

"I know what should happen," he said. "You should get a divorce and we should get married."

"Is this real?"

"It's real," he said, stroking her hair. "There's a name for it. A *coup de foudre*." He knew how to pronounce *coup de foudre*. They were constrained by the console between the driver's seat and the passenger seat.

Mike told her the story of how his grandmother and grandfather got together, his father's parents. They'd known each other socially, but they weren't attracted. Just like Mike and Barbara. Then, when they were both married to other people, they saw each other in a restaurant in Paris, and they knew in an instant they belonged together. That is a *coup de foudre*. Struck by lightning. They both got divorces, and then they married each other and lived happily ever after.

"This is the grandmother who had three presidents at her wedding?" Barbara asked.

"Her first wedding."

"Did they really live happily ever after?"

"Happier than most couples," Mike said. "It was a little rough on the children."

He touched her cheek tenderly and got out of the car. The headlights from a car passing on East Valley Road cast a beam of light on the pyracantha bushes behind the metal building that housed the Lakester.

"Good night, sweetheart," he said, leaning into the car, one hand on the door. The moonlight made dark shadows.

"We have a lot to think about."

"Get the Corvette running," Barbara said.

"We'll take it on a test drive."

CHAPTER SIX

Paradise Store

THE SECOND DAY IN New York, Rawson turned against Ted. Sooner or later, this happened with almost everyone he came in contact with—although not always permanently. They were in the coffee shop at the Midtown Hilton having breakfast. Rawson was reading *The Wall Street Journal*. There was an article about a hedge fund manager who had been indicted for lying to investors about his fund's investment performance. The photograph accompanying the article was of an overweight man with thatchy graying hair. Rawson showed the article to Ted.

"He's one of my fraternity brothers. Lived across the hall," Rawson said. "He was a real wild man. He managed the rugby team."

"UCSB had a rugby team?" Ted said. He was eating a Denver omelet and reviewing the day's schedule, which he kept in a small spiral notebook, and not paying attention. A box of books that they'd shipped was missing. What to do?

"It was a club team, okay?"

"Show me who your friends are, and I'll tell you who you are," Ted said. It was an absentminded jest.

Rawson slammed down the newspaper and said, "Show me who your friends are, and I'll tell you who you are? What's that supposed to mean? That's crazy. Who my friends are? You're saying I'm a crook? Don't patronize me, Ted."

The people in the next booth looked at them.

No amount of abject backpedaling, apologies, or explanations on the part of Ted made a difference. The downward spiral of Rawson's sense of grievance had to run its course. This was real to Rawson. Ted was the enemy. Rawson called Barbara three or four times a day to complain. As Barbara told Ted, when he called her, "If it wasn't that, it would have been something else. You've seen him turn on people."

Ted said, "Yes, but not when this trip is super important for Bird of Paradise and he's insulting people we want to do business with. This book fair at the Armory is important."

"Just get through it. Don't quit. Please," Barbara said. Not only did they need Ted to manage the bookstore—what was she going to say to his aunt if he quit?

While Rawson was in New York, Barbara and Mike did not see each other again after that first night. Nor did they talk to each other on the telephone. Barbara thought about Mike all the time. And Mike thought about her. Both felt on the brink of a tectonic change. But to see each other while her husband was out of town—even to talk on the phone—was not what either of them wanted. For them, the irresistible temptation was to make a life together. Not to sneak around.

Rawson and Ted got back on Sunday night. Rawson was still aggrieved. The next morning, Barbara took Betsy to school and then went back home and drove in to the bookstore with Rawson. When they drove past the Montecito Garage, Mike was outside. Rawson, at the wheel of the Lincoln Town Car, didn't notice him. He was still fixated on what he saw as Ted's attack on his honor.

"We need to fire Ted. He's useless," he ranted.

Barbara did see Mike. She waved a little wave through the window—just her hand back and forth, as the car swept past. She looked as if she was being kidnapped. He waved back at her, and her heart soared at the sight of him. The sight of the beloved.

"Ted's good with the catalogs. He's really good with the customers," she said to Rawson. "Can we get anyone better? That's the question."

When Barbara and Rawson arrived at the bookstore, Ted,

invariably punctual, had already opened. He was wearing a button-down shirt with no tie and a tweed jacket, and he had a small gold hoop earring in his right earlobe.

Rawson was pissy to him. "You do know the hate literature acquisition is still 'pending'?" He liked saying "hate literature."

Ted's jaw clenched. Barbara, standing behind Rawson, clasped her hands in supplication and mouthed, "Don't quit."

Ted took a deep breath. "I'm going to work at home this morning," he said.

"What are you working on?" Rawson demanded.

Ted said he was working up a spy literature catalog. He wanted to feature *The Riddle of the Sands*, the first spy novel in English, which he'd picked up at a good price in New York. He also planned to hype *The Great Impersonation*. Barbara said she'd taken *The Great Impersonation* to give to someone. Ted said he'd take it off the list. Rawson was incurious as to whom she'd given *The Great Impersonation*.

Reality had no place in Rawson's possessiveness. Over the years, he had many times accused Barbara of being unfaithful—his accusations always unfounded, always with a man whom Barbara would never in a million years have considered. Or who would never have considered Barbara. The only time he physically threatened Barbara was after she danced a sedate cha-cha-cha at the Valley Club with Howie Putnam, a popular man about town who was openly homosexual. After brooding a week, Rawson stood in front of her in the upstairs hall and told her that he wouldn't let her pass until she admitted that she was screwing Howie.

Barbara looked Rawson in the eye and said in a voice that meant business, "I will press charges."

Rawson never tried anything like that again.

"I'll be in at one," Ted said and left with a shopping bag full of books.

Rawson went into the Bird of Paradise office and started composing a letter on the computer to the indicted hedge fund manager, expressing solidarity with a fraternity brother. He had his home address on an Excel sheet. The office was the inner sanctum where favored customers and potential customers were offered refreshment and made privy to new acquisitions. Signed first editions of *The Great Gatsby* and *The Sun Also Rises* were displayed in a walnut bookcase.

Barbara occupied herself with tidying and restocking the Oak Group cards on the card rack in the main room. Originally the Oak Group cards had been in the Californiana room, but Barbara had decided they would sell better in the main room. Which they did. The walls of the main room were lined with bookcases, and three large tables had books displayed face-up. Dark burgundy wall-to-wall carpet covered the refinished hardwood floors. A brass shopkeeper's bell was attached to the paneled main door. When it rang, Barbara looked up.

Mike was in the doorway.

It was a moment before Barbara could speak. Then, in a glad voice, she said, "Hello." She was wearing a pink T-shirt with the Bird of Paradise logo, a Liberty scarf around her honey blonde hair.

"I've got the Corvette running," Mike said, smiling at her. He was looking sharp. Hawaiian shirt, tan cords, huarache sandals.

Neither of them would have predicted how very strange it was to see each other in this bastion of Barbara's life with her husband. They felt shy.

The phone rang in the office. Rawson picked up and could be heard plainly. "Bird of Paradise Books, this is Rawson." He covered the receiver and called to Barbara, "It's Chas Hanson. I'm getting this straightened out."

"Good for you!" Barbara called back.

Mike said, "Should I go? I was going to ask if you want to go for a test drive."

She said, "No, no, stay. I'll tell you about it later."

She picked up a copy of Gordon Forbes's *Too Near the Sun*, a 1955 roman à clef set in Santa Barbara, thinly disgused as the fictional San Felipe.

"It belonged to Owen Cathcart," she said, handing it to Mike.

"I remember him. The riding teacher."

"Arguably still the only real Santa Barbara book," Barbara said.

Mike opened the book and read aloud: "Property of Owen Cathcart. Who is ashamed at once having been a friend of the Author."

"He's penciled in the real names of the characters in the margins. Mrs. Homer Gibson is Mrs. Tom Storke. Homer Junior is Charlie Storke. The psychiatrist Sebrof is Dick Lambert."

"My parents had a copy," Mike said, leafing through it. "My mother said there was such a stink he had to move to Vienna."

Their stilted conversation was against the backdrop of Rawson's loud, aggrieved voice: "What the hell. I have buyers. I'll take you to court. Don't tell me nothing was signed. We had an agreement." A pause. He slammed down the receiver and stalked into the main room.

"Asshole." Then he saw Mike. He always wanted Mike to think he was cool. Because Mike had never taken Rawson seriously as a person, and over time had come to feel disdain for him, it was easy for him to jolly Rawson along. Ironically, Rawson perceived this as Mike's being a cool guy who had never patronized him. "Just had a hell of a disappointment. Major book deal fell through. Important hate literature collection."

"Bummer," Mike said.

"What happened!?" Barbara asked, as if she didn't already know.

Chas Hanson had sold the collection to another dealer, whom he refused to name.

"You're probably glad," Rawson said to her peevishly. "She didn't want us to buy it," he said to Mike.

"It is probably for the best," she said. "But I know how much it meant to you, dear heart." She only called him dear heart in public.

She asked Rawson if he wanted her to call the prospective buyers with whom he'd had breakfast at the Plaza. Rawson told her no, let Ted call them. She said again she knew how much the collection meant to him. Mike was picking up books, glancing at them, putting them down.

"You don't know who bought it?" he asked Rawson.

"Some asshole bought it."

"That's a drag," Mike said. "I came by to tell Barbara that I got the Vette running."

"It's all about the car show," Rawson said, chuckling.

Barbara said, "It's a great car. It'll be the centerpiece of the fifties section." She sounded entirely normal, but her heart was pounding.

"Has Barbara been harassing you?" Rawson said to Mike. "You know how she is when she gets the bit between her teeth."

"It's in a good cause," Mike said, in a between-us-men way. "I thought we'd take it on a test run," he said to Barbara. "You don't mind if I borrow your wife?" he said to Rawson.

"Mike, that sounds awfully antediluvian. You can't just borrow me. You men!" Barbara said. "And when you say test run, does this mean we're going to end up calling Triple A?"

"Have a little faith in Mike," Rawson said. "She's always undermining me, too," he said to Mike.

"Not true, dear heart," Barbara said. "I'm your biggest fan."

It was Rawson who suggested they take the Corvette up the Pass. Give it a real workout. They could have lunch at the Paradise Store.

"What fun," Barbara said. "But I have to be back in time to take Betsy to soccer practice."

Rawson walked out to the car with them. He was completely oblivious. Rawson could not conceive of an actual rival, a top-caliber guy.

The yellow Corvette—washed and waxed, the chrome polished—was parked under one of the ancient olive trees, next to the Town Car. They were only four blocks off State Street, but Bird of Paradise Books was an island of quiet, up a sloping driveway from Laguna Street.

"Rawson, I have an idea," Barbara said. "Why don't you call Mitzi Bevan? She's gung-ho about starting a collection—but she hasn't the foggiest what she wants to collect. Tell her about *The Riddle of the Sands*."

Mike was waiting, car key in hand. He wanted to get the hell out of there. He hated seeing Barbara manage Rawson.

"First editions of spy novels? I like it. I'm calling her," Rawson said after considering. The off-on switch had toggled. He was expansive, in a good mood. "Have fun, kids," he said and went back in the bookstore.

Mike held the car door for Barbara, and she slipped into the low bucket seat. Mike came around the car and got in. Without talking, they fastened their lap seat belts. They looked at each other ruefully, then clasped hands, their fingers intertwined. Mike gave Barbara's hand a squeeze and relinquished it. He turned the key in the ignition.

"I'm never doing that again," Mike said. "I felt like a creep."

"It was demeaning," Barbara said.

There was a comfortable familiarity between them, as they drove up State Street. They'd made their escape. Shamrock palms in concrete planters bordered the flagstone sidewalks in front of white stucco buildings with red tile roofs. For several blocks, the traffic was stop-and-go.

"Where do all these people come from?" Barbara said.

"A lot more people live here than when we were kids," Mike said. "Gotta get used to it."

The population of the city of Santa Barbara had increased by only fifteen thousand in the past twenty years, but if one included Goleta, Carpinteria, and Montecito, the population on the narrow coastal plain between the Rincon and Gaviota had almost doubled. Where in 1970 there were eighty or ninety thousand people, now there were a hundred and fifty thousand people.

Highway 154 is the two-lane highway over the Santa Ynez Mountains from Santa Barbara. San Marcos Pass is at the summit. The highway had been widened and improved with turnouts and reflectors on the center line, but even with the banked curves and the guardrails it was still a mountain road. The tires on the asphalt made a shush-shush sound. Mike passed a Winnebago recreational vehicle laboring up the grade. There was an easy, looping rhythm to his passing: pulling out, accelerating past the slower vehicle ahead, swinging back across the line. The suspension had a slightly arthritic feel; the beige leather of the bucket seats was cracked.

"I love how you pass," Barbara said.

"Nothing to it." Mike smiled his rascally smile. "In and out."

Rawson Palmer was the world's worst passer. He would speed up, come up on the rear bumper of the car ahead—then tailgate for miles without passing.

"What were you going to tell me later?" Mike asked.

"What really happened with the hate literature acquisition," Barbara said. "I did not want Bird of Paradise Books to buy that collection. Neither did Ted. But you just try stopping Rawson."

"Did you think it was immoral?" Mike asked.

"Immoral? It was garbage that pandered to sick bigots. I don't know if it's immoral, but it's tacky. What kind of customer is going to buy *The Bitch of Buchenwald*?"

"Rawson likes that crap?" Mike asked, as he passed a Volkswagen bus. Again, the easy looping rhythm.

"His favorite movie is *Triumph of the Will*," Barbara said. "Not because he thinks Leni Riefenstahl is a great filmmaker."

"Jesus," Mike said. "It's your marriage, but come on, Barbara."

"I know, I know. But let me tell you about what happened with the collection."

While Rawson and Ted were in New York she had enlisted her sister's help, and Sheila had found an out-of-work actor in Los Angeles, the friend of a friend, whom Barbara hired to pose as a book dealer. The actor called Chas Hanson and made him a cash offer of double the amount that Bird of Paradise Books had proposed. Take it or leave it. Chas Hanson accepted, and Barbara arranged to get the cash for the purchase to the actor. He rented a U-Haul truck and drove to Bakersfield. He paid for the books with hundred-dollar bills. He and Chas Hanson loaded the truck, and the phony book dealer drove off.

"He was supposed to dump the boxes in the Tehachapi landfill," Barbara said. "I bet some of those books are going to show up at Hollywood Book City. Frankly, I don't care. So long as we don't have them at Bird of Paradise."

"Resourceful," Mike said.

"You don't think less of me?"

"It got the job done. Same principle as Kip Voorhees paying off the fiancé. Except you're married to Rawson."

Coming off the Pass, Highway 154 swings to the left. Paradise Road is to the right, a paved road that follows the Santa Ynez River. The now dry Santa Ynez River. Paradise Store was a short distance down the road. Mike parked in the gravel lot in front of the store, and he and Barbara went in. The parking lot was empty except for a Coca-Cola delivery truck. Inside was the country store, with two narrow aisles, crowded displays of groceries, sundries, and camping supplies. The Coca-Cola delivery man was stocking shelves, and an older woman in a powder-blue pantsuit was behind the counter. Her bleached-blonde hair was teased into a cotton-candy bouffant, and she was wearing blue eye shadow; her lashes were heavily mascaraed. A blackboard displayed the day's menu. The special was meatloaf. They ordered meatloaf sandwiches. Mike paid. A radio was playing country-western music.

They sat across from each other at a picnic table on the porch. The Santa Ynez Valley stretched before them. This time of year, the valley floor should have been green and lush with new grass, but in this drought year there was only dry brown grass. Mike drank black coffee from a Styrofoam cup; Barbara drank milk from a pint carton. They shared a bag of potato chips. The Coca-Cola driver came out of the store wheeling his hand truck.

Mike said to Barbara, "Once when I was in third grade at Cold Spring School, some little girls ganged up on me on the playground. They kept saying: 'Are you rich or are you poor? We can't tell and it's making us mad.'"

Barbara repeated: "'Are you rich or are you poor? We can't tell and it's making us mad.' Your father was broke; he wasn't poor."

"True. And I'm not broke. I have the garage; I have investments. But I'm not in your league."

"Hardly anyone is," Barbara said. "What difference does it make?"

He thought about it. "No difference. Not to me." The crow's feet around his eyes were like the rays of the sun. "I love you, Barbara. What's happening with you getting a divorce?"

"I made an appointment to see a lawyer. But, Mike, I canceled it."

"Why? What's going on?"

"Please don't be mad at me. I hate the idea of getting a divorce. Rawson will be horrible."

"I don't imagine he'll take it well. Anything in particular? Money? Custody of Betsy? Do you think he'll get violent?"

"None of those things. He wouldn't dare hit me. And the family has good lawyers. Sheila's first husband didn't get a penny."

"What is it then?" Mike asked.

The Coca-Cola truck rumbled out of the parking lot in a cloud of dust. A hawk circled high overhead. The sky was blue. Not a cloud in the sky. A pale green Forest Service truck drove past on Paradise Road. Outside on the porch, the radio was a soundtrack in the background. Dwight Yoakam singing "The Streets of Bakersfield."

"It's Rawson," Barbara said. She never cried, but she was almost crying now. "He will always be a drag, and I will always have to deal with him. He's Betsy's father. He'll be in my life forever."

She gave an example. Crane only went up to eighth grade, and Betsy wanted to go to Cate, a coed boarding school in Carpinteria, for ninth grade. A lot of her friends were going there. There was an option to be a day student, but Betsy understandably wanted to get out of the house. Rawson didn't want her to go to boarding school. He said that people would think he was a bad father. He wouldn't listen when Barbara said she'd gone to boarding school and she'd liked it.

"We're coming up on the application deadline," Barbara said. "I'll finesse it. But if we were divorced, things like that will be a hundred times harder."

"Barbara, please," Mike said. "I'm not trying to give you a hard time."

"I wish he'd just disappear."

George Jones was singing "The Wedding Ring."

A dusty tan double-cab pickup truck with the Rancho Alameda logo on the door drove up, and a man in jeans and a long-sleeved work shirt got out. He had the swagger of the ranchers in the valley who still ran cattle and raised horses. Coming up the steps to the store, he recognized Mike. "Hey. How's it going?" he said, pausing on the steps. "I thought that Vette looked like your yellow turbo."

Mike said, "I put in a new transmission."

"This is the test drive," Barbara said.

"Barbara, this is Bill Anderson," Mike said. "Bill, Barbara Palmer."

"How do you do?" Barbara said.

"Barbara and her husband used to have Palmer Orchards," Mike said. "Barbara roped me into keeping their International Harvester running." He didn't like saying, "... and her husband."

"Mike gave me a hard time, but I loved that truck."

The skeleton peaks and ridges of the San Rafael Mountains rose up in the far distance. Shadows cast by the scattered valley oaks were black on the ghost blond bleached grass. They talked about the drought. How the ranchers were getting starved out, no grass for the cattle, going broke buying feed, in over their head at the bank. Barbara said she lay awake at night and listened to the wind blow the rain clouds overhead. The two men knew each other from high school. They'd both been into drag racing. Bill asked about the Lakester, and Mike said he should come out to the desert sometime and watch the speed trials. Barbara felt relaxed in a way that she never did when she was with Rawson. Maybe because Mike was respected.

The three of them talked for a few minutes, and then Bill said, "Later," to Mike and "It was good to meet you" to Barbara, and went into the store.

Mike and Barbara put their trash in the garbage can on the porch and got in the Corvette. Mike punched a preselect button of the Blaupunkt AM/FM. It was the jazz station. "Desafinado"—Stan Getz on tenor saxophone. A bossa nova. Neither spoke until they had turned onto Highway 154. As the Corvette powered into the wide curve of the grade, Barbara turned sideways in her bucket seat, steadying herself with one hand on the dashboard.

"I'm sorry, Mike. I dread the whole process of getting divorced. Just thinking about telling Rawson makes my skin crawl. I wish he'd just disappear. Poof."

"It would be nice. But it's not going to happen."

They were halfway up the mountain at a place where there is a scenic vista point overlooking the Santa Ynez Valley. The entrance to the vista point was across the lane of oncoming traffic. "Someday My Prince Will Come," the Bill Evans version, was on the car radio. Mike steered into the turn lane, pulled into the vista point, and switched off the ignition.

"What are you doing?" Barbara said.

Fast-food wrappers and soft drink cups littered the parking area. Names were spray-painted on the rocks, and trash had spilled out of a metal garbage can chained to a steel post. Far below, the wide valley stretched for miles and miles. The mud flats of Lake Cachuma glittered in the sunlight. Before the drought, Lake Cachuma had been a sapphire-blue expanse. Barbara smelled of cucumber soap and Blue Grass dusting powder and Chanel No. 5.

"Barbara," Mike said, "are you afraid that if you divorce Rawson, you'll be just another divorced woman with money in Santa Barbara?"

"A little bit," she said, not looking at him. "Betsy will be one of the kids whose parents have two listings in the school directory, and her mom is peppy and involved, but at the end of the day she's alone."

"Sweetheart…" Mike said.

"It's stupid. I know I should divorce Rawson no matter what. He's screwed up and it's screwing up Betsy. It's screwing me up."

Mike took her hand and raised it to his lips. He kissed her hand, biting gently the plump mound of flesh at the base of her thumb. Above them, the span of the Cold Spring Arch Bridge arched over a deep wooded canyon. There was a gust of wind, and a dust devil stirred up food wrappers and dry leaves. The dust devil swirled off into the manzanita and scrub oak, then disappeared into thin air.

Mike looked into her eyes. "Barbara, will you marry me? The minute you are free, will you marry me?"

"Yes," she said softly.

"We'll have a good life together."

"I want to come out to the desert and watch the speed trials." Then she added, under her breath, "I don't believe it will ever happen."

"It's going to happen," Mike said, fiercely. "If Rawson's a drag about the divorce, so be it. I'll be there for you. Now let's get you back before Betsy's late for soccer practice."

Coming over the Pass, there was a grand panoramic vista of ocean and coastal plain—the chaparral smell of mountain laurel. Mike told Barbara about an old man named Johnny Romero. When Johnny was a child he had heard the stories of the aged vaqueros who, as young men, had roped grizzlies from horseback at Los Osos and hunted mountain lions in Romero Canyon. Now Johnny was ninety-six. He lived in a house trailer at Paradise Camp where he grew marijuana plants between the rows of corn in his vegetable garden.

"We should go visit him," Barbara said.

"Next time we will," Mike said.

"I feel like I'm in a movie," she said.

"We write our own scripts," he said.

At that moment, they were completely happy.

♦♦♦

It was two thirty when Mike dropped Barbara at Bird of Paradise Books, pulling in between the Town Car and a Range Rover with a Bay Club tennis club decal belonging to a customer. Bird of paradise plants grew in the border against the adobe building, their blue and orange flowers like exotic birds above the bluish-green leaves. There was an aloe tree with red hot poker flowers; the stalks were partly bare and the tips of the orange-red flowers were faded.

"Mike, you haven't asked, but I want to tell you: I don't sleep with him. Not ever again. You don't have to think about that."

Mike was quiet for a moment. Then he said, "I won't say I haven't thought about it. God, I want to make love to you."

"Me, too," Barbara said. "I will get a divorce. I promise."

"You can do it. We'll have a wonderful life."

They said goodbye, and Mike watched Barbara walk up the brick entrance path to Bird of Paradise Books. He remembered the enormous silence the afternoon their two souls spoke to each other.

CHAPTER SEVEN

Freak Accident

THE NEXT MORNING, WHEN Betsy was at school, Rawson was at the bookstore, and she was alone in the house with only the housekeeper, Barbara went in the home office, the former breakfast room, and sat at an oak desk that had belonged to her grandfather. She looked up the number for the lawyer on the Rolodex. On the white-paneled wall over the desk there were three framed animation-sequence drawings from Walt Disney's *Fantasia*, the *Pastoral Symphony* segment with the Pegasuses. Three almost-identical ink-and-watercolor drawings show a wise Father Pegasus and a loving Mother Pegasus swimming side by side like swans in a pastel prehistoric sea, surrounded by their frolicking Pegasus babies. The cartoon sky was the color of orange sherbet.

The first time she brought Rawson to visit her grandmother, when they were first engaged, he studied the drawings, impressed that they were the originals. Pointing at the winged horses, he told Barbara, "That's us, my sweet. We'll be mated for life, like the Pegasuses."

Barbara had thought, *Maybe…but I can always get a divorce.*

What a sap she'd been.

It was a simple matter to make an appointment with Mr. Childs at Allen & Childs. The receptionist put her through to his assistant. Barbara explained to the assistant, who knew the family, that she wanted to consult Mr. Childs on a personal matter, and she was given an appointment for eleven a.m. the next Tuesday. Then she called her mother and asked if she was free for lunch on Tuesday.

"I'm coming down to meet with Mr. Childs," she said. "I'll tell you about it when I see you."

"Tuesday is completely open. You don't want to give me a little hint?" her mother said.

"Probably what you think it is," Barbara said, and they made a plan to meet at the Chronicle, the Pasadena restaurant where they always had lunch. Barbara's mother invariably ordered a Manhattan and a Cobb salad with blue cheese dressing.

At noon, Barbara had a lunch meeting at the El Encanto. She was on the board of trustees of the Music Academy of the West, and this was a meeting of the instruments, building, and grounds committee. On her way, she stopped at the Montecito Garage to show Mike a mock-up of the poster for the *Concours d'Elegance*. The publicity committee had decided on a witty drawing of a 1930 Duesenberg convertible in the style of Al Hirschfeld. Johnny Cushing, the artist who designed the Palmer Orchards logo, drew it. Barbara had offered to have Mike vet it for automotive accuracy.

When Barbara drove up, Mike was working on the Lakester. The black BMW that looked like an SS staff car was still up on the lift in the service bay. The yellow Corvette was parked at the side of the building. Mike put his tools down and they went into the office. He cleared a surface on the metal desk and unrolled the poster. They stood close together. Barbara was wearing a pink Chanel suit with large gold buttons.

"Looks fine to me," he said, holding the poster flat. "He's got the big round headlights and the side-mount spare tire down pat. Whose car is it?"

"It belongs to a collector in Hillsborough who's on the *Concours* circuit," Barbara said. "I knew the drawing was perfectly fine. I just wanted to see you. I have an appointment next Tuesday with our family lawyer. I'm having lunch after with my mother. I'm going to tell her. Mike, I dread it. The divorce, not telling my mother."

"You can do it, sweetheart," Mike said, rolling up the poster. "I had a dream about you last night. We were riding beach cruiser bicycles."

That made Barbara laugh. "That's not very romantic."

"Hey, it was a dream. I love you, Barbara."

"I'm on automatic," she said. "I just have to get through this."

"We'll get through this."

The wall phone rang, and he answered it. He listened to the caller, an old customer, go into detail with what he believed was a problem with the hydraulic clutch in his 911 Porsche. After a few minutes, Barbara picked up the poster and mouthed, "I have to dash."

Mike said to the caller, "I'll call you back."

He walked Barbara to her car. The red Volvo station wagon was parked under the pepper tree. The sky was a clear cerulean blue, the color of the Madonna's robes.

"Can I give you some advice?" Mike said.

"Of course."

"Don't say anything to Rawson until you talk to the lawyer."

"I couldn't agree more," she said.

"We're going out to the desert with the Lakester. Just for a couple days. I'll be back Saturday night. If you need me, we're staying at the Nugget Hotel in Wendover. I mean it, Barbara…call me if you need to. I'll be back Saturday night."

"It will be wonderful when I can go with you," she said.

♦♦♦

THAT WEEK, RAWSON WAS in one of his good periods. He didn't get angry. He didn't talk incessantly about what an imbecile Ted was. He didn't get drunk on Glenlivet after dinner. Mostly, after dinner he was holed up in the home office at the computer. Grandparents Day at Crane Country Day was a big event, and infirm grandparents were ferried around the school grounds in golf carts donated for the day and driven by dads. This year Rawson was one of the golf cart dads, and he was creating an Excel spreadsheet of the schedule.

On Thursday night, he said wistfully, "I'm not a bad fellow," when Barbara stuck her head in the game room, after she'd helped Betsy with her homework. Betsy was writing an essay on *The Scarlet Letter.* "I'm not a bad fellow," he repeated.

Barbara couldn't bring herself to reassure him. It was worse when he was like this. It brought it home that he couldn't help being the way he was—and he would never change. His almost-handsome face with its peevish too-small mouth and pale blue eyes was pathetic. She dreaded telling him that she was divorcing him.

On Saturday, Barbara stayed out of Rawson's way. She was out and about, and he was puttering around at home until late afternoon when he gave Betsy a ride to the house of the friend with whom she was spending the night. It was starting to get dark when he got home. Barbara was in the kitchen with a glass of pinot grigio, talking to her sister on the cordless phone. She waved her fingers at Rawson and kept talking.

Rawson went upstairs to their bedroom, took off his shoes, and lay on the bed on top of the bedspread. The opulent scent of the Chinese narcissus in a bowl of gravel and water on the mantel filled the room. He was feeling amorous. He unzipped his fly and waited for Barbara to come to him. It had been too long since they'd done what he liked in bed. He heard Barbara's voice going on and on. He became more and more angry. Why did Barbara do things that she knew would make him angry? She knew he couldn't afford to get angry. After twenty minutes, he got up and went downstairs without zipping his fly or putting on his shoes. He was in an aggrieved rage.

"Keep your pecker up," Barbara was saying to Sheila. It was something their grandfather used to say, meaning Remain cheerful, keep your head up high. When they were girls, they thought it was hilarious. Barbara listened a moment, laughed. "Moi, aussi," she said and hung up.

"What was that about?" Rawson said, the muscle in his jaw twitching.

"I was talking to Sheila. She's back from Mustique. Mick Jagger wasn't there."

"Barbara, I lay on the bed for half an hour waiting for you, you humiliated me."

"I was on the phone. How was I supposed to know you were waiting?" Even if she had known, she wouldn't have gone to him. All the times she'd had sex to keep the peace…never again. She wondered if Mike was back yet.

"I lay there with a hard dick like an idiot. While you acted like I don't exist."

"Why don't you just shut up?" Barbara said in a tone he'd never heard in all the years he'd known her.

Rawson recoiled.

"Why are you such a shit?" he said.

He stormed out of the kitchen and went upstairs. He described it to himself as "stormed out." Barbara, in her mind, used the words "flounced out." She stood at the kitchen window. Whatever had made her reluctant to go ahead with a divorce, that was over. Bring it on. But God, she wished he'd just disappear. The blue gum eucalyptus tree that she was poisoning showed definite signs of decline. The blue-green leaves of the tall tree were not as glossy as the leaves of the neighboring trees. Barbara was confident of success. She would again have a view from the kitchen of Montecito Peak, hazy purple against the sky above the dark-green foliage of the Valencia orange trees.

Rawson came back downstairs. He had deck shoes on, his fly was zipped, and he was wearing a tan suede bomber jacket. He was jingling his car keys in his pocket.

"Drive carefully," Barbara said.

"Why are you so cold to me?" he demanded.

She didn't answer and he went out through the laundry room. She heard him drive too fast down the driveway. She went in the game room, sat at the poker table, and played game after game of Klondike solitaire with an old pack of Bicycle cards. She thought about calling

Mike, but he might not be back yet and what would she say? This was just the beginning.

♦♦♦

The Tee-Off was a bar and steakhouse in Ontare Plaza, a strip mall on Upper State Street, between Modern Nails and Spudnut Doughnuts, not far from the Santa Barbara Municipal Golf Course. The Tee-Off sign advertised *Where the drinks are stiff, but we aren't* in red neon, next to a yellow neon martini glass with an aqua neon olive. Rawson parked in one of the diagonal head-in parking spaces that faced State Street, and, feeling purposeful, went inside. The main room of the Tee-Off had oxblood red leather booths and a bar at one end. Golf-themed photographs and drawings decorated the walls. Rawson sat at the bar and ordered a double Glenlivet on the rocks. Behind the bar, tiers of liquor bottles were like jewels in the darkish restaurant.

"I appreciate a generous pour," he said to the bartender.

"You got it, buddy," the bartender said and added an extra double jigger, the Scotch sloshing over.

The woman on one side of Rawson, a tipsy brunette with a gold cross necklace in her deep décolletage and a little girl voice, was telling the man next to her that she was a people person; on his other side, two men were arguing about whether Wayne Gretzky had sold his soul to the devil. Rawson felt like he was in a Fellini movie. He was proud of himself for the allusion. The bartender was busy, otherwise Rawson would have told him it was like a Fellini movie. He finished his drink and signaled for another. He considered ordering a hamburger, but he wasn't hungry.

"I've never been popped. Never had a DUI," he said to the bartender, somewhat later, after he had signaled for a third drink. "'Course, usually Barbara drives."

"Gotta be careful," the bartender said.

Santa Barbara had strict anti–drunk driving enforcement—people whom Rawson and Barbara knew socially had been fined, had their driver's licenses suspended for a year, had to do six weeks in the county jail. Rawson got on a favorite topic: the ridiculously, ludicrously low allowable blood alcohol percentage.

"One drink mixed by a bartender with a generous pour, and you're over the limit," he said. He liked the sound of generous pour.

The brunette with the gold cross necklace said in her little girl voice that probably everyone who went out in the parking lot and got in their car was legally drunk. The man she had been talking to seemed to have left. Rawson asked her what she did, and she said she was a legal secretary. The man came back, and she turned to him. Rawson was on his fourth drink with a generous pour. He hadn't run a tab. With each drink, he'd proffered a twenty—keep the change. He thought about Barbara. He missed her terribly. She was all he had. Why was she so mean to him? He had the thought of calling her from the pay phone, but it would be a drunken call from a bar. Better to go home.

Rawson got down off the barstool. He held on to the bar for a moment to get his balance, then gave the bartender a jaunty salute and walked out of the Tee-Off without weaving. The bartender didn't try to stop him. California had not had a dram shop law since 1978. The anti–drunk driving laws were strict, but a bar or restaurant was not liable if the establishment served an intoxicated customer alcohol and the customer then caused harm. Drunk driving accidents? Bar fights? No liability. Once outside in the cool night air, Rawson leaned for a minute against the building. Then, weaving a little, he made for the Town Car. The neon sign announcing *Prime Rib—Cocktails—Fried Chicken* cast a colored light on the sidewalk.

He was unaware that he was observed by Mike.

Mike, on his part, had had no idea that Rawson was in the Tee-Off.

The Lakester expedition had been a success. They'd gotten back that afternoon. After the Lakester and the racing gear were returned to the Montecito Garage, the owner had taken everyone out to dinner at the Tee-Off. Mike drove his own car. When he arrived at the Tee-Off, Rawson was already at the bar, but Mike, following the hostess to the back room where the Lakester group had a table, did not see him. It was a convivial group—the owner, his wife, their twenty-year-old son (he'd been the driver) and his girlfriend, another mechanic, and Mike. They all had prime rib, except the girlfriend, who ordered fried shrimp. Mike missed Barbara. He had lain awake in the motel and imagined that she was there. He had a single glass of red wine with his prime rib. The waitress came for their dessert orders. Cheesecake or mud pie? All of a sudden, Mike wanted to be alone. He said he was going to pack it in, he was tired, and he got up from the table.

"Is he all right?" the owner's wife said, after he exited.

"He broke up with Cissy," the son said.

"I don't think it's that," she said.

That was how it happened that Mike came out of the Tee-Off and saw Rawson in his suede bomber jacket weaving his way to the Lincoln Town Car. Mike's 1978 Toyota was parked two cars down from the Town Car. This was the second time in a month that Mike had, through no fault of his own, observed Rawson, unobserved. Rawson got the car door open with no difficulty. But once he was in the Town Car, and the car door was shut, he had trouble fitting the key into the ignition. With any other drunk, Mike might have interceded. He'd done this before. "Buddy, you're gassed. Let's get a ride for you. You don't want to get pulled over."

He didn't like people driving drunk.

But Rawson? He didn't want to deal with Rawson. Watching him, Mike understood in a way that he had not before what Barbara meant by *he'll always be on the scene, he'll always be a drag*. Rawson finally got the car started. But instead of backing out of the parking space, he steered the Town Car straight ahead over the concrete parking bumper. The underside of the car scraped on the six-inch bumper. The progress of the Town Car was majestic. First the front tires, then the rear tires, as the car nosed onto the sidewalk. Rawson gave it gas. The big car plowed through the fortnight lilies in the narrow planting strip between the sidewalk and the curb and landed in the roadway with a bounce. Rawson turned on the headlights and drove slowly and carefully down State Street.

He'd make it home, if he didn't get stopped, was Mike's assessment. Unless he'd scraped a hole in the oil pan, in which case he'll be dead in the water in two blocks. Mike was of two minds on calling the sheriff. *I'm not going to do it,* he decided. *I hope he drives into a telephone pole. I hope he doesn't take anyone with him.* Barbara could handle herself, but he hated the thought of Rawson drunk and in the same house with her. He'd told her to call him if she needed him. He had to stop himself from following Rawson and having it out with him.

♦♦♦

RAWSON MADE IT HOME safely. He drove all the way down State Street to Cabrillo Boulevard, the beach boulevard, and took Cabrillo past the Bird Refuge and then Hot Springs Road into Montecito. He was seeing double, and he covered one eye with his hand. He kept the car windows down so the night air would revive him, and he stayed awake by belting out "The Battle Hymn of the Republic."

Mine eyes have seen the glory of the coming of the Lord
He is trampling out the vintage where the grapes of wrath are stored
He have loosed the fateful lightening of his terrible swift sword
His truth is marching on....

He remembered the time when they were first married—one night he marched around the house buck naked singing "The Battle Hymn of the Republic," and Barbara thought he was cool. When he drove past the Montecito Garage, he thought what a good fellow Mike Brooke was. It was a feat of endurance, but he made it home. He steered the Town Car past the stone gateposts with the pineapple finials and up the driveway. The lights were out upstairs; there was a light in the kitchen.

"You're a grand old flag, you're a high-flying flag," Rawson sang, as the Town Car idled outside the garage. All three garage doors were closed. He couldn't remember the other words. "You're a grand old flag." He rummaged in the console and found the remote. He punched it, and the middle garage door opened. Open sesame. The overhead light went on automatically. It was set to stay on for five minutes. Rawson drove in, his full attention on not hitting the garage door frame on either side. Threading the needle, he said to himself. Threadin' the needle. The stupid red Cadillac convertible on one side, Barbara's red Volvo on the other. Why did she like red cars? With a final effort, he stopped the Town Car in exactly the right place. He put it in park and put on the parking brake. He punched the remote to shut the garage door, and it slid down.

"Made it," Rawson said. It had been a terrible strain to hold it together. He was really drunk. The effort of getting home without mishap had exhausted him. He opened the car door and started to get out. He fell back on the upholstered seat—just need to rest a minute—and passed out with the door open and the engine running.

♦♦♦

Barbara played solitaire in the game room for almost two hours, mechanically dealing the cards, moving the cards from one row to another, shuffling the deck for each new game. She took a break to eat a bowl of Raisin Bran cereal with a sliced banana and brown sugar and wondered if Mike was back yet. She imagined being in bed with him.

At nine o'clock, she went upstairs, got ready for bed, and took a Nembutal capsule. She got the Nembutal from her sister, who had them mailed to her from Denmark. Barbara rarely took one, but there were times when what she wanted was, as Sheila put it, "the respite without effort from consciousness that a short-lasting sedative hypnotic provides." This was definitely one of those times.

She was fast asleep by nine thirty. In her sleep she listened for Rawson's return. He was going to wake her up, and she'd have to deal with him. The garage was on the other side of the house, but the bedroom window looked out on the driveway. She halfway awoke when the Town Car drove in the driveway; she heard it creeping erratically down the driveway, tires crunching on the asphalt. She glanced at the clock and floated back into sleep. It was eleven thirty.

At midnight, Barbara was suddenly wide awake. She was thirsty, and Rawson hadn't come to bed. This wasn't all that unusual, but she felt uneasy not knowing where in the house he was. She got up and put on her robe. The house felt haunted. A wind had come up. The lights were still on in the kitchen and in the main hall. The game room was dark and empty. She went through the kitchen and opened the door into the garage. She was starting to wonder if she'd dreamed that she heard him drive in. But no, the Town Car was in the garage, and Rawson was passed out in the front seat with the car door open. The only light in the garage came from the interior light of the Town Car. This had happened before. But he'd never left the engine running. The car was idling.

Barbara was good in an emergency. She could hear Rawson's stertorous breathing. It was how he sounded when he was passed-out drunk. The best course of action would be to (a) open all three of the garage doors—all she had to do was hit the buttons that were just inside the door into the kitchen; (b) go into the garage and turn off the Town Car ignition; (c) wake up Rawson and get him into the house. He'd only been back half an hour or so. She highly doubted it was enough time for the carbon monoxide to reach a dangerous level. The whole thing would be a non-event.

Instead, Barbara did nothing. *You may not get another chance,* she thought. She shut the door into the garage and went back in the kitchen. She got a glass of water from the purified water tap in the sink. The wind had picked up. She looked out the window and saw clouds scudding across the night sky. High overhead, battalions of clouds marched. It was in God's hands.

Barbara went back to bed. She didn't think she'd go back to sleep, but soon she was in a dreamless sleep. The best sleep she'd had in a long, long time. It was in God's hands.

When she found Rawson in the morning, the engine was still idling. She called 911 immediately, and the paramedics came, but it was too late. Rawson was dead. The cause of death was carbon monoxide poisoning. He was drunk when he died. BAC 0.18. The bartender at the Tee-Off confirmed that Rawson had had four double Scotches.

Barbara told the coroner that she blamed herself. She was sound asleep. If she'd woken up and realized he hadn't come to bed, she would have gone downstairs and found him passed out in the Town Car. She might have been in time to save him. The forensic investigator assured her that she couldn't blame herself. Ordinarily, what happened wouldn't have been fatal. The catalytic converter on a 1989 Town Car reduced the amount of carbon monoxide emitted to a negligible amount. The car had recently had a tune-up and passed a smog test. But a forensic examination revealed a new hole in the exhaust pipe just before where it connected with the catalytic converter. The undercarriage of the car had been scraped. Rawson must have driven over something recently—most likely that same night. It was a freak accident.

CHAPTER EIGHT

Concours d'Elegance

THE *CONCOURS D'ELEGANCE* WAS the first weekend in June. It was beautiful weather; no morning fog cast a pall over the Polo Field. Everything went swimmingly. Barbara, fetching in a flowered silk garden party dress and a garden party hat, was one of the committee members at a table at the entrance, taking tickets from people who had advance tickets and selling tickets to people who did not.

In the first weeks after Rawson's death, she had been subdued and in shock. Everyone was understanding. Rawson's death was completely unexpected, for heaven's sake. But her grief wasn't conspicuous.

"I just want to put it behind me," she said. "I'm not stepping down from the *Concours* committee. It's good for me to keep busy. I'm still going in to Bird of Paradise Books."

No one thought this was odd. How Rawson had treated her was common knowledge. *He wouldn't be dead if he hadn't been a drunk* was the consensus. "A mean drunk," someone would add.

Sheila came to help with the practicalities of a sudden death in the family and stayed for six weeks. The memorial service was the Friday after Rawson died. It was in the chapel at the Santa Barbara Cemetery, where the urn with Rawson's ashes was interred in the columbarium. Barbara asked one of Rawson's fraternity brothers, a car dealership owner in Paso Robles, to give the eulogy. It was all platitudes and generalities. Entirely appropriate. Mike was there in a dark suit.

"The fifties classics is still on," Barbara told him, when he offered his condolences outside the chapel. Mike had sent a formal condolence note, but otherwise this was their first contact.

"Let me know when you want to get together," Mike said. "Anything I can do to help."

They started seeing each other, at first for little visits at the Montecito Garage, ostensibly to talk about the fifties classics. Then they started taking the Corvette out to the Dutch Garden on Upper State Street for lunch. One day they drove over the Pass and visited Johnny Madrid at Paradise Camp. He told them that when his grandfather was a boy, the creeks flowed all year round. One weekend, at Mike's invitation, Barbara and Betsy went out to the desert, where the Lakester racing team was testing a new brand of tires at Dry Lakes. They shared a room at the Nugget Hotel—Mike was in a room down the hall. Betsy had a good time, and Barbara hit it off with the wife of the owner of the Lakester. She was a member of the 300 mph Club and had her eye on the women's land speed record. Barbara told Mike she thought she might like to try racing herself.

Sheila, before she flew back to Aspen, told Barbara, "I think Mike likes you."

"And I like him," Barbara said.

"Barbara…I mean he likes you."

Their courtship was discreet but not clandestine. "Are you glad I didn't have to get a divorce?" Barbara said more than once.

The fifties classics section was a big hit. There was an old-school reunion feeling. Mike was devastatingly handsome in a white linen suit, standing by the yellow Corvette. He had realized that morning how very happy he was, and he dared to think it would last. All the fifties cars were local, and the owners remained by their cars. A woman told Ron Gamberini that she used to date the original owner of his turquoise Bel Air. They'd cruise State Street and then park at Leadbetter Beach and make out. She said the *Veni Vidi Vici* on the dash was her idea.

"I came, I saw, I conquered," Ron said. "Whatever happened to him?"

The woman said she didn't know.

"Good times," Ron said.

There was a pavilion with refreshments, including catered box lunches. At noon, Barbara took a break and found Mike. They got box lunches and sat on folding chairs at a round table where another couple was sitting already. Their son and Betsy had been in the same class at Crane since kindergarten. He was the boy with the decoy locker. Earlier, the man had been talking Corvettes with Mike.

"May we join you?" Mike said.

"Have a seat," the fellow said.

"How are you?" the wife said to Barbara.

"I'm fine. I'm trying to keep busy," Barbara said. "Life is for the living, I tell myself."

The two women talked about schools; the two men talked cars. *How wonderful,* Barbara thought, *to be in a couple and not have the unremitting tension of not knowing if something was going to set Rawson off.* When the other couple finished the sandwiches and brownies in their box lunches, they went off to look at the silent auction.

Mike said, "The *Concours* was how it all started—and now here we are."

"Have I mentioned that I'm glad I didn't have to get a divorce?" Barbara said.

"I believe you've mentioned it," Mike said, smiling.

"The freak accident was pretty amazing, wasn't it?"

"A confluence of the accidental," Mike said.

He had not yet told Barbara that he had witnessed the Town Car, with Rawson at the wheel, drive over the parking bumper. Barbara had not told him that she'd made the decision not to rouse Rawson and not to turn off the ignition. It was not a barrier between them. They were taking things slow. There in the pavilion at the Polo Club, both of them happy, the future before them, as Mike's father used to joke—it was the right time. Mike went first.

"Barbara, I can tell you how the exhaust pipe got a hole in it."

"Really?" she said, a shiver going up her back. Their fates were entwined.

He told her what happened at the Tee-Off.

"If I'd stopped him from getting in the car … Or if I'd called the sheriff …" Mike was informative, not remorseful.

"But you had no way of knowing what would happen."

"None."

Then Barbara said, "I can tell you how the garage filled up with carbon monoxide."

She told him what she had done. Or rather, what she had not done. "It was windy, and I went back to bed. I hope you won't think any less of me."

"You know what I really think, Barbara? I'm thinking, *what a woman!*"

It might seem that Mike's take on what was, not to put too fine a point on it, a murder, was out of character, that he had come under Barbara's influence, but that would not be true. Everyone was better off with Rawson gone. He was a drag. He was always going to be a drag. He was cursed with a low set point of happiness and a permanent sense of grievance.

"It was good teamwork," Barbara said.

"Especially since we didn't plan it."

"Exactly."

Their hearts were glad.

Two other couples joined them at the table, and Mike and Barbara ate their sandwiches and brownies and made conversation as a couple. Betsy, who was one of the runners at the silent auction, came and found them. She wanted to tell Mike that she'd decided to be a day student for her first year at Cate. Mike said he remembered when Cate was all boys.

Betsy had confided to her Aunt Sheila that she was a little bit glad her father was dead. She hated the way he always had tantrums. She was always tense in her own house. She couldn't ever have her friends over. She always had to go to their houses. Sheila—and

Barbara—had reassured her: Rawson was a sick person, and it was only natural to feel relief that he was gone.

The green polo field in the sunshine, the ticketholders walking in little clusters from one gleaming automobile to the next, stopping to talk to acquaintances, kids running around, occasional loudspeaker announcements. It was a lovely afternoon.

"Come the revolution," Mike said to Barbara.

"The great unfairness of life," she said.

They were married at Christmas. That winter, the winter of 1991–92, was an El Niño year, and Lake Cachuma filled up. In the decades to come, the wet years were more and more infrequent. But Barbara and Mike lived happily ever after, as Mike had predicted.

There is no more loving, friendly and
charming relationship, communion or
company than a good marriage.
—Martin Luther

THE POLO CLUB

To the memory of
Catherine "Kitty" Payne
March 1994–May 2012

2000

CHAPTER ONE

Chamber Music

IT WAS FATE, A complete coincidence, that Lydia Graham sat next to Hunter Evans at a "Tuesdays at Eight" Music Academy of the West chamber music concert at the Lobero Theatre, the last concert of the summer series. At first, they didn't recognize each other.

Lydia had decided on the spur of the moment that she'd rather hear "The Trout" than accompany her husband, Peter Bolin, to a Surfrider Foundation meeting. She was in favor of the work that the Surfrider Foundation did to clean up the ocean, and she fully supported Peter as a longboard surfer—her daughter's obsession with surfing, as well. But as Peter was getting ready to leave the house, she had a God-spoke-to-me moment. She really did not want to sit through an interminable discussion of public access to Hollister Ranch and why it still hadn't been implemented. More than one person had remarked that when Lydia had a God-spoke-to-me moment, it was amazing how in tune God was with what Lydia wanted.

"Probably just as well," Peter said. Lydia had a history of making outspoken remarks in public meetings. "You have a good time with Mozart."

"Schubert, sweetie."

Although Hunter also bought his ticket at the box office the night of the concert, he'd had it in his date book for a month. He liked to plan ahead, but he didn't like to be tied down. Before the concert, he had dinner at the Wine Cask across the street, then, as he put it, wandered over to the Lobero. All his life, Hunter enjoyed sitting alone in a restaurant, having a few drinks and eating a solitary meal. When he was a boy during World War II, his father briefly owned a tony Santa Barbara restaurant called the Palm Room in the El Paseo, a shopping arcade modeled on a street in Spain: cobblestone paving and wrought iron grillwork. Ten-year-old Hunter would sit by himself at a table on the balcony overlooking the dining room and have the waiter bring him a Coke. He'd sip his Coke and watch the Montecito society crowd eating lunch. Later, in the fifties, he had his usual table on Thursday nights at Perino's on Wilshire.

The Lobero Theatre, with its red plush seats and wrought-iron chandeliers, the Spanish Revival ceiling with gilt panels, the gray-haired volunteer ushers with their sashes and flashlights handing out thick glossy programs, was where Lydia had been going to concerts and plays and ballets all her life. The first ballet she ever saw was at the Lobero: *Swan Lake*. Her father took her when she was four, and she spent the entire ballet trying to figure out if the muscular male dancers in their flesh-colored tights were naked from the waist down.

There was almost a full house—the summer chamber music series had a lot of season-ticket subscribers. Lydia's last-minute ticket was for a seat up front in the third row of the right section, the undesirable section where you can't see the pianist. She had to edge past two Music Academy students—a blond young man with Slavic features in a white dress shirt and jeans, and a dressed-up young Asian American woman. Lydia's seat was next to the young man. On her other side was an empty seat, one of the few empty seats in the house. A distinguished-looking older man with a shaved head, wearing a seersucker jacket with a red bow tie, occupied the seat on the other side of the empty seat. At first glance, Lydia thought he might be one of those cosmopolitan homosexual men who is excellent company and appreciative of women. He looked up as Lydia took her seat.

"We're in for a treat," he said, across the empty seat. He had a low, urbane voice. He smelled cleanly of gin and lime aftershave. She revised her first impression. In a suave way, he was checking her out.

"The first time I heard 'The Trout' was at an art gallery in SoHo," she said, turning toward him. "On a snowy Sunday afternoon."

"The first time I heard it was on an RCA Victor 78."

"I remember 78s," Lydia said. "When I was a little girl my mother used to put on a 78 of 'Swedish Rhapsody,' and I'd dance around with an eggbeater."

There was a buzz of conversation around them. Lydia genuinely liked chamber music, and she would have been perfectly happy to sit by herself and not interact with anyone. But it was always nice to have a congenial seatmate.

Hunter's face had deep etched lines, and he shaved his head to disguise that he was going bald. But he had been terribly attractive as a young man, and he was still terribly attractive.

Lydia was interesting-looking, not conventionally pretty, certainly not beautiful, but she had always been attractive, especially to men. When she was a girl, she liked the boys, and the boys liked her. It wasn't something that had diminished with middle age. She'd never been unfaithful to her husband, but she had a carnal nature and the natural attribute of imbuing a quite proper conversation with a man with a subtext of *if only…in another world…what might have been.* Her husband trusted her. He was amused by her flirtations.

"My aunt was one of the founders of the Music Academy," Hunter said.

"Really?" said Lydia. She couldn't think of any of the founders of the Music Academy who might be this man's aunt.

"A distant aunt," he said.

She was charmed by this. A distant aunt?

The house lights dimmed.

"We'd better pipe down," Lydia whispered, sotto voce.

He put a finger to his lips conspiratorially, as the buzz of talk around them subsided. They each turned their attention to the stage. The musicians came out, all in black tie. The straight chairs in which the string players sat were lacquer red. The pianist settled himself on the piano bench and consulted with his page turner, a young man in a suit. The bass player wiped his bow with a white handkerchief. The violinist nodded. The tender rippling violin and piano of the first movement. Followed by the swelling, aching romance of the second movement. Lydia loved chamber music for the emotion. This evening the emotion was heightened by her awareness of Hunter. As he was aware of her. The smell of lime aftershave and gin stirred a memory in Lydia. As if she already knew this man.

The lights came up at the conclusion of the quintet. Applause. The musicians came back and took a bow. It was the intermission.

"That was wonderful," Lydia said. "I was transported."

"Transported by Schubert," Hunter said.

They smiled at each other in complicity across the empty seat. On the other side of Lydia, the young man in the white dress shirt was telling the young woman that a Russian pianist, a fellow Music Academy student who was attracting a lot of attention, dyed his hair. "His hair is not black. Blond," the young man said firmly. He had a thick Russian accent. "He thinks the black hair makes him more romantic. More Romanticist. I know him in Moscow."

"No way!" the young woman said.

Hunter interrupted Lydia's eavesdropping. "Why don't you move over?" He patted the empty seat between them.

"Why not," she said, smiling, and stood up, then sat back down next to Hunter.

"Hunter Evans," he said, introducing himself.

She heard the name and looked at him. It was the most extraordinary sensation. Like falling into a tunnel of time. She saw this man as he was in 1963. Then, through the telescope of time, he was transformed back to the present. A handsome old man in a seersucker jacket and a red bow tie.

"Lydia Graham," she said. "We've met, you know. Years and years ago. You were staying in the gatehouse at Campos Eliseos. I used to walk by when I walked home from the beach."

For a moment, he was at a loss. Then recognition dawned. The same process of telescoping time. "The summer of 1963. Your father is a psychologist."

There had been two Graham families in Santa Barbara then: the jeweler Grahams of Hope Ranch—they owned an upscale jewelry store on State Street—and Lydia's parents, the psychologist Grahams of Parra Grande Lane. Her father was a clinical psychologist with a private practice.

"You haven't changed a bit," Hunter said.

"Nor you," Lydia said, laughing.

"We were younger then," Hunter said.

"We were, indeed."

They looked at each other with complicit smiles.

She had been a barefoot fourteen-year-old girl with smooth, long, tan legs, wearing a beach shift; a young teenage girl with a bold manner, very curious. Now she was a rangy middle-aged woman in black silk pants, a green silk tunic, and a rope of faux pearls, with strands of gray in her dark blonde hair. Red lipstick and the lush scent of Carolina Herrera perfume, a fragrance of tuberose and jasmine.

He had been a man of thirty-two, not all that young but not yet middle-aged. Lydia had a memory of him sitting at a metal patio table on a deck under an oak tree, typing on an Underwood portable typewriter, smoke drifting from the cigarette in the ashtray, a gin and tonic by the ashtray. The smell of his lime aftershave and gin.

That summer, Lydia and her friend Annie went to the beach at the Miramar almost every day. Like going to a job. Annie lived in a big, white-stucco Spanish-style house at the top of Hot Springs Road. In the late morning before the fog burned off, she'd walk down to Lydia's house, and they'd walk to the beach together to meet their friends, "Moon River" and "Will You Love Me Tomorrow" on Annie's transistor radio. Boys and girls together, swimming out to the float.

The float rising and falling on the summer swell. They'd sit on the edge, the sun warm on their backs and their feet dangling in the cool Pacific. The cocoa-butter smell of Bain de Soleil. Whitecaps on the blue-green ocean. The *jeunesse dorée* of Hunter's generation were on the horizon of their lives. On the crumbling concrete of a seawall, *Royal Order of the Pipe Smokers 1947* was lettered in Delft blue paint, the Gothic letters rendered like calligraphy.

Lydia was a virgin and she had two boyfriends.

One boyfriend was a high-school intellectual who was into Lenny Bruce and drove a 1957 pink Lincoln Continental. If someone asked him what time it was, he'd say, "It's jiving time." The other was a surfer with a little Morris Minor wood-paneled station wagon. In the afternoon at the Miramar, the surfer boyfriend and Lydia would swim out to the buoy beyond the float, and Lydia would wrap her legs around his waist and put her arms around his neck, and he'd hold onto the mooring rope with one hand and hold her with the other, and they'd kiss—saltwater soul kisses. The coolness of salt ocean water, the warmth of the sun, the rise and fall of the ocean.

The lost paradise of summers at the beach at the Miramar is a set piece in memoirs of Santa Barbara.

In the afternoons, Lydia and Annie would walk home up Hot Springs Road, a wide, straight road lined with hedges and stone walls. Annie had porcelain-white skin that burned—she always had zinc oxide on her nose. The resiny fragrance of rock roses in the heat of the lazy afternoon, only the occasional automobile passing. The roads of Montecito were country roads then. Lydia would take her leave of Annie at a private lane that was a shortcut to her house on Parra Grande Lane. The iron gates to the lane were perpetually open, the hinges frozen with rust. Grass grew between the cracks in the asphalt.

The lane had been the entrance to Campos Eliseos, one of the old Montecito estates. Now the main house, a grand Italianate villa, was abandoned and boarded up. The grounds were in romantic decay. The owner lived in straitened circumstances on an almond ranch in Merced.

The summer that Lydia was fourteen, Hunter was going through a divorce. Adults said "going through a divorce" as if it were an illness or a rite of passage. His Japanese wife was divorcing him. His first wife had died in a tragic accident when her sports car went over the edge on Mountain Drive.

Hunter was in the category of adults that Lydia and Annie called by their first names. Friends of their parents who were younger or artistic and unconventional. Annie's mother knew his godmother.

Sometimes Hunter would be outside on the deck, working on his novel, when Lydia walked past the gatehouse in the afternoon, and, like a cat making itself at home, she would come up on the deck, sit cross-legged on a chaise longue with green-and-white striped cushions, and chat. It was a thing with Lydia and her friends to converse nicely with adults.

Writing a novel was something else adults did.

Hunter was amused. Lydia was curious and forward. But he liked grown women, not young girls. The first time he offered her a Coke, she asked pertly if she could have rum in it.

"You cannot," he said. "What would your mother say?"

Now they had met again. They hadn't seen each other for thirty-seven years.

Recalling that summer, Lydia said, "Didn't you take a job in Japan?"

He had been waiting to hear about a job. Waiting to hear about a job was another adult rite of passage.

"I did. Good memory."

Now that Lydia and Hunter had recognized each other, their interaction was animated in the way of two people who have discovered that they were in the same place at the same time in the past. Hunter said he was retired from the State Department. His delivery of "retired from the State Department" was practiced. It was also not strictly true. He had only briefly worked for the State Department. For most of his career as a civilian contract specialist, he had worked for the military.

"After my wife died, I relocated to Santa Barbara. My beloved third wife. Sharon was twelve years younger than me and drop-dead gorgeous. It makes me sad to remember… She'd buy middle-of-the-road white wine. She didn't drink much at all. I'd say, 'Buy a really good wine…' But she never did."

"I'm sorry," Lydia said.

"After she died, a friend told me, 'Hunter, remember the boulevardier in you. Sharon is dead and you are alive.' We were married twenty-six years, and I was always faithful."

This, too, sounded practiced. Like a man saying he is happily married. Which means, "I want to fool around, but I'm not going to leave my wife."

"Are you married?" he asked Lydia.

She said she was married and she had a fifteen-year-old daughter. "My one and only," she said. "She's a sophomore at Thacher."

Thacher was a boarding school in Ojai, originally a boys' ranch school. A feature, still, was that each freshman had his or her own horse to take care of.

"Do they still have horses to teach them responsibility?" Hunter said.

"They do. But only freshman year. Sally didn't bond with her horse. Her thing is the surf club."

Hunter said he had a condo at the Polo Club. It suited him, he said. There was a tennis club, and on Sundays he could wander over and watch the polo. "The polo players are a pain in the ass. I have an Argentinian polo player upstairs, and his wife hangs their beach towels on the balcony railing. They have two little girls who leave their little pink bicycles in front of my door. The patron owns the condo."

Lydia said she was a consultant for a landscape contractor. "I'm a muse."

"Landscapers have muses?" Hunter said.

"This one does," she said.

"I remember you were interested in geraniums. You took cuttings. Snapped off the stems."

"I remember." The green chlorophyll smell of the leggy, dusty geraniums, their salmon-pink flowers, crimson flowers, pink flowers. The velvety lobed leaves, warm in the sun. When she was seven, her father helped her make a circular bed bordered with sandstone rocks around the trunk of a feather oak tree. She planted cuttings from geraniums that grew on the neglected grounds of the old estates. Her favorite had salmon-pink flowers. Her father was a great gardener. His compost was unsurpassed. Even in great old age he had plants in pots on the balcony of his apartment at Vista del Monte.

She still had a list she made in 1968 of fruit trees she wanted in her garden when she had her own house: Meyer lemons, Fuyu persimmons, Mission figs, pineapple guavas, navel oranges and Valencia oranges, Blenheim apricots. All of these now grew in her garden.

The buzzer sounded to signal the end of the intermission. The seats around them started to fill up. Lydia didn't move back to her original seat. They consulted their programs—Lydia had the big glossy season program that the usher had handed her. Hunter took two pages folded together out of the inside pocket of his seersucker jacket. He'd torn them out of the season's program he had at home. That evening's program. Lydia raised an eyebrow.

"I like to travel light," he said, unfolding the pages.

The second half of the concert was Brahms's *Trio in A Minor for Clarinet, Cello, and Piano* and Mendelssohn's *Songs Without Words*.

As the lights dimmed, she whispered to Hunter, "Cello is my favorite instrument."

The musicians came out. Lydia was again transported by the music. The music was pure sensation, pure emotion and association. A monkey puzzle tree with stiff, pointed leaves on upward-sweeping branches, an illustration in an old book of fairy tales, silhouetted against a summer evening sky. The music evoked a place of green meadows and fields of wheat, pale blue skies with puffy white clouds, and quiet roads lined with hedgerows and a house like a house in a Vermeer painting furnished with dark, polished furniture and gleaming silver. A golden afternoon, redolent of dappled sunlight.

Someone applauded after the first movement of the Brahms, and Hunter said, "Moron."

In the brief interlude between the Brahms and the Mendelssohn, he and Lydia made appreciative comments to each other. At the end of the Mendelssohn, the audience gave a standing ovation, clapping and clapping. Hunter and Lydia had an eye meet, then stood and clapped, too. The musicians came back out for a second bow. No encore. The lights came up.

Lydia gathered up her purse and her sweater. She left her program on her seat. Hunter put his two pages of that evening's program back in his jacket pocket. Ordinarily he would have left them behind, but he wanted a memento.

People were filing up the aisles.

"That was wonderful," Lydia said to Hunter, as they edged down the row. The two Music Academy students were ahead of them, deep in a discussion of the next day's master class.

"Extraordinary that we sat next to each other," Hunter said. His hazel eyes were flecked with gold.

"It was a pretty amazing coincidence," Lydia said.

"I'm going to duck out the side door. I'm parked on the street," he said.

"I'm in the parking garage," Lydia said.

When they reached the carpeted side aisle, Lydia said, "Good night. It was very nice sitting next to you. I imagine we'll run into each other again."

Not missing a beat, Hunter handed her his card. It was a gentleman's calling card—narrow, smaller than a business card.

"Call me," he said.

She ran her finger over the name: *J. Hunter Evans*. Raised letters. Engraved. On the back, written with a fountain pen in black ink: 684-6798.

"Old school," she said, examining the card as the departing concertgoers eddied around them.

"Call me," he repeated. "We can have lunch."

All his life, Hunter had loved to be in love. He was very carnal. It had resonated with Lydia in a subliminal way in 1963. Now the attraction was conscious. He was also amoral. To be truly amoral is unusual.

CHAPTER TWO

The Girl Who Loved the Night

It was a quarter to ten when Lydia got home. Peter wasn't back yet from the Surfrider meeting. She changed into jeans and a pullover, put on tennis shoes, and went for a walk. She left a note on the kitchen counter: *10:02 p.m. Gone for a walk. Back soon. Much love.*

Sally was at Tahoe with her Bolin cousins.

Lydia loved the night. The night was her natural element. She loved the night smells, the sensation of the night air, the brilliance of the stars. Cats were out at night. The cats had their own world. Skunks, raccoons, possums, palm tree rats, gray foxes. When she was little, she'd let herself out the kitchen door and stand on the patio at night. When she got older, she roamed around Montecito at night by herself. The grounds of the grand old estates, the orchards, the gardens of houses up long driveways were her territory. Once, when her father was very old, she asked him about it. How could he not have known? He said, "It would have been cruel to keep you in the house."

She could see in the dark—not pitch dark, but like a cat can see. Colors looked different. She soon learned it made people uneasy, if she said anything. They denied it was true. "You have good night vision, Lydia. You can't really see in the dark."

She was very young when she realized she lived in a different world from other people—she was aware of layers and layers of sensory information that other people were oblivious to.

Recently she had smelled gas and called the gas company. The SoCalGas technician went under the house with his gas leak detector. "There's a hairline crack in the furnace firebox, but it's not humanly possible that you smelled it," he told her.

No point in contradicting him.

When she and Peter were first living together, Peter had followed her on a full-moon night. They were living in a ranch house in a new housing tract in Goleta, the first property he bought when he got into real estate. He'd borrowed money for the down payment. She heard his footsteps behind her. Even if she hadn't, she had his scent. She could easily have slipped out of sight, but she stayed in plain view on the curving sidewalks and cul-de-sacs. After a while, Peter turned back. Lydia kept going, into an abandoned lemon orchard where the land was being cleared for more houses. The dead lemon trees had been bulldozed into piles. A white cat was watching a gopher hole. This melancholy place made Lydia nostalgic for Santa Barbara before she was born. When she got home, Peter was watching TV, as if he'd never left. That he would follow her made Lydia love him all the more. Far from feeling that he didn't trust her, she admired his enterprise. She never told him that she knew he'd followed her.

When people said, "Isn't it dangerous to go for walks at night?" Peter would laugh and say, "She's the one to be afraid of."

Their house was on the Mesa, the neighborhood up from the harbor on Santa Barbara Point. Separated from downtown by Carrillo Hill, the Mesa was often foggy when the rest of Santa Barbara was in bright sunshine. Their house was on El Camino de la Luz, a little street that ran along the ocean cliff and dead-ended at a ravine. The Santa Barbara Lighthouse was on the other side of the ravine. Before World War II, the Mesa was plant nurseries and a few oil wells, and there was an artist colony.

When Lydia set off on her walk after the concert, a full moon was high in the night sky. The revolving beacon of the lighthouse shone on and off, on and off, cutting across a silver trail of moonlight on the ocean. The moist night air smelled of the ocean and star jasmine and the dry grass on the ocean cliff. Lydia was walking along Edgewater Way, around the corner from her street, when a Buick LeSabre came cruising slowly down Mohawk Road, one of the little streets that run from Cliff Drive to the ocean.

At the same time, two big white dogs with thick coats came trotting down Mohawk Road, both wearing red leather collars, their tags jingling. She and the dogs had a nodding acquaintance. When she was out at night, she'd see them, going about their business, clearly on their way somewhere. If they encountered her, they would woof and politely cross to the other side of the road. The Buick LeSabre stopped. The driver rolled down the window. Lydia stood in the light of a buzzing streetlight.

"I'm lost," the man said. He was in his fifties with a beefy red face and the glad-hand manner of a salesman. "I'm trying to get to Cabrillo Boulevard."

Lydia gave him directions. "You have to go back up to Cliff Drive. Turn right on Cliff Drive, then take a right at the traffic light."

Twenty feet away, the dogs stopped and watched. Their cars perked up and they seemed to consult each other, watching in the way of concerned bystanders who are trying to decide if it is a situation in which they should intervene.

"Right at the stop sign, left at the light? I'll get lost," the man said in a candid bluff way, as he shifted the car into park. He patted the passenger seat. "Why don't you hop in? I'll buy you a drink."

"No, thank you," Lydia said, stepping back.

"Ah, come on," the man said, opening the car door, making as if he was going to get out of the car.

Lydia smelled the flop sweat of a human predator. All of a sudden, the dogs went crazy. Barking, they rushed at the car. They came in fast. Growling and snarling, snapping their jaws, the big dogs leaped at the car, crashed into it, their front paws hitting the car door and pushing it shut against the man.

"Holy shit," the man said, recoiling inside the car. "What the hell's wrong with them?"

"They don't want you to get out. You better put up your window."

"Bitch," the man said and floored it, driving off with a squeal of tires.

Lydia and the dogs watched the red taillights out of sight up Mohawk Road. Then the two big white dogs trotted off in tandem and Lydia continued on, walking in the direction of Mesa Lane, where a long flight of wooden steps with concrete landings and steel pipe railings provided public access to the beach. Peter didn't like for her to go down on the beach at night. He thought it would be too easy for her to be trapped. The mile and a half of beach from Hendry's Beach to Leadbetter Beach was a narrow strip of sand between the cliffs and the ocean. At high tide some places were completely cut off. This was the beach below Lydia's house. There had been two unsolved murders there.

Sometimes, though, Lydia couldn't resist. This night, she stood at the top of the steps. The horizon was black velvet. The night beckoned. The night wind stirred the leaves of the eucalyptus trees. The menthol smell of eucalyptus. She was not fazed by the Buick LeSabre parked with its lights off on Mesa Lane in the shadows. The creep had circled back around. She knew he could see her. The moon was bright, and there was a streetlight.

She started down the concrete steps. There was the thud of a car door shutting. She heard the man's footsteps approaching. She kept going. He started down the steps behind her. The wind off the ocean smelled of iodine, and Lydia's every sense was alive. She paused at the first landing and waited for him. She was enraged. What if Sally was at Mesa Lane checking out the surf, on a night when this man came snuffling around?

In other situations, Lydia would have dropped off the concrete landing into the lemonade berry thickets below and vanished. There were night people who were crazy and dangerous. She kept out of their way. But this man was a coward. She could smell it. If she had been a cat, she would have been clicking her teeth. He gave a start when he came to the landing and she was there.

"Looking for someone?" she said, her voice steely.

"We meet again," he said, jocular and menacing at once. He took a step closer.

Instead of retreating, she advanced on him, her lip curled.

"Crazy bitch," he said and turned and stumbled up the steps.

Lydia waited until she heard the car drive off, then made her way home along the trail that ran along the top of the cliff, skirting the houses on the cliff. She didn't go down on the beach that night. There were cypress trees at the edge of the bluff.

♦♦♦

When Lydia got home, Peter was reading in bed. He and Lydia were both lanky and rangy. They could have been brother and sister—as sometimes in bed they pretended they were. They both had dark blond hair. Dishwater blond with strands of gray now. They both had prominent noses. Distinguished noses. But Peter had blue eyes, and Lydia had gray-green-hazel eyes, the eye color of the Afghani girl in the famous photograph on the cover of *National Geographic*. Peter had white Northern European skin—he burned easily. Lydia's skin had a subtly golden tone—she tanned without burning. Her mother's parents were both from Sweden—she spoke Swedish before she spoke English. Her mother said there were people in the far north of Sweden, where the witches and shape-shifters come from, who had Lydia's coloring.

Peter had his reading glasses on and he was focused on a report by the Asheville Planning and Urban Design Department on the revitalization of downtown Asheville. The book on his night table was on the stock market: *Dow 36,000: The New Strategy for Profiting from the Coming Rise in the Stock Market*. The books on Lydia's night table were *Gentlemen Prefer Blondes* and Eleanor Perenyi's *Green Thoughts*. She was rereading the books that she liked.

"How was your walk?" Peter asked.

"It was a great walk!"

This was a family joke. Never, not once, had Lydia come back from a walk and not reported a great walk. "It was a great walk," she'd say, after she misjudged the tide and came in wet from the waist down, her shoes squishing, having had to wade through the waves breaking against the cliff. She saw no point in mentioning the creep in the Buick LeSabre.

"How was the chamber music?" He mimed playing a violin and sang, "La-la-la," in an imitation of a lieder singer.

"Very funny," she said and told him about the Music Academy students. "'He thinks the black hair makes him more romantic. More Romanticist. I know him in Moscow,'" she quoted.

Peter laughed.

"How was the Surfrider meeting?" she asked. She didn't mention that she had sat next to Hunter Evans. Someone she'd known when she was fourteen.

"We're going to appoint a committee to investigate an amicus brief for the Coastal Commission to implement the Public Access Program for Hollister Ranch."

Lydia sat on the bed and Peter regaled her with an account of the in-fighting at the meeting.

The plaster walls of the bedroom were painted a peach color. There was a Charles Walch painting of a garden and a vase of flowers, a French modernist painting that Lydia's father had bought in Berlin when he studied at the University of Hamburg in the early 1930s. The painting concealed a substantial combination-lock wall safe. Sometimes Peter had a lot of cash on hand—he sometimes did business off the books.

The foghorn at the end of Stearns Wharf was bleating. With the window open, they could hear the waves breaking on the rocky beach below the sea cliff. Our Mother the Ocean, the surfers said. The shrilling of crickets and the smell of star jasmine reminded Lydia of summer nights when she was a little girl.

Lydia and Peter were in their thirties when they got married, but they'd known each other all their lives. Both sets of parents were pillars of the community, as opposed to social. The first time Peter and Lydia met was when their mothers co-chaired Trick or Treat for UNICEF in 1959. The mothers had their photograph in the *Santa Barbara News-Press* and they got crank calls from members of the John Birch Society. Their husbands were proud of them.

Peter was two years ahead of Lydia in school. She remembered a party where Peter and Andy Barker—in later years the landscape contractor she worked for—jumped up on a table and sang along to "Papa-Oom-Mow-Mow" while doing the surfer stomp. He remembered her as an intrepid member of the Montecito Sneak-Out Crew, climbing up the beach cliff below the Santa Barbara Cemetery at midnight, hiking up to the Tea Garden in the foothills, with a bunch of boys and girls. Her night vision was a running joke. She never brought a flashlight, and the kids would say, "La Gata is here." Although sometimes someone would say, a little bit scared, "I think she really can see in the dark."

The Montecito Sneak-Out Crew was in a separate compartment of Lydia's life from her solitary roaming.

Lydia went in the bathroom and washed her face and brushed her teeth, and Peter resumed reading the report. She came to bed naked, and Peter put aside the report and took off his T-shirt. Lydia did not consciously feel amorous, but she knew from much experience that once they touched each other, once they started kissing, the sex would be good. One of the good things about their marriage was the sex. They were well attuned to each other. They knew what worked for each other. Afterward, Peter said, "I love you, babe," and Lydia said, "I love you, too."

If in any good marriage there is the lover and the beloved, Peter was the lover and Lydia was the beloved.

Peter turned on his side, and Lydia curled up against his back, her arms around him. She had friends who had good marriages who had separate bedrooms, but she and Peter slept together. She liked the feel of his skin, the smell of his body. They had been married seventeen years. When she'd told her parents they were getting married, her father said, "I have a high opinion of his character and determination."

It was a good marriage. Not perfect. They had their ups and downs. It drove her crazy that he was a shopper. He'd wander around the hardware store looking to see if there was anything he needed. He had a broad definition of need. Once he went to the plumbing supply store in the minivan to buy a new toilet for a rental property they had, and he came back with six toilets. They were on sale.

The houses on the Mesa are on small lots, enclosed by hedges and fences. On the other side of the pittosporum hedge, their neighbor was outside in his garden playing his flute. The notes carried in the damp air, plaintive and fey like a Pan pipe. A mockingbird trilled and was silent again.

As she drifted off to sleep, Lydia thought of a scene from the novel that Hunter was writing that summer. He'd read it to her in a resonant voice. The narrator meets a Japanese banker in a nightclub and the banker invites him to climb Mount Fuji with his son, who is the same age as the narrator. The narrator accepts the invitation, and the two young men climb Mount Fuji with a guide. It is summertime. On the descent, the guide outfits the young men with special shoes like snowshoes made of straw and they slide on a grassy path from the summit to the start of the trail.

Was that possible?

She wondered if Hunter remembered the last time they saw each other, in 1963.

CHAPTER THREE

Golf Cart Polo

LYDIA SAVED HUNTER'S CALLING card in the zippered compartment of her purse where she kept an emery board and loyalty punch cards from Mesa Video and Deano's Pizzarama. She was still friends with Annie. There had been a period in their twenties when they lost touch. Annie married her Stanford boyfriend and they lived in Italy. At the same time, Lydia was in New York. But they both ended up back in Santa Barbara. "Like salmon returning to spawn," Annie said.

Annie would have loved to know that Lydia sat next to Hunter at the chamber music concert. Nostalgia and name-dropping galore. However, Lydia didn't mention it when they had lunch at Carlito's, a restaurant on State Street, a few days later. Peter always said, "For someone as outspoken and candid as Lydia is, she's the most secretive person I know. When I try to imagine what she is thinking, at the end of the day, when she thinks about her day as she brushes her teeth…I have no idea."

The first week in October, Peter had to be in Asheville for five days. He was the silent partner in a partnership with two local real estate developers who planned to revitalize downtown Asheville. Private meetings were scheduled with civic leaders, and they were in discussions to buy several boarded-up Art Deco commercial buildings. In Santa Barbara, Peter steered clear of major projects. He didn't want to be vilified as a developer. He was a local. He'd gone to Carp—Carpinteria High School. He wore Hawaiian shirts, and he organized an annual longboard surf competition at the Rincon in benefit of Transition House. *Keep Santa Barbara the Way It Was* was his vibe. He made his money as an out-of-town developer in places like Austin and Asheville.

He took an early flight out of the Santa Barbara Airport. Lydia didn't get up—she would have been perfectly happy to get up and drive him, but he liked to drive himself and leave the car in the long-term parking lot. Drowsy and warm in bed, she heard Peter take a shower, get dressed, and zip shut his carry-on suitcase. She heard an urchin fishing boat, the sound of its motor growing louder as it approached the Point, then receding as it headed out into the Channel. The smell of coffee. In the kitchen, Peter sang, "Hi-ho, hi-ho…it's off to work I go."

He came in the bedroom to say goodbye.

"I love you, babe," he said, bending down to kiss her. Lydia put her arms around his neck and kissed him on the mouth. He broke away with theatrical reluctance. "Gotta go, babe. Gotta go. You go back to sleep."

"I love you, too. Call me."

He conga-ed out the bedroom door. "Money, money, money," he chanted. One two three—kick.

♦♦♦

At ten o'clock that morning, Lydia called Hunter. She'd been saving him for a little treat, a luncheon engagement when she had a free day. She called from the telephone in the kitchen. There was a view of the ocean through the cypress trees at the cliff's edge; the focal point was a lemon eucalyptus that she had planted when they first bought the house. The blue-green ocean sparkled in the sun. The louvered windows in the sun porch were open to the onshore breeze.

She examined the calling card, ran her finger over the name: *J. Hunter Evans.*

"Call me." A classic move, Lydia thought appreciatively. If she was single, she'd have handed him back the card and said, "No, you call me." Let him figure out how to get in touch. Otherwise, you've just handed over the power. Although, "Call me" is the correct move to make with a married woman. For even such an innocent invitation as a lunch engagement with an old acquaintance.

She dialed the number. 684-6798. At the time, you didn't have to dial the "805" area code.

The phone rang three times.

"Hello," he answered in his low urbane voice. Hunter never picked up on the first or second ring.

"Hello. It's Lydia Graham," she said in her social manner. A long line of pelicans flew up the coast, like a procession of enchanted princes, their wingbeats syncopated. "We were transported by Schubert at the Lobero."

"Of course. How are you?" he said.

"I'm fine. I was absolutely swamped with work and family, but I've surfaced. Sally's back at school. I was wondering if you'd like to get together for lunch some day this week?"

"What about today? There's a golf cart polo match. Santa Barbara is playing Palm Springs. We can watch from my terrace. It's the height of the season. I'll make lunch for us."

"Golf cart polo?" she said. "What is golf cart polo?"

"Morons with three million dollars of liability insurance."

"How can I resist?"

She'd assumed they would meet at a restaurant. Somewhere like Morishima on State Street or the Café del Sol. The Paradise Café. Carlito's. Nice restaurants but nothing fancy. Nothing *intime.* Places to meet for a chaste dalliance in the middle of the day. Hunter's condo at the Polo Club was not quite the same. Lydia thought about it. Briefly. She decided the golf cart polo defused any appearance of impropriety. She wanted to watch the golf cart polo, and he was giving her lunch.

♦♦♦

The US Air Force Tactical Air Command Band's rendition of "America the Beautiful" was playing on the classical station as Lydia drove in the main entrance of the Polo Club. It was high noon.

Oh beautiful, for spacious skies / For amber waves of grain / For purple mountain majesties / Above the fruited plain.

Peter and Sally sang "America the Beautiful" in the car. They also liked "Barnacle Bill the Sailor."

The landscaping dated from the early seventies, which was when the condos were built. The grounds were well kept, but the ivy ground cover needed rejuvenation and the lawns were sparse in places. The ficus trees, however, were flourishing. People from out of town, including the polo patrons, owned condos as *pieds-à-terre*, and the polo patrons kept condos for the players to stay in during the season. In Santa Barbara the Polo Club was a respectable address for people who were keeping up appearances. "The escorts live at the Polo Club," Annie's mother always said.

There was a parking kiosk at the entrance, but it was unattended except on Sundays in the summer when there was a polo match. At night, you had to punch in a code to get in, but in the daytime, the electric gate was open. Lydia parked in one of the visitor parking slots in front of the tennis club and followed a pathway of pebbled concrete to Hunter's block of condos. Agapanthus with globes of deep purple flowers lined the path. She remembered walking through the rusted gates of Campos Elíseos and down the enchanted lane in the golden afternoon, wondering if Hunter Evans would be there.

The condo was the end unit on the ground floor of a three-story stucco building that was built into the slope. Hunter's front entrance was down three steps. No little pink bicycles. The polo season was over. Lydia rang the bell, and Hunter came to the door.

"Come in, darling," he said. He was wearing a blue Oxford cloth shirt and khakis. In the light of day, she saw the skin below his earlobes was slack, and there were deep etched lines at the corners of his mouth. He was old. "They're lining up for the first chukka. We don't want to miss it. You have to see for yourself to get the full impact."

He ushered Lydia into a little entry hall with a console table. Black-and-white family photographs in silver frames. His fashionable parents with bicycles in Bermuda in 1930. Hunter as a handsome baby in a christening gown with his fondly smiling mother. A color photograph of Hunter in black tie and a pretty brunette woman in a long dress—presumably the wife who was twelve years younger and drop-dead beautiful. The one he was never unfaithful to. A Japanese erotic print on the wall: *Lovers in the Upstairs Room of a Teahouse.* There were good rugs—a red and midnight blue Persian runner in the foyer, a large blue Chinese rug with gold dragons in the small living room—but these were laid on top of beige wall-to-wall Berber carpet, rather than hardwood floors. The fireplace was a gas fireplace.

It was classy, very nicely done. But it didn't escape Lydia that Hunter was keeping up appearances. It didn't make her not like him. She was curious.

Hunter led her out a sliding glass door onto a terracotta-tiled terrace with a low balustrade. Below the balustrade was an ivy-covered bank, and then the emerald-green polo field. Concrete planters divided the terrace into a separate patio for each condo. There was a bougainvillea with magenta flowers on a trellis in the planter between Hunter's patio and the adjoining patio. The adjoining patio was furnished with a teak table with a market umbrella and big glazed pots in which jade plants and aloes flourished. Hunter's section of the terrace was bare. They stood at the edge of the terrace in the glare of the noonday sun.

"They trucked the golf carts up from Palm Springs this morning," he said.

"What won't they think of next," she said.

On the polo field, four golf carts were faced off at the center line, two carts on each team. Each cart had a driver and a player. The players brandished mallets. A referee in a black-and-white-striped shirt threw the ball in and the carts wheeled into action, the drivers and players whooping. The game was ludicrous. The carts could race forward and make wide, careening turns, but in reverse they bucked while the motors whined.

"Now I've seen everything," Lydia said, as a beefy white man with a red face in a US Polo Association–compliant helmet toppled out of his golf cart.

"I think the word is *decadent.*" Hunter used *decadent* in the old sense of the word, as in marked by decay or decline—rather than scrumptious and self-indulgent.

The sun beat down. The golf carts careered around. There was a high myoporum hedge between the polo field and the frontage road beyond. Like boats floating on a canal in Holland above the level of the land, the tops of big trucks on the highway could be seen above the top of the hedge. Across the highway, there were tall eucalyptus trees, and then the flat expanse of ocean, Santa Cruz Island on the horizon. White pigeons wheeled and banked over the empty grandstand.

"Let's pack it in," Hunter said. Two crows flew down to the balustrade and strutted in tandem in the stiff-legged human way of crows, then flapped their wings and flew away. *Caw caw caw.* "Crows are such unattractive birds," Hunter remarked. Lydia thought that was funny.

They went back inside. Lydia sat on a bar stool at the counter between the dining alcove and the kitchen and talked to Hunter. The menu was cold soba noodles with chopped green onions and minced ginger. The chopped green onion and minced ginger were ready in Pyrex ramekins sealed with plastic wrap. The buckwheat noodles were cooked and waiting in a colander on the counter. The setup was very sixties *Playboy.* The background music was the Bill Evans Trio: "Someday My Prince Will Come." "When I Fall in Love." Hunter's CD player was hooked up to old-fashioned big stereo speakers. A sound system from the seventies. On the summer afternoons when Lydia had called on Hunter, she listened to his jazz in the spirit of talking nicely to adults. Grown-ups listened to jazz.

Her parents drove down to Shelly's Manne-Hole in Hollywood to hear Chet Baker and Miles Davis.

Hunter poured Kirin beers for them into two Pilsner beer glasses and put out slate blue rectangular woven coasters that he said he had made to order in the Philippines. "They absorb the condensed moisture from the glass," he said.

The round mahogany table in the dining alcove was set for two with beige linen placemats and matching napkins. Each place had a small jade green pottery bowl for the dipping sauce.

"When were you in the Philippines?" Lydia asked.

He said he was in the Philippines when he was a contract specialist for the Navy. At Subic Bay, the Navy base in the Philippines, there was a terrific problem with thievery. The Americans paid the Negritos, the hill people, to patrol the perimeter of the base and hunt the thieves.

"You didn't work for the State Department?"

"Indirectly," he said as he divided the cold buckwheat noodles into two Seikaiha bowls—porcelain bowls in a blue pattern of overlapping concentric circles. "I was a civilian contract specialist with the army in Singapore during the Vietnam War—that was the job I was waiting to hear about that summer. I stayed over there in Asia for thirty years.

"I liked living overseas. We lived in Tokyo, Singapore, Manila. It was an interesting life. I went to Afghanistan once to oversee a government plant that reconstituted milk. I had seventy people working for me when I retired. Twenty lawyers. In all that time, I never took a kickback."

Really? thought Lydia. "Never took a kickback" had the sound of "never unfaithful to my wife." *What happened to the money?* she wondered.

"Where does the money come from" and "what happened to the money"—perennial topics in Santa Barbara. How could she not be interested?

♦♦♦

THE LUNCH WAS LEISURELY. They ate their noodles with black lacquer chopsticks. When they finished, Hunter went into the kitchen and got two more beers out of the refrigerator. He refilled their glasses, and they retired to the living room area. Hunter sat on a black leather couch, and Lydia sat across from him in a wing chair upholstered in teal green velvet, an antique gilt coffee table between them. The tall, tapered beer glasses filled with the golden beer. The slate blue woven coasters. Twelve long-stemmed apricot-yellow roses in a white and Delft blue porcelain vase. Lydia appreciated the *mise-en-scène*, the feng shui. She was amused by his pretensions.

"So… do you have a girlfriend?" Lydia asked. She was curious—as if she was a bold fourteen-year-old girl.

"Yes and no," he said. "Do you remember Rosalind Flynn? She's Rosalind Forester now."

"Of course I remember her. I saw her not long ago at a memorial service. Her phone number is my parents' old number. One of my father's old patients called at some ungodly hour wanting to talk to Dr. Graham, and the next day Rosalind called my father at Vista del Monte to let him know."

"We have all these connections, darling," Hunter said.

Rosalind was Hunter's contemporary. She had been famous for being the prettiest girl in Santa Barbara. A judge who was a friend of Lydia's father remembered getting into a fight over her at the Valley Club. A Texas oil millionaire gave her a Studebaker convertible for her sixteenth birthday. It was parked in the driveway with a pink satin ribbon around it. She married him when she turned eighteen. The summer that Lydia was fourteen, Rosalind was divorcing the oil millionaire to marry a movie star old enough to be her father. Her divorce was almost final. The movie star's divorce was proving to be messy and expensive and drawn out. That summer he was on location in Spain filming a western, and they had expensive, frustrating, hour-long long-distance calls. Rosalind had rented one of the beach houses on Miramar Lane—narrow, tall houses on pilings, with no space between them. Now she was a widow, and she, like Hunter, had returned to Santa Barbara and the social circle of her girlhood.

"People think we're a couple," Hunter said. "We're invited places as a couple. Everyone says I should marry her. Rosalind is a dear friend. She understands me better than anyone else. I love her, but I'm not in love with her."

"What does 'I love her but I'm not in love with her' mean?" Lydia asked.

"She doesn't turn me on."

"That's too bad," Lydia said drily.

Unchastened, Hunter said, "It's like kissing your grandmother. When I take her home, she'll want me to come in, and I have to tell her, 'I can't.' She was the prettiest girl in Santa Barbara. Now she's an old lady in the buffet line at the Coral Casino."

"I can see it would be a problem." She wasn't going to scold him. If women his own age didn't turn him on, he wasn't going to change.

"It's different for a man," he said. "You're old, but you know more things."

"What do you mean?" Lydia asked wide-eyed. She knew perfectly well that "more things" was sexual experience.

Hunter said, "Don't be disingenuous, darling."

"Am I too old?" Lydia asked, being a minx.

"No, darling." Then he said, seriously, "It makes it awkward that Rosalind's rich, and my tiny amount of money has to last me the rest of my life. There isn't any way to add to it, unless there's a miracle. She wants to pay for things, but I can't let her."

They contemplated each other across the twelve long-stemmed apricot roses on the gilt coffee table. Hunter's yellow-hazel eyes, satyr's eyes. Lydia's blue-green-gray eyes, atavistic eyes. Quiet jazz and the smell of the rose petal potpourri in a crystal bowl on the console table.

"Hunter, do you remember the last time we saw each other?" Lydia said, no longer flirtatious. This was a serious question.

"The elephant in the room," Hunter said. "Lydia, let me show you something."

At that point, the doorbell rang. Ding-dong.

Lydia gave Hunter an inquiring look.

"We'll ignore it."

Ding-dong again, followed by loud knocking. "Hunter? You there?" a man's voice called out.

Hunter got up. "It's a jerky guy I knew in Vietnam." The doorbell rang again.

Hunter strode to the door and abruptly opened it. Lydia had a glimpse of a stocky man with curly gray hair.

"I've got a girl here," Hunter said, as if it were 1957.

"Don't avoid me, Hunter."

Hunter said to Lydia, "I'll get rid of him," and stepped outside, shutting the door behind him. Lydia got up and went out on the terrace. The golf cart polo was still going on. One of the golf carts had overturned onto its side, the other golf carts now parked around it, like worried herd animals around a fallen member of the herd. She walked to the end of the terrace. She heard the man say, "What the fuck happens to your money, Hunter?"

"Keep your voice down," Hunter said.

After that, Lydia heard only a murmur. Later, she thought she should have dropped down off the terrace and gone around the corner of the building to listen, but at the time she didn't want Hunter to catch her eavesdropping. Five minutes later, when Hunter came out on the terrace to find her, she was taking a polite interest in the golf cart polo. The overturned cart had been righted, and now the players were taking a break.

"Here you are," Hunter said. "Sorry to abandon you. The guy's an art dealer. I knew him in Da Nang. He travels all over the world now. He's doing a show in LA and wanted us to get together. I left a message at his hotel that I wasn't available, but he drove up anyway. The last time he was here, he kept talking about my cool pad."

"Perfectly okay. You missed the overturned golf cart," Lydia said.

They went back inside.

Lydia asked, "What did you want to show me?"

"You sit down, and I'll get it. Do you want something to drink?"

Lydia said, "No, thank you," and sat down in the wing chair.

Hunter put on a Brahms cello sonata, remarking that chamber music bored Rosalind. "She falls asleep."

The Brahms was passionate and yearning. Hunter went to a closet with louvered doors in the foyer and opened the locked trunk where he kept his important papers and the keepsakes of his life. There was the *Playboy* magazine in which a girl he'd dated was Playmate of the Month. The two pages of the Lobero program were on top. The smell of old documents, old newsprint, and gun oil. Lydia imagined a well-oiled revolver wrapped in a soft cloth. When Hunter came back, he handed Lydia a 5-by-7-inch black-and-white matte photograph. A high-quality print with a stiff backing. It was a photograph of her that he had taken when she was fourteen. She's looking into the camera, her lips parted, her eyes hazy with sex. Hunter watched Lydia looking at the photograph.

She remembered the circumstances: an afternoon at the end of August, the tarry asphalt warm and soft under her bare feet. Hunter was outside taking photographs with his 35-mm Leica, like a foreign correspondent.

"Let me take your picture," he'd said.

She'd always liked having her picture taken. There was something about having the exterior of her be the object of attention that was freeing. Her thoughts, her interior self—those were not the object of attention. The same objectification, she supposed, that so many women find insulting. Also, she liked how she looked. It didn't bother her at all that she wasn't beautiful. True physical beauty is a rare gift from the gods.

"Let's pose you," Hunter had said, looking around. "Can you sit up there?"

Many years before, a tall blue gum eucalyptus tree across the lane from the gatehouse cottage had blown over in a windstorm. Its bare, silvery trunk rested on the steep bank of the ravine, the uprooted roots a tangle like giant grasping fingers at the bottom.

Lydia was wearing a beach shift over her two-piece bathing suit. She hitched up her shift, and Hunter gave her a boost up. She straddled the tree trunk.

The weathered wood was worn silky smooth. The afternoon was quiet. No sound of cars in the distance. No birds sang. Dry leaves scudded on the cracked asphalt, and there was the peppery smell of crushed nasturtium leaves. The tree trunk was too big around for her to wrap her legs around. Even though she pressed her thighs against it, she started to slide down.

"Help," she said, laughing.

Hunter took pictures as she made a slow descent down the steep incline of the tree trunk, her beach shift hiked up, her crotch rubbing against the smooth wood through the thin cotton of her bathing suit, as she balanced herself with both hands. She heard the clicks of Hunter's camera. He was looking through the viewfinder. The friction of the tree trunk between her legs felt good, then it felt even better, then it was pure pleasure.

"Oh," she said softly. She opened her eyes wide and looked up at Hunter.

He looked up from the camera. "That was very nice," he called down to her.

She slid off the trunk to stand in a tangle of nasturtium vines and dead leaves. She was floating, the way it feels when you do the trick of standing in a doorway and pressing your hands hard against the door frame, so that when you stand away and put your hands at your sides, your arms rise of their own volition. She scrambled in dreamy slow motion out of the ravine, as Hunter kept on snapping photos. Like a sleepwalker, she went to him and kissed him on the mouth. The kiss was like white light. Hunter did not embrace her, and after a moment he stepped back. He had an erection.

"Let's go in the house," Lydia said.

"Jesus," he said. "You're going to get me put in jail."

"Not if no one knows," she said.

"You're too young," he said.

All summer, he'd known it would be easy to seduce Lydia. She was carnal and curious. But the potential for drama and scandal was too great. It always ended badly with a well-brought-up *jeune fille*. He had enough to cope with. At that moment, Rosalind drove up in her black VW Bug convertible with the top down. Hunter had been on the short list for a grade 10 civilian contract specialist with the Navy, and he had found out that morning that he had the job. He'd called Rosalind and let her know as soon as he heard.

"We could just kiss," Lydia said, as Rosalind got out of the car.

Hunter said, "No arguing. Off you go, Lydia."

"Bye-bye," she said. "Hello, Rosalind."

It was the last time Lydia saw Hunter, until they met again thirty-seven years later at the Lobero. The next time she walked past the gatehouse cottage, it was vacant. Annie's mother said he'd taken a job.

Having contemplated the photograph, Lydia set it on the coffee table.

"You never said goodbye," she said, looking at Hunter.

"No, I didn't. But I kept the picture. Were you sad?"

"Not really. You weren't part of my real life."

Now the light and graceful *allegretto* movement of the Brahms cello sonata was playing.

"Did you know I had an orgasm?" she asked Hunter.

"Look at the picture, darling."

Hunter's calculation was that if, at the moment, he got up and went over and kissed Lydia, she would let him. But she wouldn't go to bed with him. And she probably wouldn't see him alone again. Better to wait.

Lydia felt the sex in the air. It was a subterranean, emotional, erotic connection that had lasted thirty-seven years.

She had never in any of her flirtations felt that she couldn't trust herself. Now, she wasn't certain.

"I should be going now," she said, standing up. She did not want him to make a pass. "I'll let you keep the picture."

Hunter said he'd walk her to her car and then get his mail. They walked up the pebbled concrete path lined with agapanthus. They discussed the coincidence that Rosalind had Lydia's parents' phone number.

"Thank you for the lunch," Lydia said, when they got to her car. Tennis players were playing mixed doubles on two of the tennis courts. "We'll have to do it again sometime."

Hunter said, "Give me a ring."

They both knew that "We'll have to do it again sometime" meant: Our lunch, while delightful, was a one-time thing.

♦♦♦

IT WAS LATE AFTERNOON when Peter called from Asheville. Lydia was out in the garden. Snails had been eating the tender new shoots of her sweet peas down to the ground. Barriers of wood ash and dishes of beer having proved useless, she had put out snail pellets. Now the sweet pea bed was littered with the empty shells of dead snails. The new green shoots of the sweet peas were intact and undevoured, but the flower bed had a distinct elephant graveyard look to it.

"It was the snails or the sweet peas, Kitty," she said to the little cat stretched out under a rosemary bush, camouflaged by her glossy black-and-white tuxedo coat. Her sharp teeth and sharp claws were not in evidence.

Peter said the business socializing was a drag. "I want to say, 'You know, dude, our mutual goal is for all parties to make money. We don't have to be bros.' "

He was about to have dinner at the home of a civic-minded idealist on the planning commission and his wife.

"Well, it is a business trip," Lydia said. "I miss you."

He said he missed her, too. He was coming home the day after tomorrow. He'd probably have to go back, but *c'est la vie*. Maybe she would go with him, and they could go to the Outer Banks. Lydia didn't mention that she'd had lunch with Hunter.

CHAPTER FOUR

Financial

Hunter and Joel Frank, the man who came to the condo, first met in a high-stakes poker game in the officers' club at Da Nang Air Base. Hunter was in Da Nang to inspect airfield construction that the Navy had contracted for, and Joel was a fighter pilot who supplemented his military pay by playing poker and dealing in Vietnamese artifacts.

Joel was from Montauk. In college, he'd played a lot of poker, and his uncle Jacob, who was in the garment business in New York, brought him in on some high-stakes games. His uncle was known as a solid poker player, a little bit of a high roller. No one suspected him of being a cheat. He didn't cheat all the time—only once in a while to win the pot. Collusion is the easiest way to cheat, but you need a trustworthy partner. When his longtime friend and poker partner died of a heart attack, Jacob recruited Joel. Jacob Frank's smart nephew who played baseball at Cornell was a welcome addition. On his own, Joel paid a magician to teach him sleight of hand—how to deal from the bottom of the deck, palm a card, that sort of thing.

In Vietnam, he didn't cheat all the time—only, emulating his uncle, once in a while to win the pot. He observed Hunter cheating in a game at the officers' club. Hunter didn't have the card-sharper skills that Joel had, but he was a cool customer. Soon—neither could remember exactly how it came about—they became occasional partners. Joel went on to be an art dealer with an international clientele, specializing in Asian art. He sold to private collectors and museums. He and his wife had houses in Santa Fe and Marrakesh. More than thirty years later, he and Hunter were still occasional poker partners. A game in a suite at the Hôtel Meurice in Paris, a game at a retreat on Cumberland Island. Usually, Joel found the games through his wife. He and Hunter were invited, they made money, they split fifty-fifty.

He showed up at the condo because Hunter owed him money. In May of that year, Hunter had gotten them into a game at one of the Rancheros Visitadores camps—Rancheros Visitadores is like the Bohemian Grove on horseback. Ronald Reagan belonged to it. With Joel's collusion, Hunter won the pot—and then he didn't give Joel his cut. Joel was pissed. He had a lead on a game at a manor in the Swedish countryside at Christmastime, but he wasn't bringing Hunter in if he still owed him the two hundred grand.

Hunter shouldn't have been broke. During his years as a contract specialist in Asia—and also in the United States—he was a senior contract specialist at China Lake Naval Air Weapons Station—he made a good salary. He had also, despite what he told Lydia, discreetly and within bounds that didn't trigger an investigation, taken full advantage of opportunities for kickbacks. It was almost impossible not to make money during the Vietnam War. Plus, he had a generous government pension. *What the fuck happened to the money?*

For one thing, Hunter consistently made bad investments. He had a picture in his mind, from reading *The Catcher in the Rye* and F. Scott Fitzgerald, that he was the upper-class guy from the East Coast who makes it in business. The kind of guy who invests in a ranch in Argentina and gets rich. Or gets in on the ground floor with IBM. This was also his father's fantasy. His father had a brief early success in the thirties with a high-end jam and jelly business that Hunter's grandmother financed, but World War II sugar rationing put an end to that, and none of the subsequent business ventures that he financed with his own money ever made a profit. Hunter's father never grasped the concept of other people's money. He left a lot of money on the table. He belonged to good clubs and devoted a lot of thought to his clothes—he was one of the original *Esquire* Best-Dressed Men. The family had social connections. Hunter remembered in high school going into Manhattan on the train from Scarsdale to tea dances at the Plaza.

Hunter knew how to read a contract, but he didn't know how to read a brokerage statement. He would have done better putting the money in certificates of deposit. Also, he had a history of behaving badly—or impulsively. Or both. This was often expensive.

In Japan he had a Porsche that he drove at excessively high speeds. Once, when the pursuing highway patrol officers in their standard-issue police cars couldn't catch him in his Porsche—this was on a major mountain highway—the Japanese police called ahead and put up a roadblock. He lost his license for six months and had to pay an enormous fine. Another time, he and a Japanese colleague had a threesome with the friend's wife. "Two men. I am so lucky," she'd said. Hunter led the friend to believe he would repay the favor with his wife. He had no intention of following through. The colleague showed up at Hunter's house when he was away, looking for some action. Hunter's wife, Fukiko, was furious. Hunter placated her with a five-strand Mikimoto pearl necklace with a diamond clasp.

A hit-and-run accident was the most serious incident. A child was killed. He borrowed money from a yakuza loan shark at a usurious rate to pay off the family. More than thirty years later, he was still paying on the yakuza loan.

More recently, after Sharon died and before he moved back to Santa Barbara, he was involved in a disastrous real estate deal in Newport Beach with a forty-year-old divorcée and her investor father who belonged to the Jonathan Club, a members-only club in Los Angeles. On the day that Lydia came to lunch at the Polo Club, Hunter was still on the hook for hundreds of thousands of dollars.

Throughout it all, Hunter kept up appearances. His reputation was important to him. There might be rumors of insurance fraud, traffic violations, drunk driving, tax evasion, borrowing money and not paying it back—but that all came under bad behavior. No one knew about the hit-and-run death in Japan. And so while people who knew Hunter might be wary of doing business with him, they still invited him to their parties. He wasn't a criminal, for Christ's sake!

Bad behavior was the reason his Japanese wife divorced him. Not the threesome situation. In 1963, Hunter was in a high-stakes poker game at the Yokota Officers Club in Japan. This was before he met Joel Frank. Two colonels accused him of cheating. He was cheating. They roughed him up, and he had to give them all his money. All his money—not just the pot that he'd taken. Word got out, and from then on, a certain echelon of Japanese society was closed to him. His wife filed for divorce. He was fired from his good job that his father-in-law got him.

He told his mother it was a setup, and she wired him a one-way first-class ticket on Pan Am. That was all she'd do for him. This was the summer that Lydia met him. His godmother had arranged for him to stay in the gatehouse.

CHAPTER FIVE

Convergence of the Twain

THE NEXT DAY WAS hot and dry. Boulders on the mountain ridges stood out in stereoscopic relief. The day started with a call from Andy Barker, the landscape contractor Lydia worked for.

"Fire weather," Lydia said when she answered the phone.

Andy said the arrow on the fire danger meter in front of the firehouse on Foothill Road was in the red zone. He was calling to tell her that the Siegels had changed their minds about a stone wall around the master bedroom patio. Andy was meeting with them that afternoon, and he wanted to know if Lydia had any ideas. She asked if he was at the job site now. He said yes, he'd be there for a couple of hours. She said she'd come out and take a look.

"It will inspire me," she said.

This was a joke they had.

She was, after all, his muse.

Andy had gone to Chouinard Art Institute. After he graduated, he'd had a couple of shows of his photo-conceptual pieces, but then he married a woman with three children under the age of five and no child support. He'd needed to make money, and he started doing landscaping. At first, he worked for Turk Hesselund Nursery, but soon he had his own business and was hiring other people. His wife was his business manager. She had a knack for shepherding a project through the permitting process. Andy was brilliant with the hardscape, the practicalities, but his training as an artist didn't translate into an aesthetic vision. Peter, who had known Andy all his life, suggested he hire Lydia. She had an aesthetic sensibility, a feeling for the gardens of Santa Barbara. She'd designed their garden on the Mesa. Lydia was good with interior views, created views, borrowed views, and lines of vision. She also knew about plants.

Andy billed his clients for Lydia's time as a "consultant."

The job site was a property on Picacho Lane in Montecito. The original house was a four-bedroom fifties ranch house that the new owners, whom Lydia liked, were turning into a Tuscan villa.

The Siegels had started out dirt poor in Chicago and made a lot of money in the bail bond business. "From the street to the suite," Sol Siegel liked to say. Now they were in their sixties. Fran Siegel was zaftig and down-to-earth, with red hair and hoop earrings. She wore Pucci pants in geometric patterns of chartreuse and hot pink and turquoise. Sol always looked rumpled. You could imagine him going after a skip in his early days. They'd sold the bail bond business, and now they went on jazz cruises and European tours. They wanted the grounds of their Tuscan villa on an acre and a half to be like the *Giardino di Villa Gamberaia* outside of Florence. Lydia liked the concept. She drew inspiration from the terraced sunken garden at Campos Eliseos.

The transformation of a midcentury ranch house into a Tuscan villa involved adding a new wing as big as the original house, plus a second floor. When Lydia drove up, five or six pickup trucks were parked in the circular driveway. A VW Westfalia camper van with a surfboard rack on the roof and a Ford station wagon with State of Chihuahua plates were pulled up on the dusty ivy groundcover in front of the house. Lydia parked behind Andy's pickup. In the distance, over the trees, the blue-green ocean sparkled in the sunlight. A fog bank, the result of the hot air on land meeting the cold ocean water, had formed over the Channel out by the islands. The wall of fog foreshortened the far horizon.

When Lydia was a girl, there was a footpath behind this property that connected Picacho Lane to San Ysidro Road. It was a shortcut she took when she roamed about at night. One midnight, she had witnessed through the picture window of the living room the woman who lived in the house giving a man a blowjob. She was in a shirtwaist dress on her knees. He was in a coat and tie, his pants unbuttoned, the fly unzipped. His big hard dick was in her mouth. It was fashionable not to have curtains. "Who is going to look in?" A girl outside in the night, for one. *I prowl around the prowlers.*—Gide.

Lydia picked her way between a pile of builder's sand and a portable cement mixer. Two men were up on a scaffold applying a finish coat of stucco. The original persimmon-orange front door with a brass starburst doorknob had been replaced by tall monastery doors. From inside the house came the sound of hammering and the whine of a table saw, along with the smells of lumber and damp concrete. She found Andy at the back of the house. A bulldozer had already come and cut terraces for the sunken garden. Three stonemasons from Mexico were working with chisels and hammers on the stones for the retaining walls. There was a pile of sandstone blocks. The stone walls of the old estates had been built by Italian stonemasons.

Andy was talking to two young men—college age, although neither was enrolled in college—both tall, well muscled, good-looking, tanned, wearing their jeans low on their hips, bare-chested in the heat. One was blond, the other had sun-streaked brown hair. Sally called them the surf gods. Their fathers were friends of Andy's—Andy had hired them to clean up the construction debris. It was entirely likely they'd end up like their fathers and Andy, making a good living in Santa Barbara as contractors. But at the moment, they were in the marijuana business, and October is the harvest season in Santa Barbara. The plants they were growing in Los Padres National Forest were ready to harvest.

"Have to boogie, Andy," the blond surf god said. "Marauders are a definite possibility."

"We left Deedee standing guard with an air horn," the other said. Deedee was his twin sister.

"Go. Pull the plants," Andy said. "But you've got to be here next week."

"What if there's a hurricane off Mexico and ten-foot swells?"

"See you at the Rincon," Andy said.

Lydia approached and said, "Hello, Luke… Hello, Danny. Why aren't you boys in school?" This was a running joke.

"Hello, Mrs. Bolin. How's Sally?"

They were protective of Sally. They'd known her all her life. Once when she was eight, she swam out past the waves at Hendry's Beach and was afraid to body surf back in. Luke and Danny, twelve-year-olds at the time, were already out, waiting for the right wave. As Lydia was thinking she'd have to commandeer a boogie board and paddle out and get Sally, the two boys conferred with each other, then in a united effort, treading water, they picked up Sally and flung her over the crest of a wave, so that she had no choice but to body surf to shore. Sally said they hadn't exactly asked her. But it worked.

Lydia said Sally was fine, and they were off, promising they would drop some sinsemilla by the house.

"To be young again," Andy said. He was stocky and bald and had a lot of self-confidence. As he said, when you're a surfer and you go bald in your twenties, you develop a lot of self-confidence.

The master suite was in the new wing. X-marks of blue masking tape crisscrossed the glass of the windows and the French doors. The dimensions of the proposed stone wall around what would be a private patio were marked with string and stakes. Andy said Fran Siegel had decided a stone wall would make her feel like she was a prisoner. Lydia told Andy it was a failure of communication on her part. Her vision was of a walled garden with honeysuckle and rosemary, the warmth of a wall of honey-colored sandstone, glimpses of trees and of Montecito Peak over the top of the wall. It was a sanctuary, the very opposite of a prison.

"Should we try to sell them on staying with the stone wall?" she asked.

"I'll talk to them. But I want them to be sure. We can always put in a stone wall later. I don't want to have to demolish one."

One of the stonemasons came to ask Andy a question. As they communicated in a combination of Spanish and English, Lydia thought about the problem of the patio. Then her thoughts turned to Hunter. That one kiss, so long ago. How it had felt to slide down the smooth tree trunk. The stonemason went back to where he'd been working, and Andy joined Lydia.

"Okay," she said. "Forget the stone wall. A privet hedge. We can plant five-foot privet saplings close together and water the heck out of them with a drip system. They'll be a solid barrier in six months."

"Some people can't stand the smell of privet," Andy said.

"It'll be sexy," she said and described the hedge. The creamy white flowers beloved by bees. Honeybees, shiny black bees bigger than honeybees but smaller than bumblebees, tiny yellow bees, and gray bees with black stripes. The bees all drunk with nectar, buzzing and bumbling. The hedge with its glossy green leaves. "The Siegels will love it."

"What if she's allergic to bees?" said Andy.

"I'd be surprised. But definitely find out. Fernleaf clumping bamboo might work. No flowers. But not as sexy."

"You've solved it. Do you want to be at the meeting? You can be poetic."

Lydia said that she was sure he'd make a good presentation, and then Andy's mobile phone rang. It was his wife letting him know that the check for the deposit on a big job had cleared. As Lydia walked to her car, she thought about how much she liked working with Andy. If she had an affair with Hunter Evans and Peter found out, which he most likely would, it would be the end of her marriage. It would not be an amicable divorce. He wouldn't screw her over financially, because of Sally, but she'd be the bad guy. Andy wouldn't keep her on the payroll. He and Peter were bros. Something to think about.

♦♦♦

THAT AFTERNOON, LYDIA WENT for a swim in the ocean. She drove to Hendry's, a wide sandy beach a mile and a half up the coast. She could have gone down the cliff trail to the narrow beach below her house, but the ocean there was treacherous with submerged rocks. Hendry's was a family beach with two parking lots, a beach café, a lifeguard tower, and a little park with a lawn and palm trees. It was a weekday afternoon, but people had flocked to the beach in the hot, dry weather. The parking lot was full; Lydia found a parking space at the far end of the overflow lot by the estuary.

She left her beach towel on the sand by the lifeguard tower and splashed into the water, jumping over the little waves, squinting against the dazzle of the afternoon sun. Out past the waves, she paddled back and forth, then abandoned herself to the buoyancy of the ocean, sculling on her back. The tableau of the beach was like an Impressionist painting. Moms in beach chairs. People in bathing suits in line at the hamburger stand. People strolled on the beach. Children played in the foam and made dribble sandcastles. Kids on boogie boards rode the shore break. This was the beach where Sally got stuck out past the waves. Out beyond the buoys, five dolphins circled a school of fish, leaping and diving like dolphins on a Minoan frieze.

On the way home, Lydia stopped at Lazy Acres, the carriage-trade grocery store on the Mesa. She was still in her bathing suit—a fuchsia one-piece *maillot*, a beach towel around her waist, sandy feet in flip-flops, damp hair in a tangle. There is a languor after swimming in salt water. She felt a sense of pure sensual well-being.

"Can I help who's next?" the young man in the fish department asked. He had bad skin and a cheeky manner,

She said, "I'd like a quarter pound of halibut, please. It's for my supper. May I have the piece in the back?"

"You can have anything you want, ma'am."

She laughed and said, "Anything?"

He looked at her boldly. "That's what I tell my girlfriend. You can have anything you want."

When she got home, Lydia took a shower in the beach bathroom. A beach bathroom has a door to the outside, so you can take a shower without tracking sand in the house. Chilled, she stood under the hot water of the shower. She had the feeling that there was a piece of information about Hunter, something from before the summer when she was fourteen, that was eluding her memory.

She had just gotten out of the shower when Peter called. She talked to him naked with a large white towel around her, her hair still wet. He said everything was going well—he'd be back tomorrow evening at eight, if he didn't get stuck in Dallas. It turned out that he and a leader of the anti-gentrification faction were both Eagles fans. They thought maybe they'd both been at the same concert in LA in the seventies.

"We sang along to 'Desperado' in the car," he said.

"Oh, for God's sake, you are shameless. You don't like the Eagles."

"You do what ya gotta do," he said. "We bonded."

He'd seen on the Weather Channel that it was ninety-eight in Los Angeles. Lydia said it was ninety-six in Santa Barbara. She told Peter about her day—the privet hedge inspiration and the surf gods' promise to come by the house with some sinsemilla.

"I remember when Andy and I were growing plants and someone in the neighborhood didn't pull his males and all our females had seeds," Peter said.

"Talk about bad behavior," Lydia said. "I had a lovely swim in the ocean. Right now, I'm naked except for a towel."

"We could have phone sex," Peter said.

"Let's wait till you come home and have real sex."

She told him that she'd been in Turk Hesselund Nursery and the owner had gone into a tirade about how the nursery was dying on the vine because people aren't interested in real gardening anymore. The granddames took a personal interest in their gardens. They had gardeners, but they came into the nursery with their gardeners.

"The new wave is good for Andy's business," Peter said.

"True," she said. Andy had recently started a landscape maintenance service, so that the properties would be properly maintained.

After they hung up, she stood on the back steps, still naked except for the towel. A hot wind blew off the ocean. She could see a narrow racing shell, a sixty-foot coxed eight, shooting over the water, traveling parallel to the shore out maybe a quarter of a mile, the crew of UCSB students rowing in unison with long oars, pulling against the swell, appearing and disappearing and reappearing, in the gaps between the cypress trees, like a Chumash war canoe on the Channel three hundred years ago.

♦♦♦

THAT SAME DAY, HUNTER woke up before seven and masturbated while looking at a pornographic magazine he kept in the drawer of his night table—a magazine devoted to nasty girls, skanks with big breasts. The models looked like the kind of women who had yeast infections and led messy lives—completely separate from his erotic taste in women in the real world. This morning, however, his ritualized fantasy became a fantasy of Lydia. The hot, wet, moist place she had for him, her hips cocked back, her arms around his neck. "Fuck me. Fuck me."

After that, he went back to sleep. He arose at eight-thirty and ate his usual breakfast of black coffee and Kellogg's Special K with low-fat milk and a sliced banana. The round table was set with a navy-blue woven-straw place mat and a matching cotton napkin. As he breakfasted, he read the *Santa Barbara News-Press*, checking the television listings for any old movies that he might want to watch that evening.

After breakfast, he showered, and then, sitting cross-legged on the bathroom counter, a towel knotted around his waist, he shaved his head with an electric razor. At ten, he had tennis. He was on the senior tennis team at the Polo Club—they had a match against La Cumbre Country Club. Home court. About a quarter to ten, he walked up to the tennis courts in his tennis shorts.

Puffy white heat clouds piled up over the purple coastal mountains. A Forest Service helicopter racketed overhead in the direction of Ojai, following the line of the foothills, looking for fires. "Will there be a fire?" was the topic of conversation on the tennis courts. That and the rigors of tennis in ninety-six-degree heat. "We're spoiled in Santa Barbara," the tennis players kept saying. Water bottles were lined up on the courtside benches. The Polo Club team beat the La Cumbre team, and the team's standing went up a notch. Hunter and his partner won all but one of their games.

After tennis, Hunter drove into Santa Barbara for lunch with the air conditioner cranked up in his white 1998 Ford Thunderbird two-door sedan with a V8 motor. "I own stock in Ford," he'd explain, although really, he'd gotten a deal on it and couldn't afford a Mercedes or a BMW. He ate at Morishima, a Japanese restaurant on State Street a block up from the art museum, where he sat by himself at the back of the sparsely filled restaurant. Each table had a white ceramic bud vase with a single white chrysanthemum. There wasn't any air conditioning, but it was cooler than outside. The sound system played big band jazz.

The young waitress was Japanese, a student at one of the language schools in Santa Barbara. The website highlighted the beaches and the club scene on lower State Street: "Learn English, Baby." She had on a pink Hello Kitty T-shirt. Hunter ordered cold soba noodles and a Kirin. He ordered in Japanese, and she giggled. The first time he'd done this, the waitress had answered him in Japanese, and it came to light that he didn't really speak Japanese, despite having lived in Japan for many years and having had a Japanese wife. He could order at a restaurant with a good accent, and he knew how to say, "Shall we turn out the lights?"

Hunter imagined Lydia walking in the door of the restaurant. He hadn't had any further communication with Joel Frank, and he was going to have to do something about that. Ideally, he'd get his hands on two hundred grand, pay him the money, and they'd continue on as before. The sound system was playing Artie Shaw's "Stardust." Hunter recognized a man at the sushi bar, but he didn't remember his name. They'd met when he went to an orientation meeting for art museum docents—one of the things, like joining the Elks Club in hopes of finding a poker game and signing up for social tennis to meet women, that he'd done when he first moved back to Santa Barbara, before he renewed his acquaintance with Rosalind.

After lunch, he went back to the Polo Club and took a siesta. More days than not, he had a nap in the afternoon. Usually, he got under the covers in his T-shirt and boxers, but that afternoon he slept naked under just a sheet. He awoke around four, shaved and dressed, made himself a martini, and read for a little while. His book was *From Dawn to Decadence* by Jacques Barzun. He was dipping into it. His plan for the evening was to go over to Summerland and get a hamburger at the Nugget, then watch *All About Eve* on television. His martini was six ounces of straight gin on the rocks. His method was to pour the gin into the shot glass and let it overflow, in the manner of a cascade fountain, into a crystal double old-fashioned glass with two ice cubes. He kept a fifth of Gilbey's in the freezer.

When Rosalind called, he was watching the CBS news. She said the Santa Ana wind was making her nervous. Would he be a true friend and take her out to dinner? Sometimes she scolded him about never taking her out. They only saw each other when they were invited somewhere together, or when he played host for her, when she had people to dinner. This was somewhat true. Hunter said he was going to the Nugget. If she wanted to join him, he'd swing by her place and pick her up. Rosalind said she didn't want to go to the Nugget. Why didn't they go to Pete's? Pete's was Casa de Sevilla, a restaurant on lower Chapala Street. A bastion of old-guard Santa Barbara.

"Pete's it is," Hunter said. He put on a tie and a sports jacket and drove over to Montecito to get Rosalind. Her house was on the grounds of Il Belvedere.

Il Belvedere was an estate on Cold Springs Road that a gay Beverly Hills decorator had bought after World War II. In the fifties, his house parties were legendary in certain circles. He adopted as adults the two gay brothers who were his protégés and made them his heirs. The two brothers, now old men, still lived in the Spanish Revival main house designed by George Washington Smith. Rosalind, who was one of their favorite people, had been renting the guesthouse. Recently, they had sold her the guesthouse along with an acre of land. Otherwise, the original twenty-seven-acre property was intact.

Often Rosalind wasn't ready when Hunter arrived. He would show up and she would not yet have had her bath. When he protested that they'd be late, she'd say, "Hunter, they don't want us there yet." He would have a martini while he waited for her to dress. Rosalind kept a bottle of Gilbey's in the freezer for him. This evening, however, she was dressed and waiting for him. Her ash-blonde hair was in a *Town and Country* ponytail with a grosgrain bow, and she was wearing capris and a shirt with the collar turned up, like Kim Novak. There were vestiges of the beautiful, sophisticated society wife of a movie star.

"I have some news," Rosalind said in the car.

"Yes?"

"Wait till we're at the restaurant."

The dark red walls of Casa de Sevilla were decorated with framed bullfight posters. The menu was old-school: steak, swordfish, cheese enchiladas, stuffed sole, dinner salad with Roquefort dressing. In the fifties, breaded abalone was on the menu. Following the waiter to their table, Hunter was aware that he and Rosalind were an attractive, classy older couple. That was not the problem. Clyde the bartender made Hunter a double martini—straight gin on the rocks, the way he liked it—and a whiskey sour for Rosalind. A lady's drink.

"To us," she said, when their drinks came.

"To us." Hunter raised his glass.

Rosalind told him her news. That winter, Hunter had made a new will in which Rosalind was named the executor of his estate and his sole heir. He told her that, since he didn't have any living children and his half sister was ninety-four and didn't need the money, he wanted her to have the pittance he would leave. He'd asked Rosalind for her Social Security number and then gone to the bank and signed the papers for his bank accounts to be payable on death to her. Rosalind was touched by this detail. It was almost as if they were married, she said.

She had not made a new will after her husband died, although her attorney and her stockbroker had been after her to do so. She did not want to contemplate her own death. She'd had one meeting with the estate attorney. She said, "If I die..." and he corrected her: "Not if, Rosalind—when." She left the office without doing anything about a will. Now she had followed through. That afternoon, she'd signed the will and documents for a trust. Hunter was her executor and her sole heir, except for some bequests to charity. He was also the sole beneficiary of the trust.

"The original is on file in George Allen's office," she said. "I need your Social Security number to make my bank accounts payable-on-death to you."

Hunter wrote his Social Security number on one of his calling cards and handed it to her.

"So formal," she said, putting the card in her purse.

"I'm deeply touched, Rosalind," he said, as the waiter brought their dinner salads. "Odds are, though, you're going to outlive me."

"No more on that subject," she said. "Let's both live to be a hundred."

All through dinner, Rosalind was confiding and gossipy. Hunter was attentive. Thoughtful, also. Rosalind was a very rich woman, and he was now her sole beneficiary. A woman named Marianna Russo was across the room with a woman friend. Rosalind saw her and said, "Our own Jackie Kennedy." Marianna had first married a rich liquor distributor who became a congressman, and then she'd married the much richer heir to a tire fortune. In between, she brought a breach-of-promise suit against Duke Sedgwick. Hunter recalled that his father used to play tennis with Duke Sedgwick.

When Hunter ordered cheesecake for dessert, Rosalind asked for an extra fork so she could have bites. Hunter asked her if she remembered when he'd shot off a shotgun the summer he was in the gatehouse cottage. "Lydia Graham was there," he said.

He couldn't resist introducing Lydia into the conversation.

"Vaguely," Rosalind said. "Crows were attacking a baby bird? Didn't the sheriff come?"

Hunter said that was how he remembered it. Except the sheriff didn't come.

There had been a mockingbird nest in an aloe thicket. One afternoon, the parent mockingbirds were shrieking and dive-bombing two crows. Hunter and Rosalind were outside on the deck, Rosalind sitting on the green-and-white-striped chaise lounge leafing through a *Life* magazine. Her ash-blonde hair was loose around her shoulders, and she was barefoot. She had small, high-arched feet with shell-pink polish on her toenails, and she smelled of Joy perfume. Hunter was standing at the railing, smoking a cigarette, trying to see what was going on with the mockingbirds.

Just then Lydia came along and saw the baby bird that had fallen out of the nest.

The baby mockingbird was on the ground in the dry grass, flapping its wings and hopping. The two crows were swooping at it. The parent mockingbirds were going crazy.

"It's too little to fly," Lydia said, almost crying.

Hunter had come down off the deck and picked up the baby mockingbird. Lydia grabbed his arm. "Don't put it back. The parents will abandon the nest."

"Not true," he said, reaching inside the thicket and putting the baby bird back on the nest. Together, he and Lydia watched one of the mockingbird parents fly down with an insect in its beak. It whistled and glided into the aloe thicket. There was a twitter of cheeping. That mockingbird flew out again, and the other mockingbird glided in.

"See? The parents didn't abandon the nest," Hunter said.

But now the crows were trying to get at the nest.

Lydia yelled and waved her arms. “Go away! Go away!”

Rosalind continued to leaf through the *Life* magazine.

Hunter told Lydia he'd be right back. He went in the house and came out with a twenty-gauge Italian over/under shotgun, the silver stock cover engraved with a design of lilies and roses and vines. Rosalind told him he was an idiot; someone was going to call the sheriff.

He aimed high. There was a loud bang. The two crows cawed and flew away, one of them flying off-kilter, feathers drifting behind it from a tipped wing. But soon flocks of crows—hundreds of crows—came flying from all directions, rising and falling like black smoke in the sky. A great congregation of cawing crows converged in the blue gum eucalyptus trees down the lane. A murder of crows out of range of the shotgun. Lydia told Hunter that he was marked forever as an enemy of crows.

“You were mean to me that summer,” Rosalind said.

“You were engaged.”

“And you were mean to me. Did I tell you that I have Lydia Graham's father's old phone number?”

“You told me. She was a cute little girl,” Hunter said.

“She wasn't as innocent as you thought.”

“I don't know if I thought she was innocent. I just remember she'd walk by in the afternoon,” Hunter said. “Darling, you've eaten all the cheesecake.”

“I'm a weak character,” Rosalind said. “Do you think we should get married?”

“I think we should think about it,” Hunter said. “Ready to go? I'm bushed. I had tennis this morning.”

When he took her home, Rosalind wanted him to come in. “Stay,” she said.

“I can't.” He traced her cheek with a finger.

“Please…”

He shook his head. “I can't,” he said gently. “I'll call you tomorrow.”

♦♦♦

IT WAS JUST GETTING dark when Lydia went out for a walk. Neighbors were having barbecues. A hot wind was blowing, and the trees were bending and swaying. She was in her element. She felt like a cat going out to hunt. When she turned the corner onto Edgewater Drive, the two big white dogs who had come to her rescue came trotting down the street, their tags jingling. They woofed, and without breaking step, they crossed in tandem to the other side of the road and continued on their way. On the ocean cliff, a gray fox barked—a scream in the night. As if under an enchantment, she turned around and went back home. She let herself in the front door and went into the kitchen. She got Hunter's card out of the zipper compartment of her purse. Without stopping to reconsider, she dialed the number. The phone rang.

"Hello," Hunter answered in his low, urbane voice, picking up on the third ring.

"It's Lydia." The smell of the Madagascar jasmine outside the sun porch was heavy in the hot night. There was heat lightning out over the ocean—something that happens once in a decade. "I thought I might come over."

"That would be nice," he said.

What he thought was, *Baby baby baby.* He had come in the door five minutes ago. He was thinking about calling her. He knew her husband was out of town—she'd mentioned it the day before.

"Do I need the gate code?" Lydia said, her heart pounding.

He told her the code. The numbers were the same as her street address. Another coincidence.

"No one's parking in the carport next to mine. Take a left as soon as you come in the gate. It's the last one on the right. Look for the white Thunderbird in the carport next to it."

Her silver Passat was recognizable by the Thacher School decal in the rear window and the surf racks on the roof. Better not to park in public view.

If she had replied, "That sounds awfully complicated. I'll just park up by the tennis courts," her intention would not have been crystal clear. But she didn't say that. She said, "I'll see you in a little while."

The Convergence of the Twain.

Hunter said, "I'll be waiting, darling."

Ten minutes later she was in the car. Driving down the coast, she listened to Ravel's *Bolero*—clashing cymbals and swirling march rhythms. The fog bank had advanced, a blackness over the Channel, hiding the fairy lights of the oil rigs. The entrance gate was open; she drove in and turned down the first driveway. The final cacophony of *Bolero*—the crescendo of drums and the trumpets, music for the triumph of a potentate—resounded as Lydia pulled into the vacant carport and switched off the ignition.

She had the thought: *No one knows where I am.* She could smell the stables, on the other side of the property from the condos. The hot wind came in gusts. The stars were crystalline in the night sky. When she rang the doorbell, Hunter opened the door wearing a man's kimono, indigo with a blue-black pattern. She started to say something, but he put a finger on her lips. "Don't talk."

The double bed in the small bedroom was American Chippendale with turned bedposts. There was an oil painting of a ballet dancer, and a mahogany valet chair. The wind rattled the blinds. She undressed herself, and he took off his kimono. No talking. No words. Only erotic sensation. Pure desire that had existed for decades, just below their separate lives like an underground river. He was very sexual, very dominant, very experienced. She was very responsive. They took each other into other worlds. Oh God, it felt good. A hotel room in Tokyo in 1956. An old mansion house, its stone walls overgrown with giant Burmese honeysuckle, a long passage lit by candles in sconces. The eerie low whistle of a dacoit. Hunter's cock was not board-stiff but heavy and engorged. An old man's cock. Lydia's pussy was wet. It felt incredibly good; the pleasure was exquisite, and she wanted more and more. *Fuck me fuck me fuck me.* They lay side by side in the bed. He was sweaty and breathing hard. She felt like melted honey.

Hunter propped himself up on one elbow, a satyr in love, regarding Lydia in the dim light. He made certain that she was comfortable, that there was a pillow under her head. He had little tufts of hair on his shoulders, like epaulettes. So festive. On the night table was a framed black-and-white photograph of Hunter in the snow with Mount Fuji in the background. He was a realist; he knew he was never going to find sex like this again.

He said, “We’re both very carnal. Do you know, darling, how rare that is?”

“Yes, I do know.”

“Why don’t you leave your husband and marry me?” He was completely serious. “We’d make a good couple. We already know a lot of the same people. We have chamber music in common. Your daughter is at boarding school.”

“Hunter, what is this about?” Lydia didn’t think he was serious, but she was alarmed.

“Lately, I’ve been thinking about time,” he said.

“What about time?”

“It goes fast.”

“In heaven we’ll be young.”

“We’re alike, you and I,” he said.

“How are we alike?”

“We’re both cats who walk alone. We’re both very strange, darling.”

“You have no idea,” she said, in a Claus von Bülow accent.

“We belong together, Lydia.”

She sat up in bed. The small, dim bedroom smelled of lust. “It was fabulous. I have no regrets. But I’m not going to leave my husband. Please listen to me, Hunter. This is a one-time thing. It’s not going to happen again.”

“We’ll have an interesting life.”

“You don’t have any money,” she said. How had it gotten to this point? “I can’t live at the Polo Club.”

“At the moment, I don’t have any money,” he conceded.

She got out of bed and started putting on her clothes. "It wouldn't matter if you were a billionaire. If you fuck up my marriage, I'll kill you. I love Peter."

Now she was scared.

He laughed. "Darling, your secret is safe with me."

He got up and put on his kimono. Standing in the blue kimono with its wide sleeves, Hunter looked like a samurai magistrate. Lydia sat on the bed to put on her sandals.

"The marriage proposal has no time limit. Let me put my clothes on, and I'll walk you to your car."

"I'd rather you didn't," Lydia said.

He kissed her. "Tonight never happened. If that's what you want. You can trust me, Lydia."

The phone rang, and Hunter said he should get the call. The caller was Joel Frank. As Lydia let herself out, she heard Hunter say in a hard voice, "I resent this sort of shakedown."

♦♦♦

PETER GOT BACK THE next day, as planned. His plane was the last one of the evening to land before the Santa Barbara Airport was closed due to fog. The hot weather was over.

The next afternoon, they drove down to Thacher to watch Sally in a cross-country meet. Her main sport was surfing, but she was a good, solid, long-distance runner, and she was on the varsity cross-country team. She came in second, which was better than she had expected. A girl on the Thacher team—a natural runner, she was like a gazelle—came in first, as she did at all the meets. Another girl, a senior at Cate, would have come in second, except she took a wrong turn and got lost. Sally had to study for a history test, so they didn't take her out to dinner.

"We're a good little family," Lydia said, on the way home.

"We're a jazz trio," Peter said.

Peter and Lydia had both liked the idea of just one child. "We'll be like a jazz trio," he'd said. Sally was an entirely satisfactory child.

Lydia had no choice but to trust Hunter. It never happened. In the car, Peter sang "You Are My Sunshine." Lydia couldn't carry a tune—she loved it when Peter sang.

CHAPTER SIX

Jimmy's Oriental Gardens

SEVERAL WEEKS WENT BY.

Lydia got a bonus from Andy Barker when she solved the problem of a garden design for the new owners of a property in Hope Ranch, two women who were adamant that they wanted a classic English landscape garden but kept rejecting the plans. It turned out they meant an Elizabethan garden like the one at the Folger. Lydia took Peter out for sushi at Arigato to celebrate. One weekend, Sally got third place in a surf contest in La Jolla. She went with the Thacher surf club, and Lydia and Peter drove down to cheer her on. They stayed in a motel in Del Mar and had a good time. Lydia was secretly glad the waves were small. To see Sally out in big surf completely unnerved her.

The year before at Christmas, there had been a storm. In the house with the windows closed, you could hear the ten-foot, twelve-foot waves crashing. At dusk, Sally said she was going to go out at Mesa Lane. She had a cart for her surfboard behind her bicycle. Lydia wanted to forbid it. Peter said to let her go. It made Lydia anxious, but she gave way. Peter was the surfer. Together, they walked over and watched from the beach steps. The rain had stopped. The light was fading, but there was a band of luminance at the horizon. Maybe a dozen people, some of them surfers, were watching from the steps. There was the crash of the waves, the deep percussion of rocks rolling in the foam. A high wind was blowing. There were two surfers, distant figures in black wetsuits, rising and falling on the huge swells.

One of the surfers was Sally. Roiling white water came up over the bottom steps. Lydia wanted Peter to do something. Borrow a board and paddle out.

"She's fine. No one ever drowned at Mesa Lane," he said.

The surfer who was not Sally caught a wave. He rode it in to shore, was submerged in the foam of the next wave. He swam to the steps with his board on its ankle leash. He came up the steps through the water, pulling off his wetsuit hood and shaking his head to get the water out of his ears. It was one of the surf gods.

"Good ride, Luke," Peter said.

"She's waiting for the big one, Mr. Bolin," he said.

Sally was alone in the dusk. A small solitary figure in a black wetsuit on the ocean. Lydia could hardly breathe; she was so scared for her daughter. Seagulls flew past, their high-pitched mewing filling the air. Sea ducks floated far out on the swells. The surf god watched with them. A wave loomed in the dusk, bigger than the waves that had come before. Sally paddled, caught the wave, then got to her feet. She dropped to a crouch and caught a long ride to the right, across the face of the wave. The wind ruffled the white foam at the crest of the wave. When the wave crumbled behind her, she shot into the foam. For a moment, she was underwater. Then she was swimming for it, her board still attached by the ankle leash. There was a boil of dark water and white foam.

Lydia screamed, "Lose the leash," over and over.

"She's okay," Peter said, kept saying.

"You want me to go out and help her?" Luke asked.

"She can make it," Peter said.

She swam through the roiling water and scrambled onto the beach steps. Luke went down and accompanied her up the steps. She let him carry her board. Her joy was transcendent.

That night, Lydia tried to express to Peter how seeing Sally in the big waves was a waking nightmare.

He said, "She loves the ocean the way you love the night."

Our Mother the Ocean. The ocean is indifferent to plastic, the overfishing of the fisheries, the pollution—the ocean will simply wait.

All the time they were in La Jolla, Hunter was on Lydia's mind. She imagined divorcing Peter and marrying him. For what? They had chamber music in common. The sex was fabulous. The carnal fascination was still there. *Those pleasures so lightly called physical.* —Colette.

But the rest?

She loved Peter; she loved the life she had with him. If Hunter really had been like her, if he had been a night person, she would have been tempted. But he wasn't like her, whatever fantasy he might have. She wouldn't be socially ostracized if she divorced Peter and married Hunter. They weren't living in an Edith Wharton novel. Although the money was a problem. Sally would get over it (this, she wasn't so sure about). *It never happened* was the best course of action. She hoped and prayed that Hunter would leave her alone.

And for a while, he did. Hunter bided his time. He escorted Rosalind to a sit-down black-tie dinner for twenty. She told him he was the handsomest man there. He got his hands on thirty thousand and put off Joel Frank. The Polo Club senior tennis team won the league championship. He got an AOL email account and, for reasons of his own, signed up for an online dating personals service called Catholic Singles.

♦♦♦

THE LAST WEEK IN October, Lydia and Annie met for dinner in the bar at Jimmy's Oriental Gardens. Annie wanted to show solidarity with Jimmy's. The brick building with green-painted pagoda eaves that Jimmy's occupied was the last remnant of Santa Barbara's Chinatown, and the Santa Barbara Trust for Historic Preservation had recently acquired it. They were either going to knock it down or turn it into a museum. Lydia was philosophical about the ongoing destruction of historic continuity in what the Trust was calling Santa Barbara's Presidio Neighborhood. You're always going to be sad if you want things to be the way they used to be. Her father told her that once when she suffered a *crise de la nostalgie* because Santa Barbara was getting so built up. Annie did not take such a philosophical stance.

They arrived at the same time, coming from opposite directions—Lydia had parked around the corner on Santa Barbara Street, Annie was in the parking structure on State Street. It was just getting dark and there was a Halloween feeling in the air—it would soon be All Souls' Day. The days were shorter and the night was chilly. Lydia was wearing an Irish fisherman's sweater. A mural of Santa Barbara as it would have looked in 1828 had recently been painted on the outside brick wall of Jimmy's. The mural had been commissioned by the Trust. It was the view from where Lydia and Annie stood, looking over the rooftops of the town, what would have been the view if the modern town had dissolved and the viewer was transported back in time to an imagined past. The mural showed an Arcadia, a scene of grassy open land and oak trees, an Indian village, and the little adobe houses of the soldiers and their garden plots.

"Perfect timing," Annie said. Her curly hair was hennaed to hide the gray, and she had fine wrinkles, but her skin was still alabaster. She wore a paisley shawl over her flowing dress. Her husband said, affectionately, that her fashion sense reminded him of the Red Queen in *Alice in Wonderland*.

"We must be psychopathic," Lydia said. That was her father's joke.

What happened next was Fate.

When Lydia and Annie walked in the door of Jimmy's, the first people they saw were Hunter and Rosalind. They had been sitting at the bar and were on their way out. Hunter was escorting Rosalind, his hand on her elbow. The patrons of Jimmy's—the bar and the restaurant—came from all walks of life. Fishermen, doctors and lawyers, society types. One regular was a woman who trained dogs. The bar, a long narrow room with four booths on one side and two Formica tables at the back, was fairly crowded. Only one of the red vinyl booths was unoccupied, and at the bar there were only a few empty places. A sign behind the bar said, "Warning—Alcohol Can Lead to Pregnancy." Two nineteen-inch televisions, one on top of the other, were behind the bar. One had the Golf Channel, the other a Dodgers game, both with the sound turned off.

"You two look like a couple of swells slumming at Les Halles," Annie said. Her mother and Rosalind were on opposite sides of a heated controversy at the Coral Casino over whether to remodel the ladies' dressing room, but she and Rosalind were on friendly terms.

Rosalind was wearing a turquoise beaded tunic and palazzo pants. Her blonde hair was in a French twist, and she was wearing Joy perfume. Hunter was in a navy-blue suit, his red bow tie a little askew.

"We've been invited to a swish dinner party at the Pitels. The guest of honor is from South Africa—he's a former High Court judge. From the bad old days when the judiciary rubber-stamped apartheid," Rosalind said, dropping her voice. "We'll probably be the youngest people there."

"We came in for a quick snort," Hunter said. "Fortify ourselves for the fray."

"Fortify yourself for the fray—you sound like a P. G. Wodehouse character," Rosalind said.

"She doesn't let me get away with anything," Hunter said.

Lydia and Hunter had both imagined scenarios in which they ran into each other by chance. It was inevitable. Santa Barbara was a small town. Now it had happened. Hunter's primary emotions were lust and longing. The primary emotion Lydia felt was jealousy. Not what she would have expected. Neither Lydia nor Hunter gave any outward indication of their recent history, no sign of what had happened at the Polo Club.

Hunter stood politely a little bit apart, giving the impression that he wasn't sure who Lydia and Annie were. *Should he know them?* was his demeanor.

Rosalind gave him a prompt. "Hunter, you remember Annie Slocum and Lydia Graham?"

Oh yes, I remember, Hunter thought.

"My mother told me you were back," Annie said to Hunter. To Lydia, she said, "You remember Hunter. When we were fourteen, we were always trying to get him to give us a ride in his Porsche."

His godmother had lent him the Porsche to drive while he was in Santa Barbara.

"I do remember," Lydia said, as if recognition was dawning. "We used to pretend we were hitchhiking."

Suddenly the memory was vivid. She was walking up San Ysidro Road with Annie, coming home from the beach, and Hunter zoomed past them in the British racing green Porsche with the top down. They stuck out their thumbs, and he screeched to a stop and reversed, looking over his shoulder as the Porsche shot backward.

"Can I give you girls a lift? Hop in," he said. "You can both fit. Where to?"

"The Pharmacy," they said, as they crowded barefoot into the passenger seat.

The Pharmacy was the San Ysidro Pharmacy. It had a coffee shop with a soda fountain, and they liked to order lime rickeys—a gin rickey with no gin—after a long day at the beach.

There in the bar at Jimmy's Oriental Gardens, Hunter, too, was taken back in time. He was thirty-two, and he'd just heard he was shortlisted for a Grade 10 civilian contract specialist with the Navy. It was the day before he took the photograph of Lydia.

"You were staying at the gatehouse cottage," Lydia said. "I was an awful pest. I remember whenever you were outside, I'd talk to you."

"You were very loquacious," Hunter said. His hazel eyes with flecks of gold were like lion's eyes. He thought: *In the end, Casanova falls in love.*

Hanging on the wall over the booths, a carved gilt frame held a large oil painting of a 1920s Chinese vamp, with long red fingernails and wearing nothing but a filmy pink negligee, reclining in the pose of the *Nude Maja*.

"You were there sometimes," she said to Rosalind.

"I remember I came over and Hunter was reading *The Brothers Karamazov* to you," Rosalind said.

Lydia remembered an afternoon when Hunter, who was reading *The Brothers Karamazov*, dipping into it, read aloud a passage he had marked. It was one of the afternoons when he allowed her a splash of rum in her Coca-Cola. He had a good reading voice.

> "I want to tell you now about the insects to whom God gave sensual lust, …that insect lives in you, too, and will stir a tempest in our blood. Tempests, because sensual lust is a tempest—worse than a tempest! Beauty is a terrible and awful thing!"

"What can I say?" Lydia said. "I was an *intellectuelle*."

A young man in a polo coat who looked, as Annie later remarked, as if his mother was a movie star came in with two young women in tight jeans, T-shirts, and five-inch stiletto heels.

"We're blocking traffic," Rosalind said. She looked fragile and vulnerable; the decay of her beauty only made her more feminine.

"We'll let you get your dinner," Hunter said.

"It was good seeing you." "It was good seeing you." "It was good seeing you." "Say hello to your mother." "We'll have to have lunch sometime." "Have fun at your dinner party."

As Hunter and Rosalind went out the door, he said in Lydia's ear, "Call me."

Lydia and Annie took the empty booth. There was the illusion of snug privacy in the red vinyl booth, amidst the comings and goings and conversations around them. Lydia still smelled Rosalind's perfume, Hunter's lime aftershave.

"What did he say to you?" Annie asked.

"He said, 'You were a pest.'"

Annie laughed and said, "I don't think I'd have recognized him. The shaved head."

"And we thought he was old then."

"I heard that he reinstated his membership in the *Social Register*," Annie said. "He told my mother it was so he could meet girls. He's such a snob."

Lydia thought of the calling card in her purse.

The waitress came and took their orders. Annie had a glass of red wine and Lydia ordered a Heineken. They both ordered chow mein. The waitress brought their drinks right away, and Annie and Lydia got on the topic of their book club. The September book had been *The Master and Margarita*, and the woman who picked the book, also the hostess, served chilled borscht and cucumber salad, accompanied by six different chilled vodkas. She had gone to graduate school in Moscow, and she gave a disquisition on Russian names. Everyone was a little tipsy. The two divorced women in the book club discovered they had both had affairs with the same married man. The rest of the book club was audience to their revelations.

"It was my birthday and he showed up at my house with a vase, not wrapped or anything, and said…"—the woman telling the story was laughing— "he said, 'It's Ming, I'm pretty sure.' The guy collects Ming. He knew what it was. It was celadon made in Thailand in the twenties. Be still my heart."

"He's a good man on a dirty weekend," the other woman said. "But he's a rat."

As they discussed the book club, Lydia thought about Hunter. She had not anticipated how she'd feel, seeing Hunter with Rosalind, the two of them all dolled up and sparkling for each other. She was jealous. An unexpected emotion. Lydia shivered. A goose walked over her grave. There was too much she didn't know. The man who showed up at the condo, the telephone call. Hunter was a dubious character. None of that stopped her from being jealous. Not an emotion she often felt.

The waitress brought their chow mein. Annie ordered another glass of red wine; Lydia switched to jasmine tea. The two women ate with chopsticks. They were reading *Life on the Mississippi* for the November meeting of the book club. Lydia's choice. She told Annie that she planned to serve biscuits and fried chicken, along with a big pot of green beans with salt pork. Loquat chutney instead of watermelon pickles.

"There aren't any strong woman characters," Annie complained.

"The world of the antebellum Mississippi River pilot was pretty much masculine," Lydia said.

"He could have introduced a strong woman character," Annie said. "Lydia, sometimes I wonder if you're a real feminist."

"Of course I'm a feminist. How can you be a woman and not be a feminist?" Lydia said, although really, she was more of an opportunist than a feminist.

Annie got into a rant about how the Trust was gobbling up downtown Santa Barbara. All Lydia could think about was Hunter.

The waitress cleared their plates and brought the check and two fortune cookies. Lydia's read: "You are modest and courteous." Annie's read: "Soon life will be interesting."

"Hah," Annie said. "My life is already too interesting."

Coming out into the cool night from the warm conviviality of Jimmy's, Annie and Lydia said their goodbyes on the sidewalk. The reconstructed Presidio was across the street. In the glow of the streetlights, it looked like an architect's model, unreal in a bare gravel hardscape. The real Presidio hadn't been there for a hundred and fifty years. First the Mexican government abandoned it, then its adobe walls melted in the rain, and in 1854 an earthquake leveled anything that was left. This Presidio was recent. All the time that Lydia and Annie were growing up, where the reconstructed Presidio now stood had been Shalhoob's Grocery on the corner, and next to it, an adobe built in the 1870s, a private home with a little front garden, and next to the adobe a shoe shop. Real old buildings torn down for a fake old building.

CHAPTER SEVEN

A Night Made for Love

THE NEXT DAY, ANNIE called to tell Lydia that Rosalind was dead. Her mother had heard it from one of her friends. The gardener had come in the morning and found her lying on the bottom of the swimming pool in the shallow end. He pulled her out, but her body was stiff and cold. He went up to the main house and rang the doorbell, and Roddy, one of the brothers, called 911. A fire truck and an ambulance came, then two sheriff's cars, followed by the coroner.

"We told her not to swim by herself at night," Roddy told the coroner.

No one thought it was anything but a tragic accident, but any time there's a death that could have been a homicide, they have to investigate.

"Hunter was the last person to see her," Annie said. "He took her home after the dinner party. He said he didn't stay long. They had a nightcap and talked a while. He left around eleven."

"It's so strange that we saw her last night," Lydia said.

A swirling flock of cedar waxwings had alighted atop the Italian cypress outside the sunporch, and the birds were devouring the cypress berries. Lydia's little cat had a hunting blind high up in the cypress, in among the branches, where she lay in wait. Only her plume of a tail showed. Peter joked that Kitty belonged to the Audubon Society and had a life list.

"Hunter said he had a beer," Annie said. "She made chamomile tea for herself. There's going to be an autopsy."

Lydia told Peter of Rosalind's death, and that she and Annie had run into her at Jimmy's the night before.

"It's unsettling," Lydia said. "She was so alive."

Peter was understanding.

Lydia said it was doubly unsettling, somehow, that Rosalind had been with Hunter Evans. It seemed to be a good idea to mention Hunter. He was there, after all. A minor character. She told Peter that she remembered that Hunter and Rosalind were like F. Scott Fitzgerald characters the summer she was fourteen. Peter said he knew who Rosalind was, but he didn't remember Hunter.

"I was a little surfer girl," Lydia said.

"You were never a little surfer girl," Peter laughed.

"I liked 'Little Deuce Coupe.' It was so long ago, Peter."

"Golden lads and girls all must / As chimney-sweepers, come to dust," he said.

That night, after Lydia brushed and flossed her teeth, washed her face, and put on Dr. Hauschka calendula night cream, she read in bed for a while, her leg thrown over Peter's. The window was open to the damp night air. It was high tide, and she could hear the ocean. She'd known Rosalind was dead before Annie called. She'd seen Hunter drown her.

♦♦♦

Hunter took Rosalind home after the dinner party. In the car on their way to her house, as they discussed the dinner party, he reviewed the situation to himself. Two points. One: He wanted Lydia, he wanted to marry Lydia. Two: He needed money, real money. Lydia was not going to leave her husband for a man who rented at the Polo Club and couldn't afford the membership at the Coral Casino. Lydia aside, he needed money. He wanted to get Joel Frank off his back. And he finally had a chance to get out from under the yakuza loan.

The week before, he'd driven down to Los Angeles to have lunch at the New Otani with an account manager at the private loan company in Tokyo that held the loan. The young account manager had written a number on a page of a little leather notebook. "You pay this and we will forgive the loan," he said, tearing out the page and handing it to Hunter across the table. "Limited time offer."

Il Belvedere was in the foothills, and the smell of mountain laurel and chaparral was pungent in the night air. Hunter parked under the oak tree where he always parked and walked Rosalind to the door. She got her house key from under a majolica flowerpot.

"You were the handsomest man there," she said.

"You were the most beautiful woman. I'll call you tomorrow, darling."

"It's still early," Rosalind said. She'd stopped saying *Please stay.* "Do you want to come in for a little while? I'll make us tea."

Hunter made a decision. He smiled at Rosalind in a way that made her feel a new intimacy between them.

"I'll take you up on that," he said. "But I'll have a beer."

He found the former guesthouse oppressive at night, even when a dinner party was underway. It wasn't small—it had two big bedrooms with en suite bathrooms, a living room with a powder room, and a dining room. Outside, there was a terrace, a rose garden, and a swimming pool. A two-car attached garage. Rosalind felt it was a suitable setting for her widowhood. A charming little house. There was something pathetic about a single wealthy woman living alone in a big house.

The house was furnished with pieces that had been in the big house in Benedict Canyon that she sold after her husband died. The two interior decorator brothers in the main house, old war horses smelling battle, had advised Rosalind on how to arrange the furniture. It had been fun, the two elderly brothers camping it up, saying things like, "Rosalind, you're *sooo* shallow."

Hunter kept Rosalind company in the kitchen. While she made herself a cup of chamomile tea, he poured himself a Kirin. The retired judge from South Africa had thought that Rosalind and Hunter were married, and when Rosalind disabused him, he'd asked her why not. She'd said that Hunter hadn't asked her.

"Hunter!" the retired judge bellowed down the table. "You propose to this lovely woman right now."

"The man is a menace," Rosalind said. "He kept talking about the Zulu Wars."

"You told me we'd be the youngest people there," Hunter said. "Roxie Barnard was after me to water her orchids while she's in Maine. I said I was sorry, but it was impossible."

"You are the most selfish man I've ever known," Rosalind said.

"You know me better than anyone." This was not entirely untrue.

In the living room, two ivory brocade couches, too big for the room, faced each other in front of the fireplace. A Santa Barbara–style tile mural over the fireplace depicted Juan Rodriguez Cabrillo discovering the Channel Islands. It made Rosalind feel like she was in the courthouse, but the two brothers wouldn't let her get rid of it. It was an authentic George Washington Smith touch.

A framed blowup of a black-and-white publicity still of her husband from a fifties western hung on the wall. He's all in black with a cowboy hat and his six-shooter drawn. The Art Deco cocktail table had brass legs in the shape of ram's legs; a ram's head with curling horns supported the beveled glass tabletop.

Rosalind and Hunter sat at a companionable distance from each other on one of the brocade couches. Rosalind kicked her shoes off. Her well-tended little feet peeped out from the turquoise palazzo pants. The blue veins were ropey.

"When you say, 'I can't,' when I invite you in—what do you mean, Hunter?" she asked, turning sideways on the couch, looking at him as she spoke.

"Darling, you know." His tone was tender, regretful.

"Do you mean you can't physically make love? Or do you mean you don't want to sleep with me?"

"I'm impotent." A little impatient. Embarrassed.

"That one time? That doesn't mean anything."

"Darling, I don't have any libido—" He pronounced it *li-bay-dō.* "It's funny, isn't it?" he said. He wondered if she believed him. "After all those years I was such a player."

"I have to tell you a secret," Rosalind said.

"What's that, darling?"

She whispered, "It doesn't matter to me."

This was true. Not if he was devoted to her. The one time they went to bed and it didn't work, or the times that Hunter kissed her good night at the door and didn't come in, she didn't feel frustrated desire. Her feelings were hurt. Her vanity. For so long, she'd been desired for her beauty. She liked to be made love to, but she did not have a carnal nature. Hunter had always known this.

He said, "Why don't I give you a foot rub."

Rosalind said that she'd love a foot rub. She lay back against the arm of the couch, a velvet pillow under her head.

Hunter stood up and took off his suit jacket. He undid his gold cufflinks, dropped them on the coffee table, and rolled up his sleeves. Then he sat down and patted his lap. Rosalind put her bare feet in his lap, and he took her right foot in his hands. He massaged the sole of her foot, pressing with his thumbs. He did it expertly but absently, as he and Rosalind talked. Her toenails were painted pale pink.

"That was co-inky-dink, running into Lydia Graham," Rosalind said.

"I don't know if I would have recognized her," Hunter said.

"I was in love with you that summer," Rosalind said. "You broke my heart."

Hunter doubted this was true.

"We were two ships that pass in the night," he said.

He gently pinched her foot, all along the line of the arch. Then methodically—first one side, then the other—he pressed on the arch with his thumbs. She closed her eyes. More than sex, Rosalind liked to be pampered. She went every year for two weeks to a spa outside of Tucson. She had a weekly appointment with a masseuse who came to the house. She swam laps sensuously in her heated pool.

"Rosalind, will you marry me?" he said.

"Are you serious?" she asked, opening her eyes. Lying on her back like that, she had a double chin.

"Never more serious in my life, darling."

Rosalind prided herself that she had no illusions about Hunter. The summer he stayed in the gatehouse, he gave her a Liberty of London silk scarf, which she happened to know he'd charged to his godmother's store account at Tweeds & Weeds. The shop manager had excused herself and called his godmother to ask if it was okay. His godmother said, "Of course it is," but she was cross. She told a friend, and the friend told a friend, and soon it was common knowledge. That was how Rosalind knew.

"He's a little shady. But that's just how he is. I like having someone to go places with," Rosalind had said. She was engaged to the movie star, but he was in Spain.

Now she imagined a life with Hunter. They would be companions. She wouldn't alone. A husband would give her a better position. *You can take him anywhere*, as her friends said. The foot rub felt wonderful. *Fuck it, I love him*, she thought. What the heart feels and the head knows are two different things.

"Of course I'll marry you," she said.

"Do we want a wedding?" Hunter asked.

"What do you think? Maybe at our stage of life, it's a better look to get married at the courthouse and someone can give us a party after?"

This was the sort of social judgment that Hunter appreciated in Rosalind. As if they were at the court of Louis XIV.

Rosalind basked in the foot rub. The other foot had its turn. They decided it would be classier to go ahead and get married and then tell people.

"But I don't want to have some stranger for the witness," Rosalind said.

"We can ask one of our friends to be the witness," Hunter agreed.

"Think of the honor!" Rosalind said.

Hunter laughed. He massaged her calf, squeezing it progressively from ankle to knee, not on her bare skin but over the silk of her palazzo pants.

"The big question, darling, is where will we live?" he said.

"I want to stay in Montecito. We just have to find the right place. We can live here while we're looking."

Hunter lifted her foot to his mouth and kissed the arch, bending his head. "I should be going now," he said.

"Must you?" she asked lazily, but she really didn't mind.

She watched as Hunter fastened his cuffs and put on his suit jacket. She felt they understood each other. They were companions of the heart. She held out her hand, and Hunter raised her to her feet. Barefoot, she walked with him to the door.

In the foyer, he kissed her on the lips, holding her face in his hands. "Thank you for a lovely evening," he said. "Now darling, promise me you won't go for one of your midnight swims."

"No promises," she said, smiling at him. "You know that's what I'm going to do."

" I worry when you swim alone at night."

"I'll be fine," she said.

"I'll call you tomorrow," he said.

She watched him walk down the walk. The night wind rustled the fronds of a palm tree. It was the dark of the moon. The god Pan watched from the shadows. Flattering words, loving endearments.

♦♦♦

HUNTER MADE GOOD TIME from Rosalind's house to the Polo Club. All his life, he was notorious for driving fast. There was the episode in Japan. He had the jazz station on the car radio. At the Polo Club, he punched in the access code and waited as the gate engaged and slowly slid open along a track. After he pulled into his carport, he sat in the car with the engine on. "I Get Along Without You," the Bill

Charlap version, was on the radio. A rueful, worldly-wise song. He'd already made his decision. What was he waiting for? Seize the moment. He backed the Thunderbird out of the carport and drove back to Rosalind's house.

♦♦♦

Lydia didn't go straight home. After she said goodbye to Annie, she went back in Jimmy's and called Peter from the pay phone. It was the last year there were pay phones. She got the answering machine and left the message that she was going out to Montecito to go for a walk; she wouldn't be too late. It was Peter's poker night. Hunter had told her it was not a physical relationship—"She doesn't turn me on." But was it true? Ordinarily the least jealous of women, Lydia was possessed by jealousy. The essence of jealousy is to be possessed with wanting to know.

Entirely aware that her behavior was unbalanced, Lydia drove out to Montecito. It was exciting. She knew Rosalind had bought the guesthouse at Il Belvedere. Il Belvedere was one of the old Montecito estates where Lydia had roamed at night—where she still, sometimes, roamed. The guesthouse was near the main entrance, down a little driveway. She could drive in and see if Hunter's white Thunderbird was there without anyone seeing her. But she didn't just want to know if Hunter's car was there. Lydia wanted to prowl.

On Peter's advice, Rosalind's father hadn't sold the house on Parra Grande Lane when he moved to Vista del Monte. There had been a tenant for a while, but at the moment it was empty. Lydia occasionally drove out to Montecito at night and left her car there while she went for a walk, which was what she did on this particular night. Her father's gray 1986 Honda Accord was in the carport. They were keeping it for when Sally got her license. Lydia parked her Passat next to the Honda. One of her father's old tennis hats was on the dash.

The cypress hedge cast its inky black shadow. All was quiet. The night sounds and smells of Montecito surrounded Lydia as she walked up Parra Grande Lane. Five or six cars drove past before she got to the first gate at Riven Rock, the old McCormick estate that was broken up after World War II. Each time she heard a car approaching, she hid, slipping into a driveway or through a hedge, staying out of sight until the car drove past. It was like when she was fourteen.

More than once that summer, she had circled around the gatehouse cottage at night trying to see in. The curtains were always drawn, the shades were down. Hunter wasn't one of those people who said, "We never close the curtains. Who would look in?" One night Rosalind was there. Her black VW Bug convertible was parked behind Hunter's green Porsche. The bedroom window was open. The curtains billowed in the night breeze.

Lydia heard Hunter say, "Don't move. Let me do it." His voice was low and urgent.

"I'm coming. Oh sweetheart…I'm coming," Rosalind said with a swooning cry.

Then silence, murmurs.

"Do you love me?" Rosalind asked.

"I'm fond of you, darling."

"You bastard," Rosalind said.

"Shhh," Hunter said.

Lydia had been very turned on. The smell of Joy perfume and semen and cigarettes and the straw smell of the grass matting in the bedroom. The sweet smell of night-blooming jasmine and the sleepy chirping of the baby mockingbirds in the nest in the aloe thicket. It was a scene she played over and over in her head, imagining a man saying to her, "Don't move. Let me do it." The mystery of sex was incredibly exciting when she was fourteen.

Inside Riven Rock, lights were on in some of the houses; once, a motion-sensor light turned on. She turned down Ivy Lane, a steep lane with oak trees on either side. She came to a big new house with a security gate. She slipped around the gate. Inside the house,

Belle de Jour was showing on a very large flat-screen television in a great room with a cathedral ceiling and no window coverings. She circled around the house and came to the stone wall that surrounded Riven Rock. She climbed over the wall at a low place and found herself on Ashley Road. She walked down the middle of the road in the starlight, listening for cars. Where Ashley Road made a sharp turn to the left, she turned right on Ayala Lane, toward the mountains.

Andy had been the landscape contractor for the last house on the lane. It was one of the first gardens for which Lydia was his muse. Her inspiration was the Huntington Gardens in San Marino. But on a smaller scale. No camellias. Two acres instead of a hundred acres. Enough time had gone by for the plantings to be established, timeless in the foothills in Montecito. The lights were out in the house. In the dark, Lydia walked on a path of decomposed granite, between the agaves and aloes and cacti, past a Moreton Bay fig tree. The property backed up against the pink stucco wall around Il Belvedere. Standing on a tree stump, she pulled herself up on the wall, then let herself down on the other side. The wind soughed in the trees.

She was on the grounds of Il Belvedere. This was familiar territory. She soon came out on the main driveway, close to the main house, where the lights were on. A dog yapped inside the house, but no one came out. Lydia walked down the driveway past oleanders and palm trees. She had almost come to Rosalind's driveway when she saw the lights of a car coming in the main entrance. She stepped back. The car turned down Rosalind's driveway. It was Hunter's Thunderbird. Cautiously, she continued down the driveway, keeping in the shadows. She saw him park under an oak tree and get out of the car. She had assumed it was Hunter and Rosalind coming back from the dinner party, but he was alone.

Hunter had no idea he was observed.

♦♦♦

Hunter took off his suit jacket and put it on the front seat, then shut the car door quietly. He walked around to the back of the car, opened the trunk, and took out a white terry towel—the monogrammed towel he kept with his tennis things. He shut the trunk, again quietly. Towel in hand, he walked around the side of the house to the terrace. Lydia kept him in view, taking cover in a myrtle shrubbery. Myrtle had always smelled like carrion to her.

The underwater lights were on in the pool. The turquoise tiles on the bottom were distorted in the watery light. The rectangular swimming pool had a deep end with a low diving board. Rosalind was in the pool, doing a languorous breaststroke, raising her head to take a breath each time her arms moved toward her sides. She had on a black bathing suit with a skirt. Her hair was tucked into a white rubber swim cap with an embossed flower pattern. A large, fluffy, shell pink towel was on a teak chaise longue.

Oblivious to Hunter's presence, Rosalind made slow progress toward the deep end. The pool was heated; the night air was cool. Mist rose from the warm water. First Hunter took off his shoes and socks. Then he took off his pants and shirt and undershirt and laid them over the back of a teak patio chair. He stashed the cufflinks in one of his shoes. Rosalind had reached the end of the pool. She rested, holding onto the side. Hunter stood barefoot in his white boxer shorts. Lydia had a little bit of a fetish for boxers. She imagined a hard cock pressing against the white cotton. He took off his boxers.

Hunter told himself that if Rosalind turned around, he would call to her. "I came back," he would say, his resonant deep voice carrying the length of the pool. He would wait for another time. She had to be caught unaware.

Rosalind pushed off, still oblivious to Hunter's presence. The swimming pool had wide steps down into the shallow end. Hunter descended the steps. The pool was heated to bathwater temperature, and there was the smell of chlorine. He stood in the shallow end, the water up to his waist. After each kick and pull, Rosalind floated for a moment before the next kick and pull. As a result, she made slow progress. It was maddening to watch her. Leaves on the surface of the water cast dark shadows on the lighted pool bottom. Hunter positioned himself directly in her path.

Lydia, watching, smelled evil.

He waited until Rosalind was about to run into him, and then he seized her by the shoulders. He braced himself and pushed down with all his strength, forcing her head two feet underwater. He was steeled for Rosalind to fight with inhuman strength. He was taking the chance of bruises. What happened was more horrible. She flailed feebly, a few splashes, then more feebly. Her soft, fleshy thighs bounced underwater against him. He held her underwater until she went limp, a boneless thing, her legs doubled up. When he released her, her body sank to the bottom of the pool, her arms and legs white and rounded on the turquoise tiles, her black bathing suit the plumage of a dead raven.

Lydia watched.

Out of the pool, Hunter reached for the white towel. He shivered from adrenaline and the cold. Up in the foothills, coyotes howled. When Hunter was a boy, there were no coyotes in Santa Barbara. He dried himself, pulled on his boxers, put on his undershirt, his pants, and shirt. He dried his feet and put his socks on. He fastened his cuffs with the gold cufflinks and bent down to tie his shoes. Lydia stayed motionless in the myrtle shrubbery until he drove away.

Hunter drove straight home. He came to a full stop at stop signs at the unlit intersections of Montecito, instead of his usual California rolling stop. It was sad. Rosalind could be very sweet. She had understood him, one part of him, better than anyone. But he had no regrets—nor would he, in the future. The possibilities of his life opened up before him. He arrived back at the Polo Club without incident.

Lydia made her way back to Parra Grande Lane the same way she had come, staying out of sight. At no point did she consider going to the police. It wouldn't bring Rosalind back. It would completely fuck up her own life. Witnessing Rosalind's murder had made her remember the thing about Hunter that had been eluding her memory—the thing that happened before the summer when she was fourteen.

It was midnight when she got home. Peter had just gotten back from his poker night—he was listening to her message when she walked in the door.

The obituary was in the *Santa Barbara News-Press*: "Rosalind Flynn Maddox Forester died unexpectedly October 30, 2000, at her home in Montecito. The cause of death was an accidental drowning." The obituary gave her background, her education, her marriages, her community involvement—both in Los Angeles and Santa Barbara—a mention of her beauty and her generous spirit. There would be a memorial service Tuesday, November 7, at 11:00 a.m. at All Saints-by-the-Sea Episcopal Church. The photograph was a fairly recent studio portrait.

CHAPTER EIGHT

The Night the Dogs Howled

There was a full moon, and she was drawn to be outside. She was eleven years old.

At the top of Parra Grande Lane, there was a ten-acre pasture. At one time, it had been the grounds of a Victorian house, but after the house was left unoccupied for many years, it became the haunted house, a derelict shell with broken windows and rotted stairs, where tramps lit fires on the parlor floor and kids had drinking parties. The picturesque-style garden designed by Lockwood de Forest and the sweeping lawns were no more. In the early fifties, the fire department demolished it. All that was left was the stone foundation and a hitching post—two squat sandstone pillars with a polished steel pipe between them. There was a flimsy fence around the property, wide-spaced strands of barbed wire that sagged between posts set wide apart. Old Mr. Cota, who lived with his equally old wife in a small stone house at the bottom of Parra Grande Lane, where Spanish Town was before the flood of 1914, kept his two old white workhorses in the pasture.

There was a single huge boulder in the pasture, twelve feet high and set deep in the ground, swept down from the mountains in some eons-ago flood. It had been a feature in the picturesque garden. A little grove of oak saplings had grown up around the boulder. The boulder was flat on top—it was a vantage point, like a hill fort. On this particular night, Lydia had scrambled up and was enjoying the view. The two rawboned old workhorses grazed in the moonlight. The smell of horses and the sharp smell of nasturtium leaves filled the air.

Two miles away, the Coast Starlight sounded its whistle for the railroad crossing at Butterfly Lane. A car drove by on Riven Rock Road, someone driving carefully, two sheets to the wind. Then, in the direction of Mountain Drive, up in the foothills, a dog howled. It was different from the way that dogs howl when they hear a siren. This was chilling, not like anything she'd heard before. First one dog howled, then it left off and another took up the cry, then another, coming closer. As if someone—something—was making its way down Cold Spring Creek, something that enraged and terrified the dogs.

The two old white horses, wary herd animals, raised their heads, flicked their ears, nickered, and galloped around the pasture like clumsy rocking horses. Lydia, too, was spooked. She wanted to be safe indoors. She slid down off the boulder. Whatever it was that enraged and terrified the dogs was still at a distance but coming closer. She walked fast, not quite running, down the overgrown drive between two rows of monarch palms, slipped under the barbed-wire fence, and continued down Parra Grande Lane between tall cypress hedges to her house. The cool night air had pockets of warm air, like swimming in the ocean.

At the end of her driveway, she halted. The howling and barking had stopped. Faintly, then louder, she heard the sound of running footsteps.

Lydia was still spooked, but she was also very curious. Quickly, she crawled into the middle of the cypress hedge at the end of the driveway. Hidden from view by the branches, she could see out unseen. At the top of Parra Grande Lane, a man rounded the corner of Riven Rock Road at an easy lope in the moonlight. A sport jacket draped over his arm, he ran down Parra Grande Lane, past where Lydia was concealed. A shiver went up her back. But she was intrigued, not frightened. Lydia smelled what the dogs had smelled. But the evil was not real to her. Not when she was safe in the hedge and she was eleven years old.

As she watched, the man continued down the lane and disappeared around a bend.

The day after, the lead article on the front page of the *Santa Barbara News-Press* was an account of a fatal accident on Mountain Drive. There was a blurry photograph of a wrecked MG. The time of the crash was estimated to be sometime after midnight the night before. No one had reported it at the time, which was not surprising. There weren't many houses in the area. But the wreckage of the car was visible from the road above, and by midmorning someone had called the sheriff. The driver, Gloria Evans, née D'Angelico, age twenty-seven, had lost control of her sports car coming around a sharp curve and gone off the road. Mrs. Evans had died at the scene from injuries sustained in the crash. Her body was found a short distance from the vehicle. A graduate of Laguna Blanca School, class of 1951, she was a stewardess for Delta Airlines. She was survived by her son, Hunter Evans Jr., and her husband, Hunter Evans. Mrs. Evans was alone in the car at the time of the accident.

Lydia's parents talked about it at dinner.

"The D'Angelicos got their start as bootleggers," Lydia's father said. "They had fishing boats."

"Jack, you say that about everyone," her mother said.

"There were a lot of bootleggers."

Gloria Evans was the aunt of a boy in Lydia's fifth-grade class, Rick D'Angelico. She was his father's younger sister. Rick told his classmates that she had come up from Los Angeles to meet with Hunter about a divorce, and his dad said it was Hunter Evans's fault because he let Gloria drive when she was drinking. He didn't see her home. He let her drop him off at his godmother's house on Hot Springs Road. Lydia and her friends took an avid interest in grown-up gossip. But Lydia never mentioned to anyone the man she had seen the night that Gloria D'Angelico died.

♦♦♦

Earlier the same evening, Hunter and Gloria were in the bar at the Miramar discussing their divorce. Gloria was on her second daiquiri. She'd picked Hunter up at his godmother's house in her turquoise MG convertible. The top was down, and she'd had on a cream wool car coat. Hunter had driven them to the Miramar—she was the kind of woman who always handed the car keys to the man. The last time they'd seen each other was in Los Angeles County Superior Court four years earlier. Hunter had not been paying the child support required of him in the separation agreement, and Gloria had gotten a court order to garnish his salary. Hunter had flown from Japan to dispute the judgment. The judge ruled against him. Hunter committed to a payment schedule, and he returned to Japan.

It was never a real marriage. The wedding was a shotgun wedding at All Saints-by-the-Sea in Montecito. She was seventeen; he was nineteen. Hunter was in the Navy in Japan, and when he got out he stayed in Japan. She made a life for herself in Los Angeles. His son was ten years old, and he hadn't seen him since he was a toddler. They were legally separated, but Hunter stalled on getting a divorce. It would be time-consuming and expensive. Someone had to be at fault. Gloria asked Hunter why he wanted a divorce now. He said he'd realized it wasn't fair to leave her in limbo.

The truth was he had a wife in Japan. She was a beautiful Japanese girl who came from one of the kazoku families, the Japanese nobility—her father was a member of the Diet, the Japanese parliament. He'd met her at the tennis club. Her family was not pleased when she wanted to marry a Caucasian. But Fukiko persuaded them. The wedding was at the American embassy. His father-in-law helped him get a good job.

The piano player was playing torchy standards. Hunter got up from the table and requested "I Apologize," the Billy Eckstine song. He put a five in the tip jar on the piano and held out his arms. "May I have this dance?" They were the only couple on the tiny dance floor. Her full breasts pressed against him as he held her close and sang the words in her ear. She was wearing a sheath dress. Hunter wore a sports jacket and narrow tie.

"What if I'm still in love with you?" Gloria said.

Agree to a divorce, you moron, Hunter thought. Fukiko had started to ask questions. His father-in-law was not without resources to investigate. If the family found out he was married, the shit would hit the fan.

When they left the Miramar, Gloria wanted to drive.

"It's your car, darling," Hunter said, holding her car coat for her.

She said she wasn't cold.

She tied a chiffon scarf over her bouffant hair. She wanted to go the long way around, by Mountain Drive. She was a little tipsy, but she drove carefully, both hands on the wheel. Hunter was clearheaded. He'd had one martini. There were a lot of curves on Mountain Drive, and the grading was rudimentary. The scattered houses had long dirt driveways, only clusters of mailboxes were visible from the road. The night air smelled of sage, and there was a panoramic view, a grand sweep from the Rincon to Goleta, the lights of the town below them. Dean Martin singing "Volare" was on the car radio, lilting and romantic. In the passenger seat, Hunter had one arm over the seat back. The classic pose of a man in the passenger seat. He leaned over and fondled her breast through the fabric of her dress.

"Please stop," she said.

Hunter continued to fondle her breast. Her nipple got hard. She kept her eyes on the road, her lips parted. She felt a rush of desire. She arched her back and pushed her foot down on the accelerator. The rush of acceleration, the erotic rush. There was a sharp curve ahead. On the uphill side of the road, there was a steep rocky bank. On the downhill side, there was a straight drop into a ravine.

Hunter said tersely, "Slow down, darling."

She slammed on the brake. She should have eased into it. The car fishtailed into the curve.

"No," she screamed.

Hunter had good reflexes. As the car slid back and forth, out of control, he got up on the seat in a crouch, quick as a cat. When the MG went over the edge, he jumped clear. He made himself into a ball and did a tuck and roll. He half expected to land haphazardly on the steep rocky bank. Instead, he landed on his feet in the dry grass at the edge of the road. Gloria's scream went on and on, a banshee's scream of terror, as the car plunged down into the ravine. The MG bounced and rolled and bounced again.

Hunter got to his feet, bruised but unhurt. The MG had come to a rest right side up, its windshield shattered, the door on the driver's side ripped off. The headlights were still on. Gloria had been thrown clear. She lay in a patch of short dry grass. The headlights shone on her motionless body, arms and legs akimbo. By the light of the full moon, Hunter slid down the rocky scree. No one was going to come. No houses overlooked the ravine. Except for the rocks that he dislodged, it was very quiet. The engine had died. When he got to the bottom, he approached Gloria. She was on her back, her mouth open.

Hunter knelt at her side. Silver moonlight and black velvet shadows. Gloria moaned. Her right arm was bent against her body, blood seeping from below the cap sleeve of her sheath dress. Hunter considered. It was just possible the the brachial artery had been severed, the bleeding staunched by the pressure of her arm against her body. He had taken a course in first aid in the Navy.

Gently, he straightened her arm. Bright red arterial blood pumped from her right arm. Hunter jumped to his feet, out of range of the spurting blood. He knew what to do to staunch arterial bleeding. But he didn't make any move to apply pressure to the artery. The MG's headlights flickered and went out.

Gloria moaned again, not as loudly as before. The blood spurted more feebly, in rhythm with her failing pulse. Dark blood on the dry grass in the moonlight. She didn't moan again. Her spirit had left her body. Failure to render aid was not a crime in California.

He started walking down the ravine in the moonlight. Soon, he came to Cold Spring Creek. The rocky creek bed was dry, except for occasional small deep pools. Dogs howled and barked, howled and barked, one after another, as Hunter, rock-hopping and climbing over boulders, moved past their territories. They could smell evil. He left the creek where it joined Hot Springs Creek in Riven Rock and jogged through Riven Rock on Rockbridge Road, past sleeping houses. Dogs howled and barked. When he came to Riven Rock Road, he picked up his pace. No cars passed him. He had no idea that a hidden watcher saw him as he ran down Parra Grande Lane.

It was midnight when he walked in the door of his godmother's house on Hot Springs Road. She was still up. He said Gloria had dropped him at the end of the driveway. They'd reached an amicable agreement. The next afternoon, he told the sheriff he had no idea what Gloria was doing on Mountain Drive. He'd assumed she was going straight to her brother's house after she left him. Her driving was perfectly fine from the Miramar to Hot Springs Road. He said he'd always regret that he didn't insist on seeing her home. No one ever checked what time they left the Miramar. No one asked Hunter about the hour and a half between ten thirty and midnight. Hunter arranged for his son to live with his sister and her family in Wellesley, and he went back to Japan.

♦♦♦

THREE YEARS LATER, LYDIA knew immediately that the man in the gatehouse cottage was the same man she'd seen the night the dogs howled. She recognized him; she remembered his smell. Not the smell of evil. That was gone. But his individual smell. The lime aftershave and the gin. She already knew that the night she saw the man running down Parra Grande Lane was the same night Hunter's first wife died. But now she knew that the man she saw was Hunter Evans.

Lydia, although secretive, was truthful. But liars intrigued her. The doubleness of it. She never said anything to Hunter. Her correct instinct was that he would not like to be asked why he was running down Riven Rock Road, coming from the direction of Mountain Drive when she knew his godmother lived on Hot Springs Road. She'd been at her house with Annie and her mother. Also, she was fourteen years old, and she didn't want him to see her as a little girl who spied on people at night. All that summer, she kept her knowledge in a separate compartment.

She never told anyone, and as time went by, she forgot. When she was twenty, she was incredulous if a middle-aged person said they didn't remember something important that happened when they were a child. When she was fifty-one, she had no trouble believing it. After she renewed her acquaintance with Hunter, there was also an element of self-deception. She had a vague sense that she was forgetting something, a piece of information about Hunter, but she didn't really try to remember.

Having witnessed the murder of Rosalind, Lydia knew that Hunter had killed his first wife. She had no idea how he did it. She would never know. This was different from shady financial dealings or social pretensions. She was seldom afraid, but she was afraid of Hunter.

CHAPTER NINE

The Memorial Service

ROSALIND'S MEMORIAL SERVICE WAS exactly the sort of memorial service that Lydia and Annie made a point of going to. Ordinarily they would have gone together, but Lydia's father asked Lydia for a ride, and Annie's mother wanted to go with her, and it was easier to take two cars.

Lydia picked her father up at his apartment at Vista del Monte. He smelled of Aqua Velva aftershave. He was almost bald, with brown age spots on his bare scalp and wisps of white hair. He was wearing a navy-blue blazer with one of the brass buttons missing. Lydia took Cabrillo Boulevard to Montecito. It was a foggy morning, the sky low and gray. The flat, blue-green ocean was sullen. The boats that were anchored off East Beach rather than pay for a mooring at the harbor looked disreputable.

"Poor little Rosalind. The first husband was a real stinker," her father said, as they drove past the Bird Refuge. He'd known Rosalind since she was a little girl.

Earlier that morning, Lydia had been at Turk Hesselund Nursery on Coast Village Road. By the cash register, there was a row of penciled notes on slips of paper taped to the wall: *Dwarf mugo pine. Hank Ingram*—and a phone number. *Ferti-Lome Fish Emulsion. Mrs. Schroeder will PICK UP.* One of the slips of paper read: *6 white azaleas. Call Rosalind F.*

Lydia told her father about the reminder note. He would appreciate the pathos. He was quite deaf, and she pitched her voice so he could hear her. Not louder, but she enunciated more precisely. He had expensive hearing aids, but they amplified ambient sound, and he refused to wear them. To her, her voice sounded as if she was reading from a script.

"She'll never see the white azaleas," he said.

Poor Rosalind, limp on the bottom of the swimming pool.

"She wanted the world to be beautiful," he said.

"We all do," Lydia said.

For a week, since she witnessed Rosalind's death, she had existed night and day at a level of anxiety that made her feel disembodied. She always told Sally, when something didn't go right, "You have to remember, pumpkin, it's just one damn thing after another, and the important thing is to retrieve the situation."

But she couldn't figure out how to retrieve the situation.

With most decisions, it doesn't matter what you decide. Your life will be different depending on what you decide, but life will go on. Occasionally, however, you better decide right, because if you don't, it could be really, really bad. This was one of those situations. She'd gotten herself in over her head.

What if she told Peter everything? Trusted in his love and his shrewd realism. Trusted him to rescue her. Lying sleepless next to him in bed at night, listening to the shush-shush of the waves and the night wind, the neighbor playing his flute, she was tempted. She was the cat who walked alone. She was secretive. But, God, it would be nice to confide, to lean on Peter. However, if she told Peter, nothing would ever be the same again. Including—she might no longer be married to him.

All Saints-by-the-Sea was on Eucalyptus Lane, a block from the ocean. The parking lot was across from the church. There was a row of eucalyptus trees. Hunter was already there; his white Thunderbird was parked near the entrance. Lydia parked, and she and her father walked across the street to the church. The smell of eucalyptus and salt air. Tendrils of fog swirled around the pine trees outside the church. All Saints was in the classic Craftsman style, dating from

1900. It had brown-shingled sides and a steep shingled roof and a fieldstone bell tower with ivy growing on it.

The two brothers who owned Il Belvedere were acting in lieu of family. Suave and animated in an elderly homosexual way, they were both dressed in dark suits, white shirts, and discreet ties. In their early eighties, they had made all the arrangements. As a deacon handed out programs, they greeted people in the vestibule. There was going to be a reception afterward at Il Belvedere. The younger brother, the one who had called 911, had taken Annie and her mother aside in the vestibule.

"We're having a few people to the house after the service," he said. "Spread the word, please. Everyone welcome. We just don't want people no one knows showing up. Hunter will be there."

In the church, the organist was playing "As Longs the Deer for Cooling Springs," a hymn that spoke of Christian hope. The church smelled of clean old dust and ecclesiastical incense, frankincense and myrrh, women's perfume and men's aftershave. All Saints was not an austere church. The vaulted ceiling had ornately carved wooden beams, and the walls were smooth white plaster. The red carpet on the aisles of the nave matched the red cushions on the pews. There were Pre-Raphaelite stained-glass windows.

Hunter sat by himself in the first pew, debonair and subdued, studying the order of service, looking about. As if he were at his table at Perino's in 1957, as if he were the ten-year-old Hunter at a table on the balcony at his father's restaurant in the El Paso.

Lydia and her father progressed slowly up the center aisle, Lydia matching his pace, as one does with an old person. She was wearing the knockoff Chanel suit, lime green with fringes, that she wore to funerals and memorial services. A dressy outfit in a bright color was entirely proper in this social circle. An affirmation of life. When Hunter turned in his pew, Lydia felt alert and wary, like a predatory animal in the presence of a more dangerous predator—one that preys on her kind.

At the sight of Lydia, Hunter's heart sang. He imagined a life with her. The sex would be fabulous. They'd go first class. Thinking she was like him, he imagined them like two beautiful, amoral sharks swimming through the ocean together. As much as Hunter was capable of love, he loved Lydia. He had loved her for thirty-seven years. He had already met with Rosalind's attorney. The terms of the will and the trust were what she'd led him to expect. He'd already made a large withdrawal from one of the payable-on-death bank accounts. He caught Lydia's eye and smiled. She nodded acknowledgment.

Don't ever let him know that I know, she thought.

Annie and her mother were in a pew a few rows back from the front, on the other side of the aisle from Hunter. Annie waved to Lydia that she'd saved them a place. Lydia and her father edged into the pew. Lydia's father sat on the aisle; Lydia sat between him and Annie. Hunter was in her line of vision. Annie told her that the reception was at Il Belvedere.

"It's going to be swanky," she said.

"I can't go," Lydia said. "I have to meet Andy. We're making a pitch, and I have to be there."

This wasn't true. She could have gone to the reception, but she felt strongly it was better to avoid Hunter. Without its seeming that she was avoiding him.

"Rats," Annie said. "Mr. Graham..." She leaned across Lydia, enunciating each word. Annie, too, knew how to talk to a deaf old person. "Do you want to come with us to Il Belvedere?"

"I'll put myself in your hands," Lydia's father said. He would be ninety-seven on January 17.

People talked quietly. Hunter was joined in the front pew by a dear friend of Rosalind's—a handsome woman in late middle age, wearing a pink suit, her graying dark blonde hair in a French twist, and her older husband, his face dominated by heavy jowls and framed by a leonine head of white hair. They were solicitous of Hunter.

After Hunter had left Rosalind that night, before she'd unwisely (and tragically) gone for a swim alone, she had emailed this friend, sharing the news that she and Hunter had only just that evening decided to get married at the courthouse. "We're tying the knot. We want you and Harold to be our witnesses," she wrote.

The email was a stroke of luck for Hunter. He'd hoped Rosalind had done something of the sort. It corroborated his status as the bereaved fiancé. He could confide: "If only I'd stayed. We were over the moon. We talked a long time… We agreed that we both wanted to stay in Montecito. We were already close. We'd made our wills out to each other."

As the organ played, Lydia told Annie and her mother about seeing the reminder about white azaleas—the pathos of it. Her father studied his program in a magisterial way with his thick-lensed glasses in their clear plastic rims.

"They made their wills out to each other," Annie's mother said. She looked like a feisty little gray-haired terrier in a black trouser suit and white blouse with red costume jewelry clip-on earrings. She and Lydia's father weren't especially good friends.

"Hunter is going to be a very rich boy," Annie said.

By the time the organist played the last chords of "Give Rest, O Christ," and the deacon closed the doors to the vestibule, there were forty or fifty people in the church—a mix of people up from LA, people who had known Rosalind as a girl, people in her social circle, a few people with only a second-degree connection or no connection at all, a category that sometimes applied to Annie and Lydia at funerals and memorial services they attended.

"You two crashed a funeral!" Peter said once.

"We didn't crash it," Lydia said. "Annie saw the announcement in the newspaper. We paid our respects. It was a little tricky at the reception."

The service was the traditional service for the dead from the 1928 *Book of Common Prayer*, without the Eucharist. No eulogy or sharing of memories. The rector came down the aisle in his white alb and embroidered cassock and took his place to address the congregation. He had white hair, a ruddy complexion, and a worldly assurance:

I am the resurrection and the life, saith the Lord;
he that believeth in me, though he were dead, yet shall he live;
and whosoever liveth and believeth in me shall never die...

Lydia followed along in the order of service: she stood, she sat, she knelt on the kneeler. As did Hunter in the front pew across the aisle. Her father remained seated. He was violently anti-Christian. He'd often referred to Dr. Hall, who had been the rector for more than thirty years before finally retiring, as a pompous fraud. When the congregation recited the Apostles' Creed, he harrumphed. Lydia heard Hunter's strong baritone through the mumble of voices:

I believe in God, the Father Almighty,
maker of heaven and earth;
And in Jesus Christ his only Son, our Lord;
who was conceived by the Holy Spirit,
born of the Virgin Mary, suffered under Pontius Pilate,
was crucified, died, and was buried;
the third day he rose from the dead;
he ascended into heaven,
and sitteth at the right hand of God the Father Almighty;
from thence he shall come to judge the quick and the dead.
I believe in the Holy Spirit,
the holy catholic Church,
the communion of saints,
the forgiveness of sins,
the resurrection of the body,
and the life everlasting. Amen.

Lydia wiped away tears with her bent knuckle, so her mascara wouldn't smear.

The rector concluded:

O God, whose mercies cannot be numbered: Accept our
prayers on behalf of thy servant Rosalind, and grant her an

entrance into the land of light and joy, in the fellowship of thy saints; through Jesus Christ thy Son our Lord, who liveth and reigneth with thee and the Holy Spirit, one God, now and forever. Amen.

The recessional was "Ye Watchers and Ye Holy Ones." *Alleluia. Alleluia.* The mourners filed out of the church. Lydia's father wasn't the only doddery old person. People, many of whom Lydia knew, stood about on the brick walk in front of the church. Who was going to the reception? Who was invited but wasn't going? They had gathered to perform a rite of the tribe. The morning fog hadn't burned off yet. Hunter moved about, a model of discreet, undemonstrative sorrow.

A woman said, "Hunter, how are you?"

"I'm bearing up," he said.

"How are you really?" she said, clasping his hand.

Lydia stood with her father and Annie and Annie's mother for a few minutes, confirming that they'd give her father a ride back to Vista del Monte after the reception. Before Hunter could break free and come over to them, Lydia left. Hunter saw her go.

"Excuse me," he said to the man he was talking to. He caught up with Lydia as she was about to get in her car.

"Darling," Hunter said in his low urbane voice. "Will I see you at Il Belvedere?"

"Alas, no. I have to work," she said, as if this was an ordinary conversation. "Andy already rescheduled so I could come to the memorial."

"When can I see you?"

"I don't know," she said rather desperately, as if she truly wished they could get together, but it was so complicated. When the truth was that not only was she afraid of him, she was repelled. The subterranean connection that had lasted for decades was no more.

There was the low-tide seaweed smell of the ocean. The smell of eucalyptus. People were drifting into the parking lot, getting into their cars. No one would think it was odd that Lydia was talking to Hunter. Annie had told everyone that they'd run into him and Rosalind the night that Rosalind drowned.

"Don't make me wait too long."

"Hunter, you asked Rosalind to marry you," Lydia said, as if she might make a jealous scene. Let him think she was jealous. She *had* been jealous, the night Rosalind died. How strange.

"Darling, I never proposed to her. It's you I want to marry." There were flecks of gold in his hazel eyes. "She sent Jane Elliot an email saying we were going to be married. God knows what that was about."

"That isn't what you told Annie's mother," Lydia said.

"I didn't deny it. I don't want it to be awkward. Why not let people think I'd asked her to marry me?"

"No. No awkwardness." Lydia looked at him with false complicity, as if placated.

"It's very sad. I loved her, but I wasn't *in love* with her." Neither of them mentioned the bequest.

Lydia wanted to say, *Oh shut up.* Instead, she said, "Please be patient. I have to figure it out. I'll call you."

"Don't take too long."

Hunter held the car door for her, and she got in. He shut the door. He rather liked all the complications of an affair with a married woman—the subterfuges and tears. Of course, this was different—in the end, they would be married. He had no understanding that Lydia was stranger than he could ever imagine.

Lydia started the car and drove off. She'd bought some time. She wasn't any closer to deciding on a course of action. All else aside, Lydia was annoyed. She was twitching her tail. The reception at Il Belvedere was exactly the sort of event that she enjoyed. Stupid murderer Hunter made it so she couldn't go.

At the last reception she'd gone to with Annie, someone said, "We're not snobs. We're eccentric." It was at a private home after the funeral of a Shell Oil heiress who was a beloved patron of the arts (and, by all accounts, a terrible mother).

Hunter was a murderer. *Whatever I do, there's no guarantee he won't murder me,* Lydia thought. *Murder me and take me down to hell with him.* She wondered what really happened to the third wife, the one who supposedly died of cancer. Unfortunate things happened to women he knew.

CHAPTER TEN

The Most Direct Course of Action

WHEN LYDIA AND PETER bought the house on El Camino de la Luz, Lydia's father gave them a Danish modern dining table for a housewarming present. It seated six but could be extended to seat twelve. Even before Lydia's mother died and her father moved to Vista del Monte, Lydia and Peter hosted Sunday dinners at the Mesa house. Ambrose and Marilyn, the neighbors across the fence—it was Ambrose who played the flute—were fixtures. Annie and her husband and one or another of their kids were often in the rotation. Sometimes at Easter or Christmas, Lydia put in both leafs and the company around the table was a crowd of friends and family—the youngest guest a baby, the oldest in their nineties.

The Sunday after the memorial service for Rosalind, Ambrose came by the house in the afternoon with a cooler full of ridgeback shrimp. Shrimp so fresh that some of them were still twitching. Ridgeback shrimp have a sharp spine down the back, big heads with bulging eyes, and long, stiff antennae. They are incredibly sweet and succulent, but they spoil fast and they're a pain to clean. You seldom find them in the fish market. Ambrose brought the cooler into the kitchen.

"Yum yum. I love you," Lydia said. "Sunday dinner is on. Where did you get them?"

"My buddy at the Harbor," Ambrose said. "We outfitted his boat with a shrimping net."

"This is your friend who had the Fresh Wish Company?"

"None other. Are you okay, sweetheart?" he asked.

"I'm fine," she said. She knew she had dark circles under her eyes.

He looked at her skeptically. Ambrose was an old-time hipster. West Coast cool. Chet Baker and Charlie Parker "Relaxin' at Camarillo." When he was a young man, he was so handsome that women followed him home through the streets of Berkeley. He looked like Paul Newman. He was still strikingly good looking and wore the mantle lightly. He'd been a journeyman printer in the last days of linotype, a commercial fisherman, a bookie, a carpenter. He did odd jobs.

"The odder the better," as Marilyn said.

Peter had asked her the same thing that morning. Was she okay? Lydia had said she was fine, just trying to figure what to do about the sunken garden at the Picacho Lane house. When in reality, she was desperately trying to figure out how to retrieve the situation. At night, she lay sleepless next to Peter. She hadn't gone for a walk at night since the memorial service. She had the feeling that if she went out, she wouldn't come back.

"You and your gardens," Ambrose said. He and Lydia were good friends. "We're half in love with each other," he'd often say in a joking-relationship way.

"Me and my gardens," Lydia said, smiling at him. "Tonight, we feast on ridgebacks."

"We'll bring tomatoes," Ambrose said. "What time?"

After he left, Lydia stood at the sink, shelling and cleaning shrimp under a thin stream of cold water. She deveined the shrimp with a sharp little Japanese knife that fit her hand perfectly.

A hundred yards away, not out over the ocean but along the edge of the bluffs, a stream of monarch butterflies traveled down the coast, a steady drift of orange and black butterflies, the black markings like the leading in a stained-glass window, crossing each other's paths, meandering, wandering off course, but always southward, following the shore. A monarch butterfly alighted on a magenta cosmos in the garden. It had the face of the Bad Fairy.

It had been five days since Rosalind's memorial service. Lydia had not yet called Hunter. Nor had he made any approach. *Dear God, please help me.* Lydia's faith was primitive. *Dear God, thank you for what I have. Dear God, keep me safe.*

Peter and Sally were surfing at Hollister Ranch. They'd made an early start. Peter had a yellow 1950 Ford station wagon with faux wood panels and a V-8 engine that he referred to as The Woodie, which Sally found incredibly embarrassing. "Dad! It's a station wagon."

The day before, on Saturday, Lydia and Peter had driven down to Thacher to see the fall play and brought Sally back with them. *Dancing at Lughnasa* was a melancholy play set in Ireland about five sisters.

"Why on earth did they pick that one?" Lydia had asked.

"Mom," Sally said, "there are lots of parts and not any scene changes."

As Lydia cleaned the shrimp, Kitty, her little tuxedo cat, sat posed at her feet, watching her intently. Every once in a while, Lydia dropped a couple of cleaned shrimp into a pan of water that was simmering on the stove, took them out with a slotted spoon when they were barely cooked, and held them under cold water. Kitty refused to eat raw shrimp.

"If you'd eat them raw, you wouldn't have to wait," Lydia said, as she deposited the shrimp on Kitty's saucer on the floor.

Kitty said, "Mew." She was a polite cat. She never jumped up on the counter.

When Peter and Sally got home from the Ranch, they showered and changed, then took The Woodie to fetch Lydia's father at Vista del Monte. Jack Graham got a kick out of The Woodie. They came in the house talking about the coyote they had just seen. He was a big handsome coyote, proceeding at a slow trot down the middle of El Camino de la Luz in the twilight, headed in the direction of the ravine, looking about him. He waited in one of the driveways for The Woodie to pass, then resumed his reconnoiter. Peter and

Sally hypothesized that the coyote was checking out the Mesa, their neighborhood, in case he had to move his family. Someone had been shooting at the coyotes in Hope Ranch.

The sunporch had louvered windows and grass matting on the floor. The sweet hay smell of grass matting. There were beeswax candles in silver candlesticks. The smell of beeswax. There were six people around the dining table in the sun porch. The family and Ambrose and Marilyn.

Marilyn was a plein air painter of minor renown. She'd been one of the hipster art babes at San Francisco Art Institute in the fifties. She and Ambrose were like young grandparents to Sally. When Sally was little, Ambrose had a job at the Harbor, and on Sunday mornings he would take her with him when he went out in a skiff past the breakwater to feed the blue fish hatchlings in a wire-mesh hatchery attached to one of the buoys.

Lydia's father sat at the head of the table, a big old man in a yellow guayabera shirt. His hands had purple splotches and liver spots. When the food was on the table, he bowed his head to say grace.

As Sally liked to say, "We can tell that it's Sunday. Grandpa's ragging on the Christians." He referred to Our Savior as Jesus Christ and that Outfit, telling Sally, "It's all made up."

Yet it was always Jack who said grace. He did it with both irony and a sense of ceremony. They bowed their heads.

"Dear God and Jesus, thank you for the food we are about to eat. Amen."

"Amen."

The salad was Bibb lettuce from the farmer's market and tomatoes from Ambrose and Marilyn's garden. The last of the tomatoes. They grew tomatoes of unparalleled flavor. There was sourdough bread, and a platter heaped with the shelled shrimp, boiled with Old Bay seasoning and lemon. To be eaten with either lemon butter or shrimp cocktail sauce. Ambrose wanted no accompaniments whatsoever with his ridgeback shrimp. "He's such a purist," Marilyn said. The adults drank dark beer. Sally had Perrier.

"When I was a kid, the closest coyotes were two mountain ranges over," Peter said.

"Now they're eating poodles in Hope Ranch," Marilyn said.

"Not only that, they're out and about in broad daylight," Lydia said.

"Mom! You're nocturnal, and you're out and about in the day," Sally said. She was pert, in the way of a fifteen-year-old girl.

Sally had a face like Chaucer's prettie maide, with strawberry blonde hair and a widow's peak, and a delicate, small mouth. She was the same height as Lydia, but she was a lot more solid. You'd think either surfer or water polo player, if you saw her. Lydia asked her once, "What if we'd lived in Nebraska and you never saw a surfboard?" She said she'd have always felt that her life was inauthentic, that something was wrong. Like the transgender people.

She felt a stab of love for Sally. The first time she read Sally *The Story of Babar*, when they came to the part where the hunter shoots Babar's mother, Sally had examined the illustration of the baby elephant sitting by his mother's dead body, and then her little face crumpled, tears welling up in her blue eyes.

"The mother is dead. The baby elephant doesn't have a mother," she said and wept with horrible desolation.

Lydia had consoled her, reassured her. "No hunter will get me, little pumpkin."

How strange, she thought, remembering. She'd never thought of Hunter's name as anything but just a name.

Sally said, "I was in third grade before I realized that everyone's mom didn't say, 'Nighty-night, little pumpkin. The wicked love the darkness,' when she tucked them in."

"It was a plaisanterie," Lydia said.

"And then she'd go out for a walk at ten o'clock at night."

"Hey, I like the night." Lydia laughed.

Lydia's father said, "I always thought she was really a cat."

"Meow," Lydia said.

Peter said, "Pass the shrimp," and Marilyn started the platter down to his end of the table.

All this time, Kitty had been there in the sunporch, sitting with her feet tucked in, at a little distance from the table. When she saw the shrimp platter passed from hand to hand, she followed it with her eyes. The temptation was too much. She carefully gauged her jump, and in one leap, she was up on the table, landing neatly, finding places for her feet among the serving platters as she came down.

"Kitty!" everyone called out.

She'd never jumped on the table before. Holding her plumed tail high, she headed for the shrimp. But then, her tail came in contact with the flame of one of the candles and caught on fire. The fur frizzled. Terrified, she raced the length of the table, her tail ablaze.

"Dad!" Sally screamed.

"Peter!" Lydia said.

As Kitty jumped off the table, Peter made a ring of his thumb and index finger, and, quick as lightning, encircled her tail, extinguishing it as it passed through the ring of his fingers. No longer on fire, the little cat landed on the floor and streaked into the back of the house to hide under a bed.

"I swear I gave her a fair share of shrimp," Lydia said.

"Fast thinking, man," Ambrose said to Peter.

Lydia's father said, "Good work."

The smell of scorched fur was strong. Lydia got up and put some shrimp in Kitty's dish in the kitchen, for when she came out of hiding. Dinner resumed. Lydia and Sally said in unison, "The carport fell in on the Jaguar."

It was a family saying.

One afternoon, Lydia's father was rejoicing that all was well with the world—the garden was in good shape; he didn't have any reports to write; all the bills were paid. When all of a sudden, there was a terrific crash. The whole house shook. A large cypress tree, its roots loosened by recent heavy rains, had fallen on the carport, crushing the carport roof and demolishing his white X-KE convertible.

"Wow," Marilyn said. "Imagine if your tail caught on fire."

"She just couldn't resist," Lydia said.

"She took the most direct course of action," her father said.

"But did she weigh the consequences?" Peter said.

"You can always take the most direct course of action, if you're willing to take the consequences" was advice that Lydia's father often gave.

"She thought she could pull it off," Ambrose said.

"Poor Kitty," Sally said, full of sympathy.

"Don't jump up on the table" was going to become another family saying, *Unless the family is no more*, Lydia thought.

The evening was cool. It was already November. Halloween had come and gone. The fog was coming in. They could hear the foghorn at the Harbor. Lydia shut the louvered windows and drew the blinds. Dessert was apple crisp made with apples from an orchard in Ojai; they'd bought the apples at a farm stand. Peter whipped the whipping cream with a rotary beater. Lydia's father ate slowly and with pleasure, spooning dollops of whipped cream on his apple crisp.

Lydia and Marilyn talked about birds. Marilyn belonged to the Audubon Society. She said she was resisting the urge to call the bird hotline and report the sighting of a penguin. Lydia said she wanted to be a black phoebe. She thought of Hunter saying, "Crows are such unattractive birds."

"Bird watching. What kind of person would watch a bird?" Lydia's father said.

"Jack! Honestly," Marilyn said. "I saw you watching the crows at your apartment."

"I just want to know what they're up to." He was fond of Marilyn.

Looking around the table, Lydia thought how desperately she didn't want her life to change. She had to do something or Hunter Evans was going to smash up her life. Sally and Peter and Ambrose talked about surfing and sixty-foot rogue waves in the middle of the ocean and the rock fish around the reef offshore. Lydia was so anxious she felt like she was going to jump out of her skin.

Peter was in good spirits. The Ashville project was almost in the bag. Money, money, money.

That was when the phone rang. Lydia got up to answer it in the kitchen. "Hello?"

It was Hunter Evans.

That evening, he'd had a hamburger at the Nugget, sitting at the bar, then gone home and poured himself a beer. He was tired of waiting. Lydia's number was in the phone book, listed under her maiden name. Damn it, he was tired of waiting. He was prepared to blow up her marriage.

"I miss you," he said, his voice was insinuating. "I want that hot, wet, dark place you have for me."

"I can't talk right now. We're in the middle of dinner," Lydia said into the receiver in the social voice that she used for clients. The people around the table in the sunporch were still talking. Suddenly, she was furious. How dare he call her at home. How dare he!

In the sunporch, Sally was saying, "Do you think the coyotes will move to the Mesa?" And Ambrose was saying, "Nah. Too poky for them. Too many little fenced yards." And Marilyn said, "Not enough poodles."

"Let me call you in the morning," Lydia said. "We can set up a time to get together."

Hunter said, "Duck out now."

"I can't talk right now. I'll call you," Lydia said, as if to a client who would not get off the phone. In case anyone was paying attention.

"Come," he said. "I'll be here."

She hung up and went back to the table. Her tail was switching. How dare Hunter Evans call her at Sunday dinner. How dare he! She was incandescent with fury. Yet she kept up the appearance of her usual self. Peter looked at her inquiringly.

"It was the specimen tree client," she said. "I'll call her in the morning."

"The client who thought a specimen tree was a variety of tree?" her father asked. He was looking at her curiously. He had good intuition.

"None other," Lydia said. "We're going to make a tour of specimen trees. I'm trying to decide if I should take her to the Botanic Garden."

"A lot of great art has been commissioned by the nouveau riche," Marilyn said.

They made an early evening of it. Lydia's father was ready to go when dessert was over. Ambrose and Marilyn said they'd give him a ride home, and he left with them. Sally had to be back at Thacher by nine, so Peter put her duffle bag in the trunk of his Audi and strapped her surfboard to the rack on the roof. Lydia told Sally that she loved her and she'd see her on Wednesday—she was coming down for a library committee meeting, and if Sally wanted, she'd take her and a friend out to dinner. Peter and Sally were singing "Amazing Grace" as they drove off. It was one of their Sunday night songs.

Peter would be back in a couple of hours.

♦♦♦

LYDIA DIDN'T CALL HUNTER to tell him she was coming. She put the leftover shrimp in the refrigerator, sprayed on Carolina Herrera perfume, and got in the car. *Maybe I'll fuck him first.* Sunday evenings, traffic on 101 going south would be backed up. The fog would make it worse. Peter had allowed extra time to get Sally back to Thacher. Lydia took the back way. Over the hill at Milpas Street, East Valley Road to Toro Canyon Road, then Foothill Road to the Polo Club. Later, Lydia had only the haziest memory of the drive. Jerry Lee Lewis on the car CD player. "Chantilly Lace." "Great Balls of Fire." "Whole Lotta Shakin' Goin' On." Turned up loud.

As she drove through the foggy night, she was resolute. Exalted. She was taking the most direct course of action.

At the Polo Club, the gate at the entrance kiosk was shut. Lydia punched in the code and the gate slid open. The code hadn't been changed; it was still the same as her street number. Lydia thought of Rosalind, limp on the bottom of the swimming pool. Rosalind sparkling up at Hunter at Jimmy's Oriental Garden. The tennis clubhouse was dark. The light cast by the pole lights in front of the clubhouse weakly penetrated the fog. She turned down the first driveway. Hunter's white Thunderbird was there. She parked in the empty carport next to his. No one was in sight. Faint voices—it sounded like a jolly party—came from somewhere, but the row of carports was dark and forsaken. The only condos with lights on were Hunter's and two of the units at the opposite end of the block. Hunter's outside light was on.

For a moment, Lydia considered ringing the doorbell. She thought better of it and made her way around the side of the building. There was a path worn by people taking a shortcut across the polo field to the tennis club house. The ground was dry and hard, and the ivy ground cover was straggly. The leggy myoporum hedge took its water and nutrients.

A small square window looked into the living room. Lydia stood in the shadow of a leafless pomegranate bush. Desiccated pomegranates like dusty rubies hung from the bare branches. She thought of Persephone and Pluto. Persephone overcome, fainting in Pluto's arms, as he takes her down to Hades in his chariot. The high-voltage power lines along Foothill Road, strung on high pylons, buzzed in the dripping fog. Hunter was sitting on the black leather couch, a Pilsner beer glass half-full of Kirin on the coffee table in front of him. Lost in his thoughts, not reading or watching television, he was listening to Julie London. Fifties torch songs. An amoral old man in khakis and a blue button-down shirt, Bass Weejuns loafers. If he had looked in the direction of the small square window, he'd have seen only his own reflection, the lighted room reflected in the window glass.

Lydia watched a minute, then continued around the corner of the building to the terrace. The blinds were closed; the sliding glass door was an opaque rectangle of light. She scratched on the door, like a cat wanting in. Hunter didn't hear. He was a little deaf, and he had the sound turned up. Julie London was singing "Wives and Lovers." The traffic on 101, a stream of red taillights, visible above the tall myoporum hedge at the edge of the polo field, was stop-and-go in the fog. The song ended. Lydia knocked.

Hunter heard her and got up, went over to the door. "Who is it?" He was prudent.

"It's me," Lydia said, outside in the night.

Baby baby baby, Hunter thought. She had come, after all. "Just a minute, darling," he said.

He opened the blinds and unlocked the sliding glass door. The lights of a car coming up Foothill Road shone through the hedge. He slid the door open, and Lydia slipped into the living room. Julie London was singing "In the Wee Small Hours of the Morning." Hunter slid the door shut and closed the blinds again. They kissed. Hunter's kiss was tender and ardent.

"I couldn't stay away," Lydia said.

"I love you," he said.

"Would you mind shutting the blinds on the little window?" she murmured.

This request excited Hunter. Somehow it made Lydia seem very young to him. He kissed her again and then went over and turned the tilt wand on the slat blinds. Now no one could see into the living room, assuming there had been anyone wanting to see.

"Better, darling?" Hunter said. "Just let me turn down the music."

He imagined they would sit on the leather couch and talk, the torchy music in the background, plan their future, go into the bedroom and have fabulous sex. He crossed the room to the CD player and turned down the volume, his back to Lydia for a moment. When he turned around, she was looking at him with eyes hazy with lust, her lips parted. She approached him like a sleepwalker. Like the afternoon when she was fourteen and she scrambled in dreamy slow motion out of the ravine, as Hunter snapped photographs.

"I love you," Hunter said, as she advanced. She was a cat stalking its prey.

He was hypnotized. He had an erection. He was a young man again.

Lydia almost fell against him, her limbs heavy with lust. He caught her in his arms. When she kissed him on the mouth, the kiss was like white light. Like when she was fourteen.

"Lydia. Darling," Hunter said, aroused but puzzled.

Her arms around him, she nuzzled his neck, her breath warm on his skin. She growled, deep in her throat.

Starting to be scared, he said, "What are you doing?"

Her answer was a low cat's yowl.

"Have you gone crazy?" he said. Too late, Hunter tried to push her away.

Lydia clamped her teeth around the layer of skin and muscle over the carotid artery, over his trachea. Hunter screamed. A cry of pain and fear. There was no one to hear. He was fighting for his life, but he was an old man and Lydia was inhumanly strong. He tried to reach a bronze vase to brain her. She bit harder, her teeth meeting through flesh and gristle. Growling, she yanked her head back, her teeth still clamped. A flap of skin and muscle and artery wall came away. She spat it out. Hunter stumbled, and Lydia twisted away, jumped back. Bright red arterial blood cascaded out of the hole in Hunter's neck. He collapsed on the thick pile of the blue Chinese rug. Lydia watched him die. It took only a few minutes, but it was not a peaceful death.

She looked at her reflection in a mirror with a silver frame. Her mouth was rimmed with blood. She rubbed it off with her sleeve. The blood didn't show on the black jersey of her turtleneck. She stepped around Hunter's body. The smell in the condo was the smell of blood and raw meat. Lydia used one elbow to push aside the blind that covered the sliding glass door. She pulled her sleeve down to cover her hand when she slid open the door and closed it behind her. She wasn't worried about DNA. She would have to be a suspect, a sample would have to be taken. This was not going to happen. But her fingerprints were on file. Her first job out of college was a textbook clerk at San Marcos High School and she had been fingerprinted as part of the employment process.

Julie London singing "Makin' Whoopee."

There was no sign that anyone had raised the alarm. Lydia walked back the way she had come around the end of the building.

The night air smelled of the stables. There was no one to be seen. At the end of the driveway, fog swirled around the pole lamps by the tennis courts. Lydia got in her car and drove away. She took 101 back to the Mesa. Traffic was still backed up going south, but going in to Santa Barbara there was virtually no traffic. She felt a little shaky and wanted desperately to wash her mouth out. She was elated. Hunter Evans was no more.

Peter wasn't home yet when she got back. She'd been gone only a little more than an hour. In the garage, she checked the car for blood. She'd imagined there would be blood from her turtleneck on the shoulder strap of the seatbelt but none was visible. A microscopic trace of blood didn't matter. She put her clothes and tennis shoes in the washing machine on the cold cycle with a capful of Seventh Generation detergent. There hadn't been time for the blood to dry. Then she took a long hot shower, standing under the shower head with her mouth open. The ghoul taste in her mouth was hard to get rid of. Brushing her teeth with toothpaste didn't help. Only after she stood at the kitchen sink and rinsed her mouth out repeatedly with hot salt water did she stop tasting flesh and blood.

By the time Peter pulled in the driveway, Lydia's clothes were in the dryer, her tennis shoes were drying in the top cabinet over the washer and dryer, and she was sitting up in bed reading *Life on a Medieval Barony* for the fifth time. It was a 1924 first edition. She was wonderfully at peace.

Hunter was amoral. But Lydia was not a human being.

CHAPTER ELEVEN

Hunter Came to Her in a Dream

Hunter's body was discovered the next morning. He failed to appear at the tennis clubhouse for a seniors match against the Knowlwood team. After the Knowlwood captain looked at his watch and suggested a forfeit, the captain of the Polo Club team borrowed the Knowlwood captain's cell phone and called Hunter's number. He got the answering machine. "I'm not available right now. Please leave a message."

"Hunter? We're waiting for you, buddy," he said in the loud voice that people like him used when cell phones first came in.

There was an underlying mood of consternation among the tennis players, milling around in their tennis whites in the wan sunlight. The morning fog hadn't burned off yet. These were men who stayed in shape and described each other as "a young sixty-eight" or "a young seventy-four." But there was always the specter of a heart attack or a stroke or a bad fall. The team captain said he'd better go check on Hunter. He was a retired Beverly Hills attorney who, with his wife, had become prominent in the nonprofit world of Santa Barbara. He was pompous and combed his graying carroty hair over his bald spot, but he was conscientious about managing the team roster and the calendar. Hunter thought he was a jerk. The team captain thought Hunter was a prima donna.

Self-importantly, he rang the doorbell of the condo repeatedly. No one came. Hunter's white Thunderbird was in the carport. He banged on the door. "Hunter? You in there, Hunter?" He tried the front door. It was locked. He went around to the terrace to see if he could rouse Hunter. The sliding glass door was unlocked. Sliding it open, he pushed aside the closed blinds and stuck his head in.

"Hunter? You there?" he called.

He stepped inside. The lights were still on. The CD player was on, but no music was playing. Hunter's dead body was on the Chinese rug, his neck horribly ripped open, blood everywhere. His hazel eyes were wide open and clouded. The living room smelled like raw meat. The team captain blanched. "Like a wild animal attacked him," he later told the sheriff. Gagging, he lurched out the front door, tracking blood on the Berber carpet. He shut the front door behind him and walked rapidly, almost running, up the driveway to the tennis clubhouse to call 911.

♦♦♦

The day after Hunter's body was discovered, the murder at the Polo Club was on the first page of the local news section of the *Santa Barbara News-Press*. Lydia read the article with her morning coffee.

"The Santa Barbara County Sheriff is investigating as a murder the death of sixty-eight-year-old Hunter Evans found yesterday morning in his condo at the Polo Club. When he did not show up for a scheduled tennis match, the team captain went to his condo. He found Evans in his living room lying on the floor with clear signs of violence and called 911. The Sheriff's Criminal Investigation Department is asking anyone with information to contact them."

The article was curiously opaque. There was the information that Hunter didn't show up for a tennis match, that the team captain found his body on the floor with "clear signs of violence." But not a word about what sort of violence.

Peter saw the article and asked, "Wasn't Hunter Evans the man you and Annie ran into? He was with Rosalind?"

"Same guy. Apparently they were going to get married. She left him all her money," Lydia said. "It's hard to imagine him as a murder victim."

"Annie will have the scuttlebutt," Peter said. He kissed Lydia and left for his office.

Peter was right. Soon after, Annie called. She told Lydia the captain of the tennis team was saying it was like a wild animal had attacked Hunter.

"What does that mean?" Lydia said. "The newspaper article gave zero information."

"I don't know. I'm locking the windows at night," Annie said. "Of course," she added, "we don't know if the captain of the tennis team is a reliable witness."

After they hung up, Lydia called the Sheriff's Department and asked to speak with the officer in charge of the investigation of the murder at the Polo Club. This was preemptive. No doubt the police would obtain a record of Hunter's phone calls and her name would show up. Also, someone may have noticed her Passat with the Thacher School decal at the Polo Club, either the day of the golf cart polo or, possibly, the night she killed Hunter. Lydia intended to come forward with a good explanation.

The receptionist asked her name, but Lydia said firmly that she would prefer to be put through without giving her name. After a brief time on hold, she was connected.

"This is Lieutenant Aragon."

"Hello. Are you the person to talk to about the murder at the Polo Club? I may have some useful information," Lydia said.

He said he was in charge of the investigation. Lydia gave her name and said she would prefer to talk in person. She sounded appropriately nervous. "Can I come to your office?"

"I can see you at one o'clock," he said.

♦♦♦

Lydia did some work on a garden design, and then she spent an hour trying on outfits. This was an important performance. She considered jeans. She considered her knockoff Chanel suit. She decided on classic black slacks and a beige twinset, sleeves of the cardigan pushed up. One spritz of Chanel No. 5. Her usual red lipstick. Pearl stud earrings, no other jewelry. Casual but polished. Not a person who might have ripped a man's throat out.

The Sheriff's Headquarters was on Camino Real in Goleta, a ten-minute drive. The sand-colored concrete building had inset panels in a contrasting tan and a red tile roof façade. It reminded Lydia of the condos at the Polo Club—the same 1970s architecture. The parking lot was landscaped with pine trees and divider beds of orange and red lantana. The spaces closest to the building were occupied by a row of black-and-white sheriff vehicles. Lydia was a few minutes early. She sat in the car and gathered herself together. This was high stakes. The important thing was to experience the rôle.

At one o'clock on the dot, she presented herself at the reception window. "I have an appointment with Lieutenant Aragon."

The receptionist picked up the phone. "Your one o'clock appointment is here," she said. She listened a moment and hung up. "He'll be with you shortly," she said to Lydia.

In a minute or two, the buzz-through door opened. Lieutenant Aragon was not in uniform; he wore a sports jacket and khaki slacks. He was a big man. He looked as if he'd played football, but he'd run to seed—still strong, but he had a gut. He had light brown hair and bushy eyebrows.

"Lieutenant Aragon," he said. "We can talk in my office."

Lydia walked with him down a fluorescent-lit corridor with a terra-cotta tile floor. She thanked him for seeing her in person, and he said a member of the public could always request to meet with a deputy.

"Did you grow up in Santa Barbara?" she asked, making nervous polite conversation. What sounded like nervous polite conversation.

"I was born at St. Francis Hospital," he said.

"Cottage Hospital," she said. They were fellow locals. "We probably know people in common."

"Most likely," he said, in a tone intended to remind Lydia that this was a murder investigation, not a social call.

Lieutenant Aragon's office had a view of the Santa Ynez Mountains over the roof of the county jail. The vinyl and chrome chair that he offered Lydia faced his desk. She put her purse on the floor and sat up attentively. She was ready. Lieutenant Aragon sat down at his desk and picked up a Bic ballpoint pen, prepared to take notes on a yellow legal pad.

"You said you had information?" he said.

She took a deep breath, making it clear that this was difficult.

"I think I have information that might be helpful. And I'd really like it if none of this is made public."

A brief silence while what she had said hung there between them.

"Lieutenant, I especially don't want my husband to know."

"I can only assure you that if your involvement isn't pertinent to the investigation, it will remain confidential," he said.

"Okay," she said, as if she were leveling with him. "Obviously I want you to find whoever killed Hunter. There's a lot of gossip about how he died. I understand it was gruesome. But I have to be honest. This visit is not entirely public-spirited. I didn't want you to call me at home."

"Why would we do that?" he said evenly.

"Because my name is going to come up. I imagine you'll request a record of telephone calls. And I'm probably in his appointment book."

"Why don't you tell me about it?" His bulky physique made him seem avuncular, although they were the same age.

Lydia launched into her story. She didn't look the lieutenant in the eye, and she clasped her hands together. She was convincing as a woman who had stooped to folly. There was a framed color photograph of the Sheriff's Mounted Unit on the wall. She said she'd known Hunter when she was fourteen. She didn't see him again for almost forty years, when they ran into each other at a concert. He invited her to lunch at his condo at the Polo Club. She said she wasn't certain of the exact date—it was the day of the Palm Springs–Santa Barbara golf cart polo match. Lieutenant Aragon was making notes; he didn't ask questions.

"Do you need to make notes?" Lydia said. She was fully aware that it was to be expected that the lieutenant take notes, but she wanted to emphasize her desire to be kept out of it.

"These are for me," he said.

"I visited him at his condo one night when my husband was out of town. It was only a day or two after we had lunch," she said. "I told him that night I didn't want to see him again."

"Did you see him again?"

"No. Well, I ran into him at a restaurant, and I saw him at a memorial service, but I didn't see him again in the context you mean."

Another silence. The lieutenant waited.

"Something happened, though," Lydia said, breaking the silence.

She said that two days ago, on Sunday, the day Hunter was murdered, he called her at home and wanted her to come and see him. That evening.

"I waited until my husband left—he was taking our daughter back to Ojai; Sally goes to Thacher—and then I drove down to the Polo Club. I wanted to see him," she confessed. "But when I rang the doorbell, no one came. I knocked on the door and rang the doorbell again, and then I went back home."

"I see," the lieutenant said. "And you saw or heard something that caused you to leave?"

"No," Lydia said with candor. "More like, I came to my senses. I thought maybe he didn't hear the doorbell. He was a little deaf. Maybe he was drinking. Now I wonder if he was dead. Maybe the murderer was in the condo." She gave a shiver. "It didn't matter. I had a God-spoke-to-me moment. I thought: *This is a stupid thing to do*, and I left."

"What is the information you thought might be helpful?" the lieutenant asked impatiently.

If Hunter had been shot or even bludgeoned, he would have considered her a person of interest. Not a prime suspect, perhaps.

But he'd have wanted to dig a little deeper. But it was impossible that this woman had killed Hunter. Lieutenant Aragon had seen the body. It was physically impossible. Lydia had a fling and she didn't want her husband to find out. That was what this was all about.

"I'm sorry. I didn't tell you the important thing," she said.

"What is that?"

She said that the day she was at the condo for lunch, Hunter had a visitor. "He went outside to talk to him. They were quarreling about money. It sounded violent. I don't mean physical violence. They weren't hitting each other. But the man was cursing Hunter. After he left, Hunter told me he knew him in Vietnam. He was an art dealer."

"Do you know his name?"

"Hunter didn't say."

"We'll look into it," the lieutenant said.

"Probably it's nothing. I don't want to cause trouble for him."

"We'll look into it," he repeated. "See if he has an alibi. Run a DNA check if we need to. You did the right thing coming in."

The interview was over.

Lydia stood up. "Lieutenant Aragon," she said. "I'm aware that it was not my finest hour. But I love my husband and I don't want to hurt him."

There was a silence.

"I don't think anyone needs to know this," the lieutenant said.

"I'm trusting you," Lydia said.

♦♦♦

THE SAME DAY, AN envelope addressed to her came in the mail. The return address on the white envelope was engraved with Hunter's name. It was postmarked the day before he died. On a single sheet of typing paper, he'd typed on the same Underwood portable typewriter he had in 1963:

Along a mountain path
The scent of plum blossoms
And, on a sudden,
The rising sun.
—Bashō

Lydia read it standing at the mailbox. Then she tore up the envelope and put it in the garbage can. It was fortuitous that she got the mail that day. Thank God Hunter was dead. He would have pursued her with increasing indiscretion. She folded the sheet of paper with the haiku and stuck it in *Life on a Medieval Barony*. For all anyone knew, the haiku could have been there for decades.

♦♦♦

Hunter had kept his life in compartments. In days to come, a wife in the Philippines who had divorced Hunter and whom no one knew about came to light—except the people who did know. It was a secret de Ponchinelle. The discovery of a Colt MK IV with two loaded magazines in a locked trunk in the hall closet, along with a receipt from a shop in Singapore, was the subject of many conversations. The photograph of Lydia didn't cause a stir. She was fully clothed. It wasn't a secret that Lydia and Annie had known him the summer he stayed in the gatehouse.

"God, it was a long ago," Lydia said, when Annie told her. "He was outside snapping photos with a Leica. How strange that he kept it."

Interestingly, Hunter had written his own obituary with the date of death waiting to be filled in. It was in the trunk. Annie said you couldn't tell when he'd typed it. The couple who sat with him at Rosalind's memorial service saw to its publication in the *News-Press*.

J. Hunter Evans, Jr.
18 Nov. 1931–12 Nov. 2000

"Of so divine a loss, we enter but the gain, indemnity
for loneliness that such a bliss has been."
—Emily Dickinson
No Services
Burial At National Cemetery
Westwood, Los Angeles

There was speculation about the meaning of the quotation. To Lydia, it sounded like a contract. Symbolically. Gain and loss and indemnity. Every time, though, she tried to parse the poem, the meaning slipped away. The same couple who saw to the publication of the obituary organized the burial.

♦♦♦

THE MURDER AT THE Polo Club was an *affaire célèbre*. In the coming years, two books and several magazine articles were written about the murder, but at no point was there a serious suspect. Joel Frank was located and was briefly a person of interest, but at the time of the murder he and his wife were at an ethnic art show in Chicago. The murder was attributed to a psychotic drifter. The murder at the Polo Club was yet another unsolved Santa Barbara murder.

For years, Santa Barbara had the highest number per capita of unsolved murders of any small city in the United States (or so people said). In the late sixties, several hitchhikers were murdered, their bodies found much later. In the eighties, a young woman met a man in a grocery store parking lot in answer to an apartment-for-rent classified. Later, her body was found off Camino Cielo with the hands cut off. In the early nineties, a man was shot in a beach house in Montecito, and the killer was never found. There were the murders on the beach—a couple bludgeoned to death, a man in a sleeping bag shot in the head, an ax murder. It was accepted that drifters were responsible for these unsolved murders. And perhaps they were.

At the time and in years to come, Lydia escaped any whiff of suspicion. Lieutenant Aragon respected the confidentiality of their conversation. Peter never knew. Life went on happily. When decades-old unsolved murders started to be solved by DNA matching with relatives, it occurred to Lydia that she should be concerned. She had cousins who were the sort of people who would order a DNA ancestry kit. But she had no doubt that her DNA was an anomaly. She was not a human in so many ways. The DNA of a relative in Minnesota would not be a near match for the DNA found at the crime scene.

♦♦♦

HUNTER HAD MADE A new will. It was signed, witnessed, and notarized the day of Rosalind's memorial service. The Music Academy of the West was the chief beneficiary, and he left a substantial sum to endow a chamber music concert annually as part of the *Camerata Pacifica* series—or another similar concert series, if *Camerata Pacifica* ceased to exist. Lydia had wondered if he would leave her anything. It would have been awkward.

♦♦♦

HUNTER CAME TO LYDIA in a dream. He was completely real. Dreams are the way the dead appear to us. He said that she could come to him, if she wanted to. They would have the life they imagined together.

"In hell we'll both be young," she said.

If she killed herself, they would be together for all time. He was persuasive, but Lydia said, "Be gone."

She watched him disappear. He was on an ice floe, drifting out to sea. The cold green sea, icebergs like an engraving in an old book, a walrus and a dead seal and red blood on the blue ice, as he disappeared.

♦♦♦

THE PAST IS SEDUCTIVE because we know how it turned out. Twenty-five years after the end of this story, in an unsettled time, the path through the forest has grown over behind Lydia, and when she looks back, the past is only there in bits and pieces.

ACKNOWLEDGEMENTS

I WOULD LIKE TO thank Tove Alsterdal, the Swedish writer, who said, “You should write that book,” on the occasion of the Festival du Roman Noir 2019. Also my first readers, Phillip Lopate, my advisor at Columbia School of the Arts, and Lukas Ortiz, who has been, along with Kim Lombardi, unfailingly helpful.

My heartfelt thanks to all my family and friends who encouraged and supported me,

Thank you to everyone at Rare Bird.

Within nearly every house was a guitar, and when evening came and twilight darkened, from all parts of the pueblo were heard the sounds of music and rich melodious voices. There was something distinctly characteristic in their songs, in most of which there was a minor tone of sweet plaintiveness. When the lamps were hung and the guitars and violins sounded the waltz, light hearts beat and merry peals of laughter floated through the old California homes. Lissome forms glided gracefully through the halls. Dark velvety eyes looked words unspoken. The hours passed rapidly by, and before the last dance had been stepped and the last soft glance given, the bells of the old Mission tower had sounded the matin call. Those were halcyon days in the fairest spot in a lotus land.

—*Walter A. Hawley, 1910*